WHAT WE BECOME

WHAT WE BECOME

JESSE KARP

HARCOURT
HOUGHTON MIFFLIN HARCOURT
BOSTON   NEW YORK   2013

Harcourt is an imprint of Houghton Mifflin Harcourt Publishing Company.

The text of this book is set in Garamond 3 LT Std.

www.hmhbooks.com

Library of Congress Cataloging-in-Publication Data
Karp, Jesse.
What we become / Jesse Karp.
pages cm
Sequel to: Those that wake.
Summary: Two years after destroying a corporate empire intent on
controlling human thinking through technology, teenagers Mal and Laura
engage in another battle to save humanity when a "corporate bogeyman"
known only as the Old Man tries to gain absolute power.
ISBN 978-0-547-55500-3
[1. Science fiction. 2. Corporations—Fiction.] I. Title.
PZ7.K1467Wh 2013
[Fic]—dc23
2012028980

Manufactured in the United States of America
DOC 10 9 8 7 6 5 4 3 2 1
4500395421

For Maren—
my teacher, my fighter,
my hero

The important thing is this: to be able at any moment to sacrifice what we are for what we could become.

—Charles Du Bos

PART I

MAL

A FIST JACKHAMMERED INTO MAL'S face and smashed his head into a brick wall. Thunder cracked through his skull, and when he groped his way back to awareness, he realized that his eyes were still open but he couldn't see. What he primarily couldn't see were the two large men in tight dark suits, a bright sheen over their eyes from the steroids that swelled their muscles and the performance enhancers that quickened their reaction times.

Mal dropped, assuming another blow was coming toward his head, opened his mouth to let the blood stream out of it. Something hard in his mouth almost lodged in his throat as he sucked in air: a tooth. A knee buried itself hard in his gut. He coughed out, blood and his tooth spraying out into the air. An arm around his throat straightened him out. Pain rang through his body, flooding all other sensation, but he realized he had thrown a punch himself when he felt hard impact against his fist, the vibration up his arm.

"Son of a *bitch!*" one of them snarled. The one holding his throat from behind used a free hand to pound into Mal's kidney.

He gagged, coughed more blood, probably spraying the one in front of him. The smudge that was his vision began to sparkle, shapes began finding their way back into Mal's rattled brain.

"Just get him in," the one in back said. "Just get him *in!*"

The blows from behind stopped. An arm locked Mal at both elbows, so he stomped down behind him, caught an instep. The man grunted, jerked back. Mal spun on him, a dark silhouette in Mal's injured vision.

The man's arms flashed up in three expert blocks, parrying each of Mal's flurried strikes.

"Are you kidding me?" The other's voice preceded a kick in the crotch, which brought Mal to his knees again and left no air to power his limbs, to get him back up. The sidewalk, clean and textured, appeared in alternating waves of dimness and light.

"Just drag him. Hurry."

Hands on his arms, his legs kicked out from beneath him, Mal's knees scraped the concrete, tearing his pants. The bright city formed around him, spinning. Sound rushed back in, traffic mostly. People walked by as he was hauled toward the big dark limo parked ten feet away. The people looked down at their cells, or their eyes were invisible behind black plastic cellenses, a man shouting red-faced at an employee, a young woman crying in racking sobs to her apathetic boyfriend, all of them trapped in the output of their technology, like insects mired in honey. Once, Mal would have thought they were trying to ignore the unpleasantness. Now he believed they simply didn't notice.

The door of the limo was opened before him. He tensed to push back, but they felt it. One punched him in the neck. Choking, more blood, less air. They stuffed him inside, onto the spacious floor. One climbed on top of him, knees in his back, forearms resting on his neck, Mal's face pressed to the floor mats. A door slammed, the limo began to move.

"This is him?" a woman's voice asked.

"Of course, Ms. Kliest," one of the suits said, not the one on top of Mal. It was a tight, clipped voice, showing no insult at the affront to his professionalism that the question implied.

"How can you tell with all the blood?"

"He wasn't bleeding when we saw him, ma'am," the other one said, the one pressing down on Mal. His voice was heavier, angrier.

"I know, Mr. Castillo. What I'm saying is, did you have to beat him so badly?"

"He's tough, ma'am." Castillo's heavy voice leaped to his own defense. "We had to put him down. He got a few good ones in, anyway."

There was a cold silence.

"Well" — the woman's tone suggested a possible thaw — "is he conscious? Is he alive?"

"Yes, ma'am, I can feel him breathing."

"Turn his head this way."

The pressure on Mal's neck eased; his head was jerked around. He resisted on principle, and the other man had to get in on it. Finally, with Castillo still on his back and neck, while the other kneeled on his head to trap it in place, Mal faced the liquid-black gloss of a pair of high-heeled shoes.

"That is truly" — the woman searched — "gross."

Nevertheless, she bent low, and Mal felt fingers pry one of his eyelids wide. For an instant, there was the woman's face, coolly exquisite, high cheekbones, blond hair pulled tightly back, the slim line of dark cellenses covering her eyes.

"Oh, for God's sake"—she glared into his eye—"you've given him a concussion."

Another uncomfortable silence.

"Sorry, Ms. Kliest," and "Sorry," they muttered.

She released Mal, sat back up, breathed out a heavy sigh.

"Mal Jericho," she said too loudly. "Do you understand me?"

He closed his eyes, let his tongue probe through the blood to the place where his tooth had been. They hadn't simply knocked it loose but actually cracked it off. He could feel the jagged root protruding from his gum into the empty space between the teeth on either side.

Fingers snapped—one, two, three times—right in front of his face. He wearily opened his eyes.

"Listen, boy," she said. "You'd better let this penetrate, because your life literally depends on it." He believed her. "There are forces in this world that make things run, that determine the direction of human life." This he knew. Better than he liked. "The weather, for instance; the geographic distribution of natural resources. And there are certain in- dividuals—individuals who sit on invisible thrones and preside over cultures, governments, societies. An audience with such an individual is more precious than a field of oil wells or a cavern shot full of gold ore. Today you will be privileged with such an audience. Do you understand what I've just said to you? Answer, or I'm going to kick you in the face."

He closed his eyes again. If she had just let the question stand, he would have answered her, but with the threat attached, he would not. A moment later her kick jarred through his spinning head, anchoring it briefly with a spike of pain, before sending him swirling down a whirlpool of nausea and disorientation.

"People kill their own families, sell their own lives, to be in the same room with such a person," she said reasonably. "And what do you do? You really ought to be ashamed. Bind him, Mr. Roarke."

The weight on his back shifted, hands moved onto his arms. He pulled away, felt Castillo's knee press down on his kidneys. While he coughed out blood and bile, Roarke bound his wrists behind his back with something thin enough to cut the flesh. Mal pulled at it, anyway, but found it utterly unyielding, though his palms and fingers became slick with blood.

The limo slowed, bumped down a ramp, pulled to a stop. The door opened, the woman got out, then the men rearranged themselves, gripped him under the armpits, and pulled. He gave them dead weight, but with the benefit of fifth-generation performance enhancers coursing through their bloodstreams, they struggled him out into a moist, echoing space. He opened his eyes briefly, but the fluorescent light from above cut into his brain like a razor. For a brief instant before he clamped his eyes closed again, he saw a huge parking garage with low ceilings, completely empty but for the limo; at its center, where they stood—where Mal hung from his wardens—was a column with a bank of elevators.

Elevator doors slid open. They dragged him in, the doors closed, the elevator moved upward. Mal straightened suddenly, threw his head to the left where a face must be, judging by the grip on his arm. He connected, and on impact, his knees buckled, he vomited, and his head blasted out of existence.

"*Christ!* Do you believe this little bastard?"

Castillo's irate voice jarred Mal awake. He might have been lying down on the floor, his face in his own vomit. Maybe. All his sensations were vague and far away now, except the light cutting through his closed eyelids, driving spikes into his brain. He squeezed his eyes shut tighter.

"He head-butts me with a *concussion!* You've got to be kidding."

Roarke was silent. The vague sense of motion stopped. Mal felt himself lifted by his shoulder again, pulled out. He kept his eyes shut. More light, he thought, might kill his brain.

"Clean him up," the woman said, her voice receding. "Then bring him in."

"Yes, ma'am," Roarke said tonelessly.

They dragged him, laid him on something soft. Water ran, something wet swabbed at his face, none too gently. As the rough passage crossed his jaw, where his tooth had been cracked, the sensation became briefly sharper. The cleaning went on for a minute, over his hands and arms.

"What about his clothes?" Castillo asked.

"What about them?"

"They're disgusting."

"So?"

"So, we're supposed to clean him."

"She didn't say give him a shower and send his things out to the laundry, Castillo."

"Screw you, Roarke. I'm trying to do what she said." The wet cloth rubbed halfheartedly at Mal's shirt, his pants, then gave up.

"Let's go," Roarke's clipped, professional voice said.

They lifted him, dragged him. A door slid open like a whisper, and they lowered him into a soft seat.

"Fine," said the woman's voice. "Roarke, wait outside. Castillo, go fix your face."

"Yes, Ms. Kliest."

"Yes, ma'am."

Footsteps, the door, then silence. Lighter footsteps, coming closer, the woman nearing.

"Let's try again," she said. "My name is Arielle Kliest. I'm employed by the Old Man."

Ridiculous. The Old Man was a ghost story they told on the streets.

"He's quite real," she said, having seen a flutter of muscles in Mal's face or having simply read his mind. She didn't have an accent, exactly, but her enunciation was so cleanly sculpted, she didn't sound American. "And he's in the next room. I'm not in the habit of murdering children, despite what it may seem like to you. I'm not in the *habit* of it, but I *will* do it. So listen very carefully. You listen to his questions. You answer his questions. You leave. Nothing else."

She did not, thankfully, ask him if he could do that.

The door whispered open. Large hands drew him to his feet. The room felt like it was teetering and swirling around him, but he found that if he kept his eyes closed, he could stumble along with assistance.

Another door opened, and he passed through into a darker space. It was humid, hot enough so that Mal felt a prickle of sweat on his forehead and down his spine. He was set down on a chair, shifted so that he didn't have to support his own weight but wasn't leaning on his bound wrists. Cautiously, he opened his eyes into slits.

The light in here was hazy red, pouring from ledges along the walls. It cast the center of the room in a dim but hot glow, like a dying ember, though the outlying areas of the room were still steeped in shadow. Before him, in that shadow, the floor rose a level, and on that platform was the wide blot of a huge desk, nearly the size of a small car. Desks were the corporate equivalent of a modern throne, and, Mal supposed, some might have believed that the bigger your throne, the greater your status. But truly, it was the vague silhouette at the other side of the desk that demanded attention. It was small enough that you could almost believe it was a trick of your eyes and did not exist at all. But then the glare of the red light would pick up a stray detail, the gentlest sense of movement, and Mal had to focus, no matter how badly it cut into his brain.

The shadow was slight, so thin as to appear almost skeletal. Hands lay upon the desk, fingers long and sharp, but unmoving. The features of the face were impossible to make out, but Mal imagined folds and creases so deep, they swallowed the shadow around it, a parchment so ancient and wrinkled and dry that if you touched it, it would crumble to dust.

When Mal was a young boy, his father had told him a story, a story that both he and his father would return to in the years before the older man had died, because the story seemed to speak to them both about something deep in themselves. This story flooded back to Mal now, the myth of Medusa, who slithered in her shadowed temple, a monster in a world of winding darkness. And if you penetrated the darkness too far, gazed on the monster's countenance, you were destroyed. Mal squeezed his eyes tightly shut again.

"There was a great city," the voice said from the shadows, a dry whisper that would have been blotted out by the gentlest noise, had there been anything but silence around it. "It was attacked and scarred. A giant dome broke its skyline . . . and that dome was made of fear. Fear infected people's minds . . . and their minds destroyed the city."

Then the room was quiet again for such a long time that Mal was not certain he hadn't dreamed the words. Maybe there was the sound of shaking breath, the monster rallying its strength to continue. Finally, it did.

"I whispered into people's ears and changed their minds. Soon the dome was made of strength, a tribute to . . . the human ability to overcome fear. Now the city is great again, people flock to it to see . . . this monument to human achievement. Minds are tools, and I use those tools . . . to shape the world. But you already know how minds affect the world . . . don't you, boy?"

Yes. Mal knew that.

A moment passed as the monster breathed.

"There is a mind out in the city. It is more powerful . . . than any mind before. I want it."

Even with his eyes closed, it was as if Mal could feel the monster's gaze turned on him. It was a long minute before the voice returned.

"Where is Jon Remak?" it finally asked.

"Gone. He's gone." Mal's own words vibrated through his skull until he gritted his teeth to stop from screaming.

"But you will find him. And bring him to me. That is all."

Hands were on Mal again. They dragged him from the seat and out of the hot darkness, leaving the monster alone in its lair.

Light stabbed through Mal's eyelids. He was brought back down a hallway, his legs buckling every few steps. They stopped, and he felt the cool tingle of a spray injector in his right bicep.

"It took us a while to get ahold of you, Mal." It was the woman, Kliest, beside him. "But now you have a chemical geolocator in you, and we'll have you when we want you.

And if you make it hard, we'll take the girl. Find what he wants, Mal. You have three days."

A door whispered open, and Mal was pulled back into the small, bright space of the elevator.

"Drop him where you found him," her voice said before the door closed, and they moved down.

Out of the elevator, into the limo. The car moved, back into the sounds of traffic, through the streets, eventually pulled over. The door opened; Mal was shoved harshly out. His knees came down hard on cement, his hands still bound behind his back with the sharp plastic. A door slammed, the limo pulled away.

Mal could picture himself, bound, his clothes stained with blood, kneeling on the flawlessly clean sidewalk, with all the flawlessly clean and oblivious people walking around, sparing just enough attention to navigate the obstacle. But the MCT were watching, always, and in no time officers would pick him up.

The city was so bright now, every skyscraper reflecting a scouring gleam onto the streets. So he opened his eyes into a squint and, through the agony of razors, found what he needed: half a block away, between a gourmet coffee super-store and an office building.

He rose, a wounded behemoth swaying to its feet. He

staggered forward, glancing against a woman who focused just long enough to say "fucker," and then hazed back out behind her cellenses and hurried along. Higher powers had polished up the city, made it bright and shiny to cover up the decay beneath, and his bloody body was an unacceptable assault on that world.

He came to the spot, fell against the wall to steady himself, then pushed off and disappeared into one of the city's forgotten places.

LAURA

"I MUST CONFESS, I FIND your credentials quite impressive, Ms. Westlake," said the man with the judgmental eyes and the thick, thick head of blond hair, styled into a fashionable sweep. "For an eighteen-year-old," he added with unconcealed distress.

"Thank you, sir," Laura said from the other side of the rich, wooden desk, inlaid with a plexi-optic surface that projected the screen and keyboard in a hovering crystalline image above it. Dr. Richard Innes, as the plaque on the door identified him, also had a large window that looked down into the hospital parking lot and the small forest of surrounding trees.

"Of course, being eighteen suggests other issues. Oversleeping, for instance."

"Um, no, sir. I am sorry to be late. There was only a single elevator working downstairs."

"Yes. We have stairs as well, you know."

"I did know that, Dr. Innes, but security wouldn't let me into the hallway."

"You might think about arriving earlier, to head off such problems."

Seriously, dude? Laura worked hard to keep it out of her face. *Seriously?*

"I'll try to remember that."

"Do." He cleared his throat, his expression proclaiming that he was doing her the favor of starting fresh. "I see you've selected your major already. I believe you're still a freshman, is that not right?"

"That's correct, sir."

"Are you not concerned with limiting your options?"

"I'm very committed to psychology. I've been committed to it for a few years now."

"Yes, I see that by your advanced placement work in high school. Yet no internships until now. We decided to shoot for the very top on our first outing, didn't we, Ms. Westlake?"

She blinked once, over her unfaltering smile.

"I had a family emergency during my senior year in high school, Mr. Innes. It didn't leave me any time to pursue internships and keep my grades at a high level. So that I could be considered for such top-level positions." Had he detected the note of sarcasm she was striving to quash?

"*Doctor* Innes," he corrected. "Perhaps this family emergency would explain why you've failed to qualify on the new Voight-Kampf Diagnostics programs."

"As you noted, sir, I'm still a freshman. We don't generally train on diagnostics software until the final term. My adviser has assured me, though, that I'll be permitted to start during the next semester."

"Impressive for you, I'm certain," Innes said. "Somewhat too late for us, I'm afraid."

"I . . . see." Laura could feel her jaw muscles tightening. She never had an easy time with officious middle-echelon corporate lackeys. Less so when her own adviser had commented that she was more capable already than many of the seniors they were sending out for similar positions. Less still, when the interview had pushed back a reunion with her boyfriend, returning today after a three-day absence he playfully but frustratingly refused to explain. Her boyfriend, who was, even now, probably waiting for her under the flag-pole back on campus. "I'd thought that the hospital might be more interested in someone with an ability to connect with people rather than hook those people into machines and dispense brain-deadening medication."

"*Excuse* me?" His judgmental eyes sharpened to an ex-ecutioner's glare.

"Well, Mr. Innes, I can see that the budget that should have been spent keeping the elevators working so that visi-tors or—oh, I don't know—your *patients* wouldn't have to wait in the lobby for ten minutes has instead gone to your antique desk and fancy computer screen."

"Ms. Westlake," he said, leaning back in his chair, his voice going low, "it's clear you're not the material we're looking for. And it's *Doctor* Innes."

"Sad," she said, rising. "Sadder still, you're clearly not the material *I'm* looking for, Richard."

She closed the door gently behind her before he could mount a response. God, these corporate bureaucrats buried in their technology. She didn't know whether it was the men or the machines she could stand less.

She found the stairway entrance up here, not blocked off by security, and went downstairs, pleased for the op-portunity to blow by the seated guard downstairs who had blocked her path before. She went out to the parking lot and got into her car and pulled her cell. Plenty of people she could call about this development, a few who would even be upset if she didn't. Or call her guy. That was most tempting. But holding the cell, even pulling it out, felt distasteful. In minutes she would actually see him, not on a miniature screen digitally sharpened until he looked more like a special effect than a person, not transmitted across miles of space, but actually *him,* right before her. Good enough to touch.

She drove the miles to campus, found a space near her dorm, started walking toward the main square, and soon found herself half running with excitement. It was just three days, but that was somehow three days too many.

There was the massive flagpole, with both the college's gold, white, and blue flag and the Stars and Stripes fluttering serenely in an early spring breeze, a glare of sun cutting majestically between them. Lots of kids gathered at the base, the college's unofficial Place Where Things Happened. Too much of a crowd to see if he was —

"Laura," came his voice, from behind. She turned into his soft smile and put herself into his open arms. "You okay, Button?"

She nodded into his chest, suddenly not sure she could speak without cracking.

"How was the interview?" he asked, his breath falling on the top of her head.

She shook her head.

"Crappy," she managed to say.

"Is that the problem?"

"No." It wasn't. She barely even cared about that now. "No problems." She looked up at him, the sun blinding her from behind his head. The sun, or just seeing him. "Just glad you're back, Josh."

He nodded.

"Glad, too." They kissed and held on to it, students flowing around them, the hubbub receding to the back of her mind. Her hands found his cheeks, cupped his face. She kept going until her finger touched something small and metal. She stopped dead.

She pulled her head back, tilted her neck so she could see it.

"You got one," she said. "That's where you were the last three days."

"Yeah, Button. Surprise." It came out a little lame.

"We were . . ." She stepped back but caught the tone in her own voice and smoothed it out. "We talked about doing it together."

"I know, Laura." Big smile. With those deep, dark eyes

and that slim, jagged scar down his cheek that brought the perfection of his features out, and that shaggy head of dark hair, it could defuse a protest before it even heated up. "Don't be upset. You kept putting it off, kept talking about how nervous you were about it. I just thought if I did it, you'd see it was no big thing, and I would still come with you when you got yours. You're not mad, are you? Don't be mad," he started with the funny wheedling voice. It usually worked. "Much better if you're not mad. Come on, come on."

She wasn't mad, not exactly. But looking at the thing, the tiny little metal disk lodged just in front of his left ear, right over the jawbone, it made her queasy, almost made her feel like she was talking to someone who wasn't quite Josh. She worked hard to put a smile on her face and keep it there.

"So," she said, looking at his eyes, looking to see if something was there—she wasn't even sure what. "How was it?"

"It was nothing at all. Like getting an ear pierced. They knock you out for, like, an hour and implant the transponder. Then they put the magnetic patch on." He reached up and touched the disk, maybe a third of an inch in diameter, and removed it, leaving a tiny patch of shiny skin beneath. "I can make and receive audio signals just by thinking about it, Laura. It's unbelievably awesome. I almost made you my first call, but I wanted to surprise you. And"—he pulled out a pair of slim, black sunglasses—"you clip it into these." He put them on, the small disk of the cellpatch on his temple clipping into a small circular interface in the earpiece of the glasses, and his deep dark eyes disappeared behind the cel-lenses. "I can get visuals on calls, Internet, watch movies. And games; with the biosync . . ." He raised his eyebrows hyperbolically. "*GTA 8* is vicious in these. It's unbelievable, Laura. I'm telling you—you're gonna love it."

She looked up, waited for him to take the cellenses off, which he did after the barest moment of silence. His smile never faltered, laboring to support hers, too.

"It doesn't hurt at all?"

"No, not at all. The implantation only took an hour. The rest of the time, they were locking the biosync and teaching me to subvocalize my calls and stuff. Didn't hurt a bit. Isn't even sore."

He sounded like the web ads and infocasts that the companies ran on the process.

"They even said they're going to have a wireless link to contact lenses in less than two years, and we can get rid of the glasses." He was watching her expectantly.

She looked around her, at the other students coming,

going, and sitting. Four, five, six, eight others that she could spot had the patches, too. They didn't come cheap. These would be the kids without student loans, with enough money to eat off campus if they wanted; the kids like Josh. And Laura.

"Dude," a student, someone Josh knew and Laura knew in passing, shouted out as he went by, pointing at the spot near Josh's ear. "Sorry about the brain cancer." He smiled and swept by.

"Nice timing," Josh's voice rose after him, then quieted. "Dick." He looked back at Laura, worried. "That's a totally false rumor," he said. "They talked all about it. The rise in brain cancer only has to do with —"

"A higher incidence of the fallout from the ozone-layer satellites, I know. I read all the same websites you did."

"Come on, Button"—his voice sounding strained now—"I'm back. I'm cool. We should be thinking of something better to do than this."

She felt the tension, wanted it to vanish.

"I'm sorry," she said, touching his face again. "The interview got me messed up. I'm so happy you're back. Meet me in an hour at the café, and we'll come up with something good."

"Okay," he said uncertainly. "What are you gonna do?"

"Just want to talk about the interview. I'm going to call my parents."

"Honey!" Laura's mother was delighted to hear from her as always. It didn't matter if they hadn't spoken in a week or ten minutes, the brightness of her mother's exuberant smile nearly blew out the screen of Laura's cell.

"Hi, Mom."

"What is it, Laura, what's wrong? Was it the interview?" Did Laura let something slip into her voice, or was it her mother's seemingly preternatural ability to key into Laura's mood even across an expanse of miles? For God's sake, did the woman have anything else in her life but her daughter?

"No," Laura said. "Yes. No. Maybe." It would be easier to talk about the interview than what was really bothering her. "I met with a guy; he talked about the diagnostic programs. They don't care about how people work there, Mom. They care about how machines work and how machines can fix people, and then they don't have to worry about dirtying themselves by acting like actual human beings." Laura was surprised to hear the anger in her own voice. She hadn't even been this angry after the interview.

"I'm sorry, honey."

"Is that how it is everywhere, Mom? I swear, half my

teachers have the same attitude. Is everyone in the world an asshole?"

"Laura . . ." Her mother's voice suddenly hushed in a tone of admonishment. She could bear the cursing if they were face-to-face, but somehow on cells it always troubled her, as though they were performing for an unseen audience.

"Sorry, Mom," she said by rote. "But I'm finding it really hard to take right now."

"I can see that, honey. Are you in your room?"

"Yeah." It was a tiny, cramped little place, which Laura loved dearly. Her roommate, absent at the moment, left her side as neat as if a maid came through every day. But it echoed her mother's obsessions and left Laura with a sense of home. Her own side was filled with pictures of Mookie — leaping up for a Frisbee, peeking out of his dog house — with a framed arrangement of dried flowers and her father's proud addition to the room, a vintage poster that screamed LET'S GO, METS GO! to cap it off. All of Laura's electronics were hidden away, under the bed, in drawers. They might not have even existed.

"Are you alone?"

"Yeah, Mom." She could hear it coming.

"Well" — her voice went quiet again, as though that would do any good if someone *was* monitoring their cell conversations — "are you having those headaches again?"

"They weren't headaches, Mom," she corrected, already exasperated.

"Well, the episodes."

"They weren't episodes. It was a transient, self-limited loss of consciousness." Always a comfort to retreat into the technical, though it turned her mother's face sour.

"Well, you know what I'm talking about, anyway. Is that happening again?"

Laura took a deep breath in and let it out in a not-quite sigh.

"No," she said, but had paused too long.

"Laura, please tell me the truth. Are you having those flashbacks to high school again?"

"They weren't flashbacks, Mom. I never had any flashbacks. I was—there was confusion about some things in senior year."

"It was more serious than that, Laura. You went to the hospital."

"For *observation,* Mom. And they didn't find anything."

"That's serious. The hospital is serious. You know how your dad and I worry about that."

"You *and* Dad, huh? I have the feeling Dad's managing okay."

"You're changing the subject."

"You noticed."

Her mother stared back at her, silent, through the miniature screen.

"No, Mom, that's not happening again. I'm just, I don't know . . . feeling uneasy about things."

"Like with those episodes."

"They *weren't* episodes. Christ, Mom."

"But like with those things."

"Yes, a little bit. The uneasiness, but without the panic attacks or syncope."

"You speak just like a professional, Laura," her mother said with equal amounts of frustration and pride. "You should come home until it lets up."

"I'm not going to do that."

"Laura, what could it hurt? You could get home by dinner. I'll fix mac and cheese with franks and—"

"That doesn't actually have an effect on brain chemistry, Mom."

Her mother's face fell.

"I'm sorry, Mom. Thank you. I don't . . ." Because no part of the small dorm room was not visible from any other part, Laura saw a small white fold of paper being slipped beneath her door. "It's not that serious." She sat, transfixed by the tiny arrival.

"You should still think about—"

"I'm not coming home, Mom. I'm seeing Josh in twenty

minutes, and I've got a paper due in two days." Laura rose from her bed but stood in place, looking at the note. Why not a text? It would have scrolled right beneath her mother's face, assured instant receipt. Who left actual notes anymore?

"Laura, what's going on?"

Laura's attention snapped back to the cell.

"Nothing. I'm fine."

"Laura. Go see the counselor. Okay?"

"I don't need to see the counselor."

"It helped last time, honey, and if you're not coming home, then at least do that. I know you don't want my help, Laura. That's a way you can help yourself. Please."

Laura was suddenly overwhelmed with a sense of how far away and helpless her mother must feel.

"I love you, Mom," she said softly.

"I love you, too, Laura. So much. Go see the counselor."

"I will."

"Promise."

"I do."

"Okay. Tell Josh I said hello."

"I will. Bye, Mom."

The screen flickered out on her mother's smiling face, leaving behind a scrolling advertisement for soothing, comforting hot chocolate mix.

Without her mother's presence, the room was filled

with Laura's growing unease. And that note wasn't helping. She wished Kari, her roommate, were here, just so someone would be around when she read it.

She walked over and picked up the note and held it, still folded, before her. What the hell was going on with her? It was just a goddamned piece of paper. *Open it.*

She did. A silly, innocuous message; probably slipped under the wrong door for all it meant to Laura. It contained only one sentence:

Where is the Librarian?

ROSE

MAL WOKE FROM A TWITCHING nightmare, his face crusted to the concrete ground with his own vomit, the glints of grim gray light pricking his brain like long needles. He was, by some way of thinking, fortunate to be waking up at all, though fortune felt as foreign to him right now as a smiling face and a warm embrace.

He pulled himself to a sitting position, his stomach somersaulting and the dry matter on his face crumbling into flakes as he winced. The space around him reflected the tone of his thoughts just now: a large room filled with toppled wooden chairs and tables, a forlorn kitchen filled with rusting pots and pans seen through a long galley window. Once it had been a soup kitchen, when such things were allowed in the city. The homeless, though, had been shipped out of the city by ranks of MCT officers in riot gear, shuffled off, and dropped into neighboring cities, into hastily constructed and just as hastily disintegrating camps. City government had mandated a shiny, flawless façade that would present an inviting picture of a hopeful future to its inhabitants. Problems like poverty were more easily denied and coated over with gleaming new surfaces than actually addressed. So, what use were homeless shelters? This one, far past simple abandonment, had been forgotten. Like the forest Mal had once woken in to find himself trapped by a power beyond his understanding, this homeless shelter had been torn out of the memory of Man, interred in the graveyard of the past, lost to everyone. Except Mal.

The walls of concrete and wood were seamed and cracked, long fissures running up to end somewhere Mal couldn't track, and they made him think of the face in the shadows of the monster's lair, its seams and cracks deep and old. The color here was old, too, old and washed out, everything merely suggesting a color; its pigment worn away and inexorably moving toward a disintegrating gray, including the scraps of produce still lying on the kitchen counter, dried and withering like dead plants. Even the light here—

pouring through a crumbling window that no longer contained curtains, pane, or glass—was dim and muffled, a dirty light that fell from muted clouds and felt like old dust on your skin.

Mal wouldn't look up at that sky now. Dim though it may be, its illumination was more than he wished to inflict on his aching brain at the moment. He knew it well, though; knew the muted colors and worn-out texture of this place as well as he knew his own scarred face. This place, places of its kind, had been a second home for nearly a year now. He was used to the sound, too, the way the thrum of traffic and quick *rat-a-tat* of thousands of walking feet blended together and Dopplered into this place in warped waves, one second far away, almost silent, the next second roaring like an angry ocean, louder than it would have been right next to him.

The nightmare he woke from still lingered, the same one he always had. It was his only constant companion in life now, this low-ceilinged dream of a man in a suit trying to drill into his brain.

He pressed his fingers into his temples—slowly, everything felt like it was moving through thick, unyielding syrup—and tried to gouge out the nightmare and the pain along with it, to absolutely no effect whatsoever. He swallowed and blinked and grunted and ran his tongue over the jagged shrapnel of tooth lodged in his soft, bloody gums, and did little things with his body, just to steady himself. It was difficult to focus, particularly on things that happened right before he went out, but he knew they had put something in him, something that would let them keep track of him. That, at least, he could counter. No technology they had could possibly penetrate into here, into a forgotten place. But, he suddenly wondered, was that to his advantage? How would they take it if their means of keeping him under tabs proved worthless as soon as they had let him go? He needed to keep this advantage in reserve, because while he was immediately safe in here, he couldn't stay in here forever. That would mean death, not only for his body, but long before that, death for his spirit, which was slowly worn away every moment he spent in one of these places, just as the surfaces of the building and ground were slowly worn away.

He gave himself another moment before he tried to stand and then, nearly toppling over, sat down again. He did this twice before he overcame the unsteadiness by a sheer refusal to fall, turned the spinning alley and tilting floor into an enemy, and then simply refused to back down from it. He shuffled to the ragged and splintered doorway, and—bracing himself for the more intense light, the more intense world of input—he stepped out.

The world roared into life around him and, again, almost knocked him backwards. He held himself with a powerful but trembling arm against a wall. People streamed by, not a single one sparing him a glance away from their cells or the images their cellenses were transmitting into their eyes. The flawlessly polished window of a gourmet coffee superstore incongruously reflected his ruin of a face back at him.

There was only one place for him, one person for him to go to. Putting her in danger made his blood boil hot, knowing they were tracking him wherever he went now. But the woman, Kliest, knew about her already. So going to her would not be putting her in any more jeopardy.

How to get there, though? With about five bucks in his pocket, he couldn't get a cab, and he stayed clear of the shiny silver subway stations patrolled by the MCT. It was moot, since barely anyone took cash anymore, anyway. He steadied himself to begin what promised to be a grueling walk across town, when a shadow fell across his path and halted there.

"Mal, are you all right?" asked a person he'd never seen before, a plump woman with frizzy hair, pushing a baby carriage. He squinted into her eyes briefly, collecting himself.

"Yes."

"What did they do to you?"

"Gave me a job."

"What? What do you mean?" the woman asked as the

baby in the carriage studied Mal upside down and kicked its legs energetically.

"How did you find me?" Mal questioned the unfamiliar woman, squinting down at the innocent, unspoiled little human like it was an alien creature.

"I saw them pick you up but couldn't follow. I waited, and they dropped you back."

"You've been watching me."

"I . . ." The plump face could not seem to decide how to end that sentence, so Mal gathered himself and began shuffling away.

"Mal," she said a moment later. "Can I help you?"

"No." He took another two steps before he realized how limited his options really were. "Wait." He turned slowly, oblivious crowds spinning around him, around both of them. "I need a cab ride."

The plump woman opened her purse and scoured through it as though its recesses were alien to her. After a moment she produced a wallet and then slipped from that a credit card, which she studied cursorily before looking up to hail a taxi.

She watched while Mal lowered himself heavily into the back seat. The driver and the woman both looked at Mal expectantly.

"Use the card," he said, not prepared to part with the address yet.

The woman, understanding what her role was to be, used the laser scanner in back to flash the card.

"Mal, if you would let me help, maybe we could—"

"You've helped." Mal used what he had left to close the door and tell the driver where to go.

As the taxi slid back into the flow of traffic, Mal watched the woman tarry at the curb, then suddenly tilt her head as if caught in the middle of a daydream and look down and notice the stroller as though for the first time. She put her hands on it and pushed it away, joining the crowd.

The façade of the apartment was a clean white, the windows reflecting sparkling light on their tinted surface. Only if you were close enough and peered in could you see that they were barred on the inside. Indeed, as Mal fumbled the key from his pocket with clumsy fingers and pushed in, surface was all the building had going for it. Inside, the hall was filthy and stank of something sour and old, airing the decaying lie beneath the pleasant veneer. The elevator was pitted and scratched as though a war had been fought within its claustrophobic confines, and it rattled angrily as it rode up.

The hallway was lined with rusting doors, many of them roughly etched with nicknames, comments, or offenses, two or three twisted and scored at the locks and slightly ajar. He used the key to open the door and nearly tumbled into the tiny, dim apartment.

He lowered himself onto the cot in one corner, leaning his back against the cold concrete of the wall. He was grateful for the tint of the Plexiglas window, which dimmed the light that stabbed into his pounding eyes. Even so, he could see the tight forest of buildings, their surfaces perfectly crisp and welcoming, which opened some few blocks away to make space for the dome. Gleaming silver, it caught the light around it, glowing like some alien spacecraft. Rising behind it were the proud Lazarus Towers, five black points reaching up like a hand trying to tear God from the heavens. In the dome's reflective surface, the buildings warped into a skewed world of barely recognizable curves and spires.

That was what he was staring at when he finally let himself go.

The quiet noise of movement nearby stirred him, but trapped in a state of groggy near-consciousness, Mal had to jab his tongue down hard onto the raw, bloody pulp of his jagged tooth to bring himself fully awake.

In the darkness, a girl moved about, her desire not to wake him clear in the tension and calculated movements of her body. It was dark out now, though the sounds of the city never slowed or wavered. He checked his muscles, flexing them slowly, one group at a time. He burned with pain in many areas, and his head still felt as though someone were leaning on a vise they'd affixed to it. There were things on his body, adhesive bandages over the worst abrasions on his chest, his face, his arms. She'd bandaged him while he slept. Of course she had. It was a wonder she could tell the new from the old, his body an homage to damaged flesh: the scar across the bridge of his nose, the rough flesh on his forearms and elbows, the deep discolorations that old bruises had left on his torso, the mad frenzy of interlaced scar tissue across his knuckles.

"Thank you," he said, and his voice sounded soft and mushy to him.

The girl stiffened and looked through the dark, then came to the cot and turned on a small lamp on the floor. She leaned into the hazy glow. Her eyes were obscured by thick locks of shaggy hair that she wore like a mask.

"Mal," she said, her voice dense with his suffering, though it always issued so quietly you needed to listen as if to a whisper. "What did they do to you?"

"It's complicated."

She put her hand gently on the side of his face and held it there, casting the barely visible slivers of her eyes into his own.

"We're going to need to get you away from here, Rose," he said, pushing himself up on an elbow and coming to a seated position, with her help.

The question passed across her uncertain features, taking time as it always did to work its way to her mouth.

"This wasn't bare knuckles down in the park, was it?"

"No."

"What's going on?"

He let his eyes close, touched the bandage on his face.

"People want something from me."

"Give it to them," she said plainly.

"I don't have it."

"But they won't accept that, will they?"

"No. Which is why you have to go."

Beneath her mask of hair, her lips shifted into a smile. It was a smile that recognized futility. *Go? Go where?* Would she be here at all if she had any choice?

"I'm going to take you somewhere safe," he said.

"And then what?"

"I'm going to get what they want."

She looked down. Partially visible, her fragile, anguished features held no doubt at all.

"But you're not going to give it to them, are you?"

The darkness pressed in on them, held back only by the meager glow of the tiny lamp.

"No."

JOSH

LAURA WALKED THROUGH THE SERENE, vaulted stacks of the university library, coming out before the grand windows with the stained-glass designs on top. Between two such windows sat the reference desk, a small island of directed knowledge among all this free-floating information.

She went up to it and took the seat at the side. A tall man with a snappy bow tie turned his glasses on her.

"Hi," she said quietly, "I think I got a message to see the librarian."

"Which librarian?" he asked at a normal volume, which

almost made Laura wince at the way it seemed to create an explosion of sound in this still place.

"Uh, didn't say."

"How did you receive the note?"

"Under my door." It sounded ridiculous when she said it out loud.

"Your door." His eyebrows raised, and the way the light caught him, it gave him the appearance of a sly cat. "Well, official notifications are voice-texted. Someone sent you a paper note?" He said it as though it was the set up for a joke.

She reached into her pocket and produced the slip and handed it over.

"This notice didn't come from the library," he informed her. "In fact, it doesn't even call on you to see a librarian, really."

"No," Laura said. "I kind of figured all that. It's just that, well, this is where all the librarians are."

"Yes," he said, and proffered the note with the tips of his thumb and forefinger and then sat looking at her.

"Sooo . . ." She drew out the syllable. "I guess I don't need to be here."

He continued looking at her.

"Okay, thanks." She rose and began to walk away when the boom of his voice caught her.

"'Librarian' is capitalized in your note."

JESSE KARP

"I'm sorry?"

"'The Librarian.' Capital *L*." He was looking at his computer as he spoke, already casting off the exchange. "Like it's not just *a* librarian, but *the* Librarian."

She looked at the note again. It was true. She had assumed it was an idiosyncrasy of the author's grammar, to the extent she'd considered it at all, and this dude struck her as a bit of stickler, but it was true. And so what if it was? Why was she wasting her time on this, anyway?

"Thanks," she said, and he nodded, already off on another adventure.

Josh was waiting for her in the café, seated with a large Coke in front of him and a sweating glass of iced tea with lemon across from him. She spotted him immediately, despite the fact that his eyes were hidden beneath black cellenses and the stem of the glasses obscured the scar down his cheek. She walked over and stopped directly in front him, and he remained immersed in the internal world created by his new toy.

"Hi," she said, "thanks for the tea." She sat down and stared across the table into his face, and it took another moment before she realized he still had no idea she was here.

"*Hello.*" She slapped him on the hand, and he jolted as if someone had jumped out of an alley at him.

"Whoa," he said, removing the lenses. "Sorry, Button, didn't see you. You could just say 'hi' like a normal person."

"I did, actually."

"Oh. Sorry. I got you an iced tea," he finished brightly, fixing one of those good smiles on his kisser.

She took a sip and regarded him silently.

"So, uh, how's your mom?" he asked.

"Worried, as usual."

"Uh-huh. And, uh . . . how are you?"

"What do you mean?"

"Well, you seem kind of—I don't know—off?"

"Annoyed, you mean?"

"Yeah, that would be another way to put it. Remember before when you were all, like, happy to see me?"

Laura's shoulders relaxed, and a smile escaped from the tension in her jaw.

"I'm sorry," she said, and reached out to squeeze his hand.

"Your mom set you off?"

"No. She said . . . nothing. It's nothing."

"Laura." He added a sideways glance to the smile. "You're gonna tell me eventually."

"There's nothing to tell. Seriously."

He gulped at his Coke, clearly dubious.

"Hey," she said, perking up, "what do you know about librarians?"

"Uh, they always want to charge me fines?"

"Nice. What else?"

"Books, research, old, musty, glasses . . ." His eyes searched around his head for a couple more. "Oh, yeah. Quiet. How could I forget that one?"

"Do you know any famous librarians?" she asked. "Or really important ones?"

"Seriously? What are we talking about exactly?"

"Just go with me."

"Okay. Uh, wasn't, like, Benjamin Franklin a librarian or something?"

"Was he?"

"I don't know, Laura, I'm trying to go with you here." He took another gulp of his drink, slightly miffed.

"I bet your new toy knows."

"You want me to look?" He sat up straighter, interested that she was maybe coming around to it.

"Yeah."

She watched him clip the lenses back on.

"Whoa, hey, I was right," he said almost immediately. "He founded something called the Library Company of Philadelphia, and he—"

"What about other famous librarians?" she asked, feeling something bubbling and urgent in her stomach suddenly.

"Lemme look," Josh said, and as he did, Laura watched his fine, strong face, as its identity was weirdly scoured away by the lenses. His lips moved gently and then stopped, and something left his face altogether. Maybe it was a tension in the muscles, but if so, it was tension that was supposed to be there, a set to the jaw line, a sense of animation in the expression. It left, like it had been sucked out of his eyes through those goddamned lenses.

"Look up Librarian with a capital *L*," she said sharply, something harsher than mere urgency in her now.

"Uh, yeah, it doesn't differentiate between lower- and uppercase, Button."

"Put it in quotes, Josh. Jesus, have you ever actually *done* any research?"

"Hey, chill out, Laura. What's the problem? I'll put it in quotes." He defended himself nominally, but his expression had not returned and his voice sounded subdued to her, as if he were speaking to her from behind a curtain, from another place altogether.

She had to clench her fists to keep herself from tearing the things from his face, and she didn't know why.

"There's a bunch of random stuff here, Laura. Beginnings of sentences and stuff. It doesn't really refer to anyone specifically, you know? Laura?"

He unclipped the lenses and looked across at an empty seat. He blinked and craned his neck to take in the whole café. Laura was gone.

Laura sat on her bed fuming, her arms hugging her knees, her forehead pressed down on her kneecaps, her entire body tight. Irritability growing into unreasoning anger was not an unfamiliar symptom to her. Her "episodes"—as her mother so charmingly put it—had begun that way. Those had been brought on by a fixation in her senior year of high school. Now, though libraries and librarians had no special bearing on that time of her life, she could feel the more extreme symptoms of her episodes sniffing around her delicate psyche. She ignored the bleat of her cell, chiming from where she'd kicked it under her bed. Ten minutes after it had given up, there was a knock on her door.

"Go away," she said into her thighs.

The knock came again.

"Fucking fuck," she hissed, and got up and flung the door open. She turned her back before she could take in Josh's slackened jaw and confused eyes. She stormed back to the bed and huddled herself into the same position. She heard the door close and Josh come over and stand there, dumbfounded.

"I'm sorry," she said without looking up. "It's not you."

"Uh, yeah, I know. Cuz, like, I didn't do anything except what you asked. Is it the cellenses? I mean, jeez, I could—"

Laura looked up; her luminous blue eyes were blazing, and tears moistened their edges.

"No," she said. "I don't *know* what it is. Do you *get* that?"

He stared down at her silently for a moment longer and then sat down and wrapped his strong arms around her. At first she remained stiff, but when he didn't let go, she rolled into him and, without returning his embrace, let him take her weight.

"I'm sorry," he said, for no reason other than he knew it fixed things sometimes.

"*I'm* sorry, Josh. It's my fault. It's bringing back some stuff." And then, shaky, "Stuff I thought I was through with."

"Are we going to talk about that stuff?" He invited as casually as he could.

"No." She may have been shaky, but her response was definite.

He held her in the quiet room, expecting there might be hard tears. But they just sat like that, for minutes.

"So, just what the hell did your mother say to you?"

Laura laughed harshly.

"She gave me some advice. And I'm going to take it."

Laura sat on the big, plush yellow sofa chair across from the neatly dressed girl in an office chair. In a sense, Laura was looking into her own future. Having already declared her psychology major and intending to follow up her degree with postgraduate work, it wasn't more than four or five years before she was going to be sitting on the other side, looking at a young freshman come to pour out her anxieties.

The office, in the basement of the student services building, was carefully modulated to present a tone of informal but caring concern. A trickle of light poured in from the high window, illuminating the small bouquet of geraniums, chosen to evoke neither thoughts of death (lilies) or romance (roses), two primary reasons a distraught college student might show up for free counseling. There was a teddy bear on the secondhand wooden shelf with all the worn psychology texts, and by the clock on the desk was a small base into which you could easily slide in or remove a nameplate. The one there now read TERRI.

"How are you doing, Laura?" Terri smiled softly, and it was the element that completed this bizarre feeling Laura had of entering a performance.

"I've been better," she said, settling in.

"How are classes?"

"Classes are fine," Laura responded. "It's my boyfriend." She regretted it instantly. "Sort of."

"A breakup?"

"No, no. Nothing like that. It's not my boyfriend, really. It's . . . he's more like the focus of something else. Something's getting me down, and I'm putting it on him. I guess."

"All right," Terri adjusted her steel-rimmed glasses. Her hair was pulled into tight braids, and she wore a blouse and slacks, working hard to kill her looks and appear professional. "What's your boyfriend's name?"

"Josh," Laura said, with a strange quaver in her voice that she hadn't put there intentionally. Taking the cue, Terri twitched a smile, trying out a touch of female camaraderie, and pushed ahead.

"College is a different experience than high school, and relationships can grow and deepen, and sometimes it can be scary. Do you feel serious about Josh?"

Laura stared back at her, struck dumb with the realization that she didn't know the answer.

"Do you feel serious about him, and that's not familiar to you?" Terri offered.

"No. I know what a serious relationship feels like."

"So, Josh isn't your first serious boyfriend?"

Except he was, really, if you were going to get right down to it. There had been Ari, of course, but she refused to count that douchebag. And her senior year of high school — the second half of it, anyway — she could look back on, pick out certain memories, but she could not make a smooth narrative of them. Individual memories floated about, but when she tried to arrange them relative to one another, they wouldn't hold. She would get trapped in an endless maze with no exit, chasing through those memories for . . . *something* that was always an inch out of her grasp, a blur on the edge of her vision. But it had become a compulsion; she couldn't stop herself. This was what had led to the anger, the panic attacks, and finally the syncope, or loss of consciousness — it had proven a cold comfort that she could diagnose it herself.

"Josh is my first serious boyfriend," Laura admitted to Terri. "But I . . ." — she was parsing it out as she spoke the words — "already know what serious feels like. I . . . already know."

"Like recognizing the taste of something and not remembering when you tasted it before?" Terri suggested.

"No." She was immediately certain. "No, not like that. Like recognizing the taste of something but knowing that you've *never* tasted it before. I don't remember it, but I *feel* it."

"Memories can fool us," Terri said.

"We're made of our memories," Laura said, something rising from deep inside her. "We *are* them. If I can't trust my memories, who am I?"

"It can happen to any of us," Terri said, catching a whiff of something much deeper here than she had expected. "But I can see how it would leave you feeling confused."

"I'm *not* confused," Laura said heatedly.

"I'm sorry, Laura. Why don't you tell me how you feel?"

"Angry." Laura shook her head to cancel that response. She searched inside her skull for the answer, and she realized in a revelatory flash that that was the very problem. She didn't know exactly what she was feeling, not now and not months ago when she'd had her "episodes." She wasn't being made to feel angry. She didn't know what she was feeling, and *that* made her angry. Laura's eyes rolled up to the ceiling, and her head swung back and forth, the muscles in her neck cording with the tension of trying to delineate the phantom emotion. It was something weird swirling inside her, an untouchable ghost that was always at the corner of her mind's eye, poking and prodding, but never in front of her where she could grab it and hold it.

Or not.

Again a small revelatory shudder.

Not like a ghost. Not like something swirling. Like nothing. Like a huge hole right in the middle of her. No wonder she had chased through that maze of memories, never able to grasp what she was looking for. What she had sensed there was nothing at all.

"Empty," Laura said, almost a sob — not of sorrow, but of relief. "I feel empty."

Terri nodded again, clearly somewhat relieved herself.

"Is this something you're picking up from Josh? Do you feel like the relationship is empty?"

"Josh isn't empty," Laura said. "I am."

But Josh was empty. It felt like the floor was dropping out from under her when she realized it. Josh was a person, of course, perfectly kind and warm. But she was using him to fill the emptiness, and it wasn't working, at least not anymore. So he *was* empty, empty to her.

It was all crashing down on her here, even though she had felt silly coming into the free clinic, like she was above it, too smart for it. Apparently, what she needed was the context, and maybe even a little gentle prodding from Terri.

Terri was saying something else, but Laura just stood up, her face a dazed mask.

"I'm ready to go now," Laura told her.

"Are you okay, Laura?" Terri asked with unveiled concern. "What just happened for you?"

"I realized why I came." She looked up at Terri. "But thank you. You got me where I needed to go."

"Um, all right. Are you sure you're okay?"

"We'll see." She came to the door and stopped and turned. "Hey. Do you know any famous librarians?"

"I'm sorry?"

"Any famous librarians."

"Not really," Terri said after a brief thought. "Why do you ask?"

"Oh, I just got a weird note about a librarian a couple of days ago."

"From Josh?"

"No," Laura said, perplexed. Why would Josh send her a note about librarians?

"Oh. Who sent it? Maybe they know."

"Who sent it?" Laura echoed, poised at the door.

"That seems like the natural question," Terri said.

Yes. Yes, it did seem like the natural question, didn't it?

SILVEN

ROSE WATCHED MAL FIGHT HIS nightmares. There was no rest for him even in sleep. The muscles in his face danced, deepening his scowl. Low grunts and snarls escaped as he wrestled them until, sweating, he roused himself.

His dark head—short black hair, dark eyes, brooding countenance—pulled slowly upward, followed by his powerful torso, slim at the waist, wide at the muscular shoulders, like a *V* of swelling strength, until he sat on the edge of the cot, minutely swaying. His arms were shot with veins and hard muscles, his torso packed solid and flat.

But for Rose, what always kept her attention rapt were the scars.

The scars were Mal's living history, a road map of where he'd been and what he'd done wrong, and to Rose, they were a constant fascination not for what they revealed about him — he seldom accounted for any of them — but that they were evidence he had a history at all. He had dropped into her life fully formed, without a clear past, and what she'd learned about him in the time since was that he might as well have existed in the world itself the same way: without real identity, without acknowledgment that he was a person who had done things, been registered in places, had ever been known by anyone else.

The cords and planes of muscle flexed instinctively in his recovering body; she realized she was fascinated by the imperfections because they seemed to make him more powerful still. They painted an image of a boy leaning into a fierce wind, pushing through a whirlwind of sharp, flying debris all his life, and managing to move slowly forward despite it.

"Breakfast," she said to him, nodding with her chin at the aluminum lumps sitting on the cracked table by the bed.

His eyes took them in bleakly, and, as though facing

up to an unpleasant necessity, he straightened his body and took the food.

Two huge hamburgers dripping with cheese, from the greasy old kitchen where she worked until early mornings, came out of the bag. He wolfed them down, wincing whenever a bite made its way to the right side of his jaw. The pain was enough to make the stoic face grimace, but it was not enough to slow down consumption, and in less than two minutes, both burgers were gone.

Sometimes she watched him work his body: pushups, crunches, shadowboxing, isometrics until his body was covered in glistening sweat and his muscles trembled as if minor earthquake tremors were running up and down his body. And still he pushed himself on, all the while his face flat, his eyes always brooding. Such effort, such commitment, never released outward. She watched him work his body, she watched him struggle with his nightmares, she studied the flat face and the brooding eyes, and she knew that something had reached inside of Mal and pulled something integral out of him, leaving a gaping hole where his will to reach out to other people — to *her* — should have been. What, she spent many restless hours unable to sleep wondering, had pulled it out of him? What had it left behind?

He blinked now, as if the eating the hamburgers had

left him in a daze, and before he could ask, Rose pulled a tall bottle of water out of the rickety miniature fridge that always hummed too loudly. He drank down half the thing, came up for air, and finished off the rest, wires of blood stretching from his mouth into the water as it quickly disappeared. Then, finally, he looked at her with something that resembled full awareness.

"Nightmares again," she said. It was not a question but an invitation; one that was, as usual, roundly ignored. She adjusted. "You're not squinting anymore."

"It's dark here."

"Still."

"Better. It's better." To prove it, he stood slowly and straightened himself without using a wall to lean on, then held himself up in place, towering over her, cross-legged on the dirty floor.

"Are we going somewhere?"

"Not yet."

She chewed on that for a moment. She hadn't been completely sure he was lucid when he spoke of taking her somewhere, had hoped in asking just now that he wouldn't even know what she was talking about.

"Why not now?" she asked, not wanting to seem as though she was resisting the idea.

"I think . . ." — he searched inside his own skull — "some things are going to happen first."

"What things?"

He was pacing slowly from one end of the small, cold room to the other, reacquainting himself with his own equilibrium. His slight limp — he'd had it since she knew him — was heavier now.

"You need some sleep," he said.

He was putting her off, but she was exhausted. She always came back from work that way. Whatever else they were waiting for, she couldn't possibly guess. It was certain they weren't waiting for him to get the medical attention he needed. He'd come home bloody and barely on his feet before and never did any more than sleep it off.

She came to her knees and reached aching arms to the cot and slithered into bed. The last thing she saw before she closed her eyes was Mal taking a gentle jab at his shadow and nearly falling over backwards.

Rose's eyes came open, and she only realized a knock on the door had woken her because Mal's face was turned toward the door, his body frozen halfway through a pushup. His body, supported by knuckles on the rough concrete, tightened.

She sat up and waited with him. Instead of the second knock she was expecting, though, a voice sliced sharply through the door.

"Open it, Mal."

She watched Mal bring himself to his feet with a muffled groan and, again, sway briefly, before stepping forward and opening the two locks that held the metal door closed.

When Mal had slurred out the bit about the people who wanted him to find something, Rose had imagined a loose-knit gang of the sort he routinely faced down in the park: kids, dirty and mean-looking, flunkies of some psychotic twenty-year-old drug dealer who fancied himself a mastermind.

The two men on the other side of the door were dressed in rich, dark blue suits more expensive than Rose's apartment and all the others on the same floor. But while the suits fit the men like they'd been stitched around them, the men did not really fit the suits. Their faces were blunt, unsubtle, harsh; one wore thick white bandages on his nose and had a red and black bruise under one eye that made part of his face look like raw meat. The muscles of their arms, torsos, and legs were so thick, it looked as though their flesh had been packed with liquid metal.

The one in front, the one with a steel-gray crew cut and

no bandages on his face, took a step in, but Mal didn't move from his spot. In nothing but his cargo pants, and almost a full head shorter even at his impressive height, Mal looked like a child blocking a steamroller.

"How's your head, Mal?" the one in back asked, the one with the bandages, in a tone of warning meant to move him. Naturally, it didn't.

"You disappeared off our grid for about an hour right after we let you go, Mal," the gray one said, and his voice was quiet and toneless. This was all just a business meeting to him. "We've got to put another one in you. Is that going to be difficult for us, Mal?"

Mal said nothing and didn't move.

"For all of us?" the bandaged one said, and his sleepy eyes fell on Rose. Rose pushed herself farther onto the bed, until her back met the cold, rough wall.

Without a word, Mal stepped back into the room, never turning his front from them. They came in, the second one closing the door behind them and locking it up. The gray man scanned the hateful concrete prison they lived in without judgment. If business called him to a five-star restaurant or into a sewer, Rose was sure his expression didn't change. The half-lidded eyes of the other one took the tactical parameters of the place in and locked them into his brain.

The gray one produced a slim silver case from inside his jacket and popped it open. His rough fingers drew a delicate hypodermic from it, and after slipping the case away, his hand whipped out—not with antagonism but not to be refused or avoided—and caught Mal's bicep.

Mal didn't flinch, stood unmoving as the needle sank into the flesh between his shoulder and neck, but Rose had never imagined such hostility could come from an unmoving figure. Even from behind, she could see Mal's entire body set with aggression.

The operation concluded, the needle went back into the case, and the case disappeared.

"Ms. Kliest is concerned, Mal," the gray one said. "You haven't moved since you got here."

"You gave me a concussion."

"Yes. Sorry about that." The business face didn't change. "But you only have two days left."

"I have some ideas," Mal said.

They stood in the room like cowboys about to slap down for their guns. The shorter one stared hard at Mal with cruel invitation.

"All right, then. I guess we'll see you soon." When the gray man said it, the shorter one opened the locks and stepped out into the hall. The gray man took a step backwards, then spun neatly, militarily, on his heel and walked out. The shorter one reached back in, leered wolfishly at Mal, and swung the door closed.

Mal stood still for a full minute, then locked the door. He went to the window and leaned on the edge and rested his head on the bars as he looked down into the street through the tinted glass.

"Do you really?" Rose asked after the silence had held too long for her.

"Really what?" Mal said, turning to her.

"Really have some ideas?"

"Yes," he said, and lifted his hooded sweatshirt from the floor and pulled it over his solid frame, which did not seem to take up quite as much space as it had before those other two paraded through.

"I'll come with you," she said, rising from the bed.

"That's"—he looked down to slip his feet into his sneakers and then back up—"not a good idea."

Rose stood across from him, quiet in the semi-dark. She watched him swaying, like he was balanced on the edge of a precipice. Through the camouflage of her hair, her eyes found his and held.

"Come on," he said, turning toward the door.

Mal walked them through the city with what appeared to be no goal. They stopped in a datacafé for ten minutes, went into a store, and moved through aisles of cell upgrades for twenty minutes, then sat down in a quiet courtyard abutting a corporate tower until after half an hour Rose roused Mal from the bench he had nodded off on.

He looked around himself and blinked at the aggravating sunlight that the high windows beamed down into the courtyard.

"That should be enough," he said. It had all been to confuse the people who were tracking him, she realized, to camouflage his real destination. He stood up and led her away, his limp exacerbated further by the downtime. He wouldn't go into the subway, despite her suggestions. They walked.

Midtown gleamed, the tall pinpoint towers reflected both in the mirrored surfaces of their neighbors and in the dark lenses of the thick crowds clogging the streets. Every third or fourth person here was wearing cellenses, doing business in the privacy of their own heads, instinctively dodging others caught up in the same distraction. Mal held his place, an unyielding stone in the midst of a flowing river. He stared hard across the street at the glass and chrome façade of a particular building. To Rose's eye, it differed in no particular way from those around it: tinted glass windows and doors, mirrored chrome frames, the address built up sculpturally over the door. Two plants were set on either side of the door, some kind of homage to the idea that actual living things were good, or at least looked pretty sometimes. Two women perched on one, eating their lunches and gazing out at the crowds in dull silence. At the other, a man finished his cigarette and stubbed it out in the soil.

Rose had known Mal long enough now to see that his reaction to this building was inexplicably extreme. There was a strain in his shoulders and jaw that, on anyone else, Rose might have attributed to fear. Mal did not want to go into that building.

"Are you sure what you need is there?" she asked him. Her voice, even amidst the din of the streets, was little more than a whisper. Somehow, he always heard her.

He turned to her with the eyes of someone lost in a memory.

"Mal?" she prodded. Staring right at her, he seemed to not be there at all. She reached over and put her warm hand around his, and his eyes immediately flooded with their dark, guarded life; then he flinched his hand away as if stung.

He turned and marched across the street, a soldier going to his death. She hurried to catch up, weaving between the cars that he simply ignored. At the doors, he stopped. The reflection of his face showed nothing, but he stood before the doors unmoving until, finally, they opened and disgorged a group of men in suits, who blew past them as though they were invisible. As the door closed, Mal's eyes flickered over the sights within.

"It's just a lobby," he said, and she was not sure he was speaking to her at all.

He gripped the handle, and as if it were an action requiring some massive exertion, he set his body and pulled.

The door opened into the cool, regulated air of what was, indeed, a lobby. They stepped onto light blue tiles with silver swirls, an ocean of them covering the entire massive atrium. Elevator banks opened up on either side; small snack shops were built into the walls, each with a uniform appearance and interspersed with HDs, advertisements, and stock reports marching along the top and bottom of each screen. At the center, down a short flight of stairs, was a gurgling fountain that felt somehow even more artificial than the lobby around it. This was a place built out of profit and trade. A body of water in the midst of it was a comment on how insignificant nature really was. *Yes, remember water? Quaint, little nature? Here's a little bit of it to amuse you.*

Directly before them was a high desk, with three big men in dark blue blazers sitting behind it. Even though all three had dark cellenses covering their eyes, it was not difficult to tell who they were looking at.

Rose felt cold and hollow when even casual eyes found her. She squirmed under the scrutiny and looked at Mal, who was oblivious to the attention. He was taking in every detail of the bland, empty artifice of the place.

"I believe you're in the wrong building," said one of the three men. Mal was in cargo pants and an old, hooded sweatshirt. Rose was in jeans and a T-shirt, huddled in a worn leather jacket two sizes too large for her. Every single other person in the lobby was wearing a suit.

Mal looked at the man squarely and stepped forward.

"A man outside, down the block," Mal said. "He's yelling at people about how oil is destroying us. He's got some spray cans."

The man's clear suspicion of them clicked into a different gear, as he yielded to his allotted role. How else could it be, Rose realized. His stiff face, his plastic eyes. The man was a robot, programmed for specific duties. Mal apparently knew how to reprogram him.

The man rose, as did another of the three, and they hurried from around the desk toward the doors. The third man's attention was hyperfocused inside his cellenses, and he started speaking into the air.

Rose moved forward, impelled by Mal's strong hand on her back, not fast, but not slowly. She saw the small black globes on the ceiling, cameras capturing them so that when this proved to be a false alarm, their images could be studied.

They stepped into an elevator with a small group of people who might have been curious about them if they had bothered to notice them at all, but each was trapped in his or her own private conversation, one of them disclosing hideously private details of his marriage, as though he were sitting in the privacy of his home.

Mal's hand came out, and his finger hovered over the single button at the top of the rows, the button for the top floor, and then pressed it.

The mirrored doors opened onto a cool hallway, all waves of blue and silver, like a stylized ocean. The waves swooshed to the end of the hallway, where the space opened into a suite of offices, a curving desk carrying the same blue and silver motif. An icily beautiful woman with precise features, cellenses, and a stiff sculpture of brown hair crowning her head sat beneath swooshing silver letters that read SILVEN ASSOCIATES.

Mal walked toward the desk, and Rose kept pace two steps behind.

"Can I . . ."—a perceptible pause emphasized the receptionist's distaste—"help you?"

Mal gave no indication of offense nor, in fact, of the woman herself, as he blew directly by her and around toward the rows of silver and blue offices.

"Excuse me," the woman's voice became shriller. "I'm calling security," she warned as Mal disappeared from her view. Rose, trailing just behind him, glanced back helplessly at her.

Rose was at once intimidated by the perfection of the space — the flawless design, the spotless tiles, the calm lighting, the luxurious couches and coffee tables in the central waiting area, the perfectly balanced climate — and weirdly disgusted by the astonishing expenditure of money on something of such sheer artifice. The cost of a single lush couch or streamlined glass and chrome coffee table could have put her in a better apartment for a year. And all to create the illusion that everything was under control, that the world was in perfect order.

Which it clearly was not, as first one, then two, then four heads turned or poked out from office doors. You could see by the flat restrained expressions that Mal and Rose were as unwelcome here as a foul smell; vulgar, sweaty reality invading the sealed-off world of privilege.

Mal stopped dead in the middle of a small open lounge space and looked around at nothing in particular.

"Who are you looking for, sir?" A young man in neat gray slacks and a crisp white shirt had deigned to remove his cellenses and was addressing Mal.

Mal turned toward him and took a step forward, causing the man to flinch back as though dodging a punch. But Mal walked right by him to meet a phalanx of men in blue blazers stepping out from the front and arraying itself before him. Was one of them the man from downstairs that Mal had lied to? With their cellenses, standard outfits, and flat, expressionless faces, it was impossible to tell.

Mal, of course, did not slow his progress. His limp grew more pronounced as his body tensed. He was intending to plow right into them, ignite an explosion when all they wanted him to do was leave.

"Mal," Rose said, her face going red as attention turned on her. "Don't." She could barely bring herself to speak now that people were looking at her. But Mal was in no condition to fight. Two days ago, she had bandaged wounds on him that would have sent other people speeding to the hospital, if not straight to a morgue. But he wasn't slowing. He just was not built to register any other choice.

The men tensed, the outside two beginning to circle around, to catch Mal between four points. Mal's hands came up. The front two men began to glide forward.

"There will be absolutely none of that in here," a voice from down the hall cut across the scene so sharply that everybody froze and all eyes shot to the source.

A young man radiating confidence from his platinum hair to his quiet, evaluating eyes to his firm jaw and gym-sculpted body beneath a rich black suit stood at the end of the hall, waiting for the world to fall into place properly.

"Mr. Silven," the receptionist explained breathlessly from behind the phalanx of frozen men. "They walked in unannounced."

Silven's eyes were already on Mal, picking him apart like an equation. Mal was looking back, unimpressed but curious, as if there was something about Silven's appearance that was not patently clear, like there was something Mal was looking for just beneath the surface.

"Well"—Silven's tone seemed enough to put the room at ease—"let's rectify this without damaging any of the furniture, shall we? Young man, why don't you come into my office?"

The calm that encompassed the room was immediately replaced by confounded concern.

"Mr. Silven?" a voice went out.

"Sir?" said one of the men in blue.

"This way, if you please." Silven beckoned Mal to the office at the end of the hall, and his eyes encompassed Rose as well.

Mal straightened, having apparently found what he was

looking for in Silven, and he walked over. Rose, caught frozen in the confusion, shook herself free an instant later and hurried after him.

They entered an expansive office that carried the silver and blue motif in from the outer halls. The wall-size window here afforded a view between the mirrored forest and onto the city itself, straight down to the gleaming dome many blocks away and the needles of the five-spired Lazarus Towers behind it. A plaque outside the door read ALAN R. SILVEN III, CEO.

Silven closed the door behind him and, without sitting down at his intimidating desk or even taking another step into the carpeted room, spoke quietly.

"Mal," he said in an urgent tone, "why did you come here, of all places?"

Mal looked around him somberly and dropped heavily on a leather couch near a bar in the wall. Rose could see that the journey here had depleted the last of his resources. He was struggling just to keep his eyes open. Rose herself was struggling to remain hyperaware, to gather every word they said and parse some meaning from all of this.

"Maybe the same reason you did. I needed to see that it wasn't here anymore," Mal said, plunging things even more deeply into mystery.

"It's not," Silven said. "Of course it's not. This isn't

even the same building. They put this up afterward. It's just what it looks like: concrete, glass, metal. Nothing else."

Mal nodded slowly.

"You knew that," Silven pressed, "as well as I did. Why are you here now?" Mal didn't look up at him, just leaned back in the sofa and closed his eyes. Silven's own eyes, unadorned by cellenses — though the metallic button of a cellpatch protruded near his ear — searched Mal's figure with sharp, mathematical precision. It was a meticulous precision, Rose realized, that did not exactly fit the surface polish.

"Mal?" he said.

"He's had it kind of hard lately, Mr. Silven." Rose's voice sounded like a thunder crack in her own ears.

Silven looked up at her as if stumbling on an entirely new piece of the equation all at once.

"My name isn't Silven, Rose," he said to her. "It's Remak. Jon Remak. And I'd very much like to help you."

ARI

EARLY IN HER SENIOR YEAR of high school, Laura's boyfriend had been Ari. Never had there been such an absolute, total, *professional* douche as Ari. Big and sleek, with the hard, streamlined physique of a track and field athlete, Ari had bright blond hair with a steel earring riveted in his ear, a quiet smile, and a low voice that never lost control. He appeared an extremely confident, tightly controlled guy. Having lost her virginity only at the end of eleventh grade, Laura was still in the throes of discovering what made sex good and what could make it better. She liked the idea of Ari's apparent discipline and control, and, some two months into their relationship, she found herself comfortable enough to take things to that level. Ari had a quiet enthusiasm for it and energy that he had earned by cutting all those math classes to put extra time in on the track. Best of all, as a result of that tightly bound self-control, he seemed only too happy to let Laura take the lead. Until . . .

Until the day he brought her home while his parents were gone for the weekend and they found their way into his mom and dad's huge king-size bed, and as she lay there, naked, he mysteriously excused himself for a minute and returned with his track-mate, Mike—no, not Mike, *Mark*. Where had Mike come from? Mark was slim as a razor, with a nervous twitch on his lips and a hazy look in his eyes. He had a jumpy energy and his speech was slightly slurred, and while he undressed, Ari came over to a stunned Laura, kissed her gently on the check, and spoke in that quiet, always controlled voice.

"Enjoy it," he said. "I'm just going to watch."

Naked, Laura came out from under the covers, slapped Ari across the face so hard that the echo of it rang off the bed frame and the lamps, and she blew right past the confused and slow-moving Mark. Never had Laura felt unsafe in an intimate physical situation, never before felt *invaded*; a very unfortunate introduction of darkness into something so playful and joyful. Her fascination in and pursuit of psychological theory had already begun, and she had an inkling of what was healthy and what was not, and that it was, to a great extent, in *how* things were done as much as in exactly *what* things were done. Ari had fucked that one up to high heaven, fucked it up unforgivably, turned himself from a strong, quiet mystery into a leering pervert in the space of less than a minute.

One might've thought that the slap and exit would have ended the story, but the following Monday, in school, after a weekend of sobbing silently into her pillow and trying to decide whether she could ever tell her mother and father about this, Ari came up to her, looking concerned.

"You seemed really upset," he said at the lockers, the rest of the student body streaming down the hallways on the way to their first class. "Is everything okay?"

She took him out back, to the slim, shady strip of grass between the PE equipment storage and the maintenance shack, and laid into him. He stared down at her, dark in his eyes, but no expression on his features until, when she felt she was about halfway through, he simply turned around and walked away; he never spoke to her again.

That had been it through the end of high school. She had searched for memories during the second half of that year: seeing him at graduation, giving him a final glance of electric hatred. But she knew not to go searching through those memories too closely now. She was fighting hard to avoid a resurgence of those problems that had plagued her first few months at Vassar, problems that were just now coming to a head. With Josh. Her latest breakup.

She sat at their favorite bench on the round, her black hair tied in a tight ponytail, sticking out from under her father's Mets cap; a little moral support for a girl diving into weird, unknown waters by sheer instinct. She was careful not to wear anything Josh particularly liked — no tight, white tank top, no capri jeans with the psychedelic flowers up the side — just a blue T-shirt and jeans. She wasn't his great love; she was just some girl about to break up with him, that he'd moon over for a bit, then remember fondly, and eventually let go of. But she was sitting on their favorite bench, just the same, to acknowledge that they had something good for a while.

He jogged up breathless, fifteen minutes late. She had spent the time, unaware of it, searching through her own spinning head.

"It was Professor Garner." He had his famous lopsided "I'm a dope" grin when he sat down and explained, giving her a swift kiss on the cheek. "He held me after class for a couple of minutes."

Her attention focused around that comment, and she turned her eyes on him. She had bright blue eyes; they almost seemed to glow at her from the mirror in the half-light sometimes. She fancied sometimes that they dimmed, grew dark when she was angry or her mood had darkened.

"Why did he do that?" Her voice was more penetrating than she'd intended.

"Oh, it was nothing. He just had . . ." Josh was looking sheepish. He had been, since she'd known him, an awful liar. "All right. He caught me on a call during class. These cell-patches are so easy to use, you almost can't help it. Guess I need a little more practice with the subvocalizing, though."

Laura looked down, shaking her head.

"Oh, come on. It's a new toy. I was just playing around."

She was one to talk. She hadn't even attended a class since yesterday morning. She could feel the weight of the work piling up and inexplicably, miraculously, didn't care, which was not like her at all.

"I know." She looked straight into his eyes. "Josh. We can't do this anymore." Right there, out with it, quick and simple like a solid cross to the face rather than a slow and painful series of gut shots. And why was it so violent in her head? Had she taken up boxing in her sleep or something?

Josh closed and widened his eyes at the same time. The lids slowly opened in sheer astonishment.

"Are you—what? Is this . . ." His head was spinning;

she would swear she could actually see it. "Are you, like, breaking up with me?"

Students walked by on the path, their faces bright, oblivious.

"Yes." Her voice was small. What else was there to say?

"Because of this?" He touched the metallic dot at his temple.

"No, Josh. No, of course not."

"Because I'll get rid of the goddamned thing. Laura, you are so important to—"

"Don't, Josh. Please don't. You *should* get rid of the thing, if you even can. It's going to, I don't know, hollow you out."

"What are you talking about?"

She wasn't even sure herself.

"You should get rid of it, but that's not what this is about."

"What, then? Please tell me, Laura. I know we can work this out."

"We can't." Sure, definite. Like the slap in the face for Ari. You needed to be clear where you stood for everyone's good. "This is not about the kind of person you are, Josh."

"You're not going to say that this is about you, not me, right?"

She was. She was going to say that, God help her.

"Josh, there's something going on with me, and it's—"

"I know. I can see that. That's what I'm here for, to help you with what's going on. If something is going on with you, do you really think shutting me out is the best idea?"

"You're part of what's going on with me. I'm in this relationship because it's filling in for something that I'm . . ."

"What?"

"Missing."

He stared hard at her. Goddamn him, there was no anger in those eyes, just desperation, longing.

"Josh . . ." She put a hand on his shoulder, though she'd promised herself she wasn't going to touch him. "You are kind and smart and funny and compassionate. You're a lovely, lovely person. But you're not for me."

He stared longer, his eyes going shiny.

"Who is?"

"No, Josh, it's not like that. There's no one else."

"I know that. Not right now. But if I'm not for you, someone else is. Who?"

She stared back at him, and all she could feel right now was his pain. The moment she saw Mark undressing and Ari standing back, preparing for his little diversion, she made a decision, one she could only fully understand in retrospect, that when confronted by boys who hurt her, she would not shed a tear. She would be strong, because if you let them do that to you, control your heart that way, then you were never your own person. But it didn't work so well when the boy in question wasn't sick, wasn't a monster, did it?

She was crying. Crying for him.

"I'm sorry, Josh." Her hand was on his face. "This isn't fair at all. But this is what has to happen to . . ." She swallowed. "To make me whole. Or something. I'm sorry."

She moved to stand, but before her fingers had completely left his cheek, he had her by the hand, and he looked up hard into her eyes.

"Don't do this, Laura." His voice was low, filled with concern. "For you, as well as me. These last few days, it's like you want to walk away from your life. You don't have to be afraid."

She took her hand away, looked down at him, the tears suddenly drying on her cheeks.

"I'm sorry, Josh. I'm not afraid. For the first time in a long time, I'm not afraid."

She turned and walked away. From behind her, there was no call, no sound of his voice at all, as though he had simply ceased to exist. She did not turn around.

With that behind her, the urgency, the immediacy of figuring out what to do next began to gnaw at Laura. By the time she was back in her room, it was practically eating her alive. She locked her door—her roommate was in class, wouldn't return for hours. She went to her cell, snatched it up. Instead of dialing her mother's number as she intended, she hurled the thing at the wall as hard as she could, where it rebounded invincibly, falling into the bed's soft welcome, its high-impact plastic construction able to withstand far worse then she could conjure.

"What do you want?" she said to the room, her vision still swimming in black. "Ask me to my face. I don't understand the note. I don't understand who the Librarian is supposed to be."

"God*damn* it," she said, focusing on nothing in particular. She picked up her cell, dropped it on the floor, and stomped on it hard. The large single plastic eye of its screen glared back at her, invulnerable in its judgment.

She looked around the room, spinning crazily, trying to find something, spot something, not knowing what. She jammed her fists into her eyes and held them, doing deep-breathing yoga exercises that should, theoretically, slowly melt her muscles and calm her nervous system until all her tension was gone. But they were useless, worse than useless. They felt like a child's tool now, an affront to this impossible and inexplicable fear and rage welling up in her.

She stormed out of the room, downstairs, across the

campus to the library. She walked into it, only barely able to keep herself in a proper state of quiet. She marched through the stacks, tracking each librarian on duty, keeping herself in the shadows as best she could so as not to be seen in return.

Follow the librarian. See where he goes, what he does. Turn the table on him.

But which librarian, you idiot? For how long?

She held her final position, watching the reference librarian stare down at his computer, direct a student, stare off into the distance.

"Hey, Laura. What you up to?" A whisper from behind. She turned: Dunphy, goofy smile, red hair, his huge frame lumbering to a stop; a student in her lit course, books clutched under an arm.

"Not now," she hissed, hurrying past him and out of this stupid, stupid place.

Outside again, she sat on the stone steps, watching students come and go, others on the green washing back and forth from classes like a tide.

A tall boy with cellenses and a leather jacket sitting on a bench in the round seemed to keep turning his dark plastic eyes on her. But after five minutes, so did a girl with braids coming up the steps and a guy jogging by the front and a couple of girls sitting on the lawn with books spread out before them. Dunphy walked past her down the steps, pretending not to look at her, a metallic dot at his temple. Did he have that last week? Did *everyone* suddenly have them now?

Now she kept thinking she was going to see Josh. Or worse yet, *not* see him, even though he was out there somewhere, watching her flail about fruitlessly for answers. Why was she so easily able to imagine enemies everywhere around her?

Panic was edging up to her brain now, like before. She knew just what that panic led to: the crowd of fascinated students gathering around her toppled body, the visit to the hospital, her breathless parents insisting that she take a break for the rest of the semester. She was not going to let it happen again.

Laura rose and walked quickly from across the green, along the path to the parking lot. She got into her car and locked the doors. An off-to-college gift from her parents, their own three-year-old Prius, it now only gave her the comfort of a locked space . . . and mobility. She nodded.

"Okay," she said, and started her up.

She drove out of Vassar, garnering a wave from the guard, and headed in no specific direction. Poughkeepsie blew past her, offering little more than its megalithic malls and the standard array of franchise restaurants between them. Its trafficked streets quickly gave way to greener areas, more expensive houses recessed from the street behind expansive lawns. She kept going until fields flanked her car, the highway far in the other direction, other cars passing at minute-long intervals.

She pulled onto the shoulder and got out and walked into the waist-length grass, soft and caressing; far, far out toward a border of trees in the distance. The only sound she heard was wind and a distant hum, maybe the highway or maybe an invention of her own ears. She collapsed, lying flat and staring up at blue.

The wind rustled the grass around her, made clouds slowly swim across her line of sight. Her eyes closed, and for no reason she saw city, tall buildings, shining reflective skyscrapers that made her uneasy.

There was a sound, a rhythmic rustling not from wind but from footsteps. She opened her eyes, focused her concentration. Footsteps for certain, coming nearer, but not exact. Observed from the road, she must have simply seemed to have disappeared in this tall grass when she lay down. Someone was trying to find her. Josh.

She stood abruptly, facing the direction from which she imagined the footsteps to be coming. Strange things were happening to her body: heart racing, yes, but muscles tightening, feet finding strong purchase, fists curling. Her father had never spared a moment to teach her to fight, if he even had any idea himself. Baseball, yes; boxing, definitely no.

The footsteps stopped; the figure spun toward her. But if he was surprised, his face remained resolutely unperturbed. He was most assuredly not Josh, but a surprisingly young—could he be more than fourteen?—thin and tall boy with a complexion that was treating him unkindly. His sharp slacks and expensive brown sweater of rich cashmere made him particularly incongruous out here in the field. But, of course, he was not just out for a walk, was he?

They stared at each other, fifteen feet separating them, standing off like it was a showdown.

"Well," he finally said in a voice that retained twangs of pre-adolescent petulance, "now what?"

"What do you mean 'now what'? *You're* the one following *me.*" She felt a bit like she was scolding an obstreperous child. "And just who the hell are you, anyway?"

He nodded, as if this sort of trouble was inevitable.

"Let's cut through the play-acting, could we? Could we, *please?*" His gaze was astute and incisive, his cheekbones rode high, and his eyebrows slanted at sharp, devilish angles. His hair was a dusty, noncommittal shade of brown, but styled as though he had a Hollywood blockbuster budget to sink into it. His lips were truculent, though whether that was a physical characteristic or a choice of expression wasn't clear.

"Listen, I don't know what you're talking about, but you'd better make with the explaining or . . ." She lost the tail end of that one. Should she call the police, or his mother?

"The Librarian," the boy said, his eyes showing how tired this all made him. "You don't expect me to think that you drove out here to lie down in a field, do you?"

"Actually," she said without missing a beat, "I came here to lure you out."

The boy faltered at that one, an obvious affront to his superior intelligence. He went so far as to take a step back, his eyes flickering from side to side, suddenly concerned that he was in danger from forces he couldn't see.

"Now," Laura pressed, "if you'll just explain who this Librarian is, I won't have to give you a spanking."

"Something is obviously wrong here," he said magnanimously. "But we'll have it cleared up in no time."

She spun around in time to see another figure closing in. He'd been summoned by cell, no doubt, though, unlike Josh, the boy looking for the Librarian was clearly quite good at subvocalizing, since Laura had neither seen nor heard any indication of the order being dispatched. Wouldn't you know, the approaching figure was Dunphy, the grass parting as he lumbered through it, his expression made far less goofy with cellenses now hiding his eyes. Behind him, down at the road they'd all left behind, was a second car, one that Dunphy must have been charged with driving, given this boy's age.

Dunphy stopped about five feet from Laura, his eyes focusing from behind those black lenses.

"Dunphy," the boy said, from behind Laura now.

There was an instant to decide: Run or not? But could she outrun Dunphy, here in an open field? If she managed to, then what? Would she have her answers? Plus, the idea of this kid being some kind of sinister mastermind was a bit too much to swallow.

Dunphy was to her by then, no hint of apology on his features, reaching out a large hand for Laura's arm. She feinted a kick to his crotch, and when his hands snapped down and his knees came in to protect himself, causing his body to hunch forward, she snapped out a right cross that cracked his nose with such precision that it didn't even knock his cellenses askew. Pulling backwards and grabbing his nose with both hands, blood spouting out between them, Dunphy opened his front up completely, and Laura actually did kick him in the crotch. He went down into the grass, folding in on himself, moaning.

Laura heard an audible gasp from the boy behind her, a bleat of consternation over the destruction of an infallible plan, though it was certain no one could have been more astonished by this development than Laura herself. Dunphy's nose had felt like a dry cracker crunching under her knuckles, which now stung fiercely. She killed the sick, nauseous look on her face before she turned back around to face the boy.

"Well," she said, "now what?"

REMAK

"WOULD YOU LIKE SOMETHING? WATER?" Alan Silven—or
Jon Remak—asked, sharp eyes cutting out of the polished
face.

Rose shook her head almost imperceptibly, her eyes
flickering back to Mal, limp on the couch.

"Why don't you sit down, and I'll try to explain," Silven or Remak said, proceeding to his desk and touching a
button on the phone. "No calls, no meetings."

"Yes, sir," a woman's voice responded. He looked back
up and smiled. The face itself smiled well, as though it was
so practiced that the muscles flowed right into the proper

places like liquid. But the smile did not reach into the eyes. The eyes seemed cast of another material, a part of sculpture formed of entirely different marble.

Rose sat, her posture stiff, on the edge of the couch next to Mal.

The man came around to face her and stood before the opposite sofa, but did not sit down. She became smaller beneath his regard.

"What has Mal told you?" he asked.

"Told me?"

"About what he's doing, what happened to him."

"I don't understand." She desperately did not want to be heard by anyone outside the room, and it made her wince slightly whenever Silven or Remak spoke in a normal voice. "He left his foster parents when he turned eighteen. He's been supporting himself by picking up bare-knuckle fights for money down at a place in the park. He's in trouble with some corporation, because he's not in their system."

"Not in their system." The man nodded, again a disassociated smile. "That's all? How did the two of you meet?"

"I work at a diner near the park. He came in."

"Did you put these bandages on him?" He indicated the strips of white peeking from beneath Mal's shirt, running up his neck. "You know what you're doing."

Rose nodded. Bandaging was something she knew. She had spent years bandaging up her mother.

The man's eyes were dissecting her, something behind them coming to a decision.

"I'm not sure exactly why Mal hasn't gone into more detail, what he doesn't want you to know."

"Mal is made out of iron," she said, her hand unconsciously brushing across his. "You just can't get inside of him. He won't let you. It's like he forgot how. Something made him this way, and I don't know what it is." She looked down at Mal, saw him sliding into sleep. If there was one thing she knew the sight of by now, it was Mal sleeping. The sight, the sound, the exact emanation of warmth from his body. Rose looked back up. "Tell me. Please."

"Mal and I already have a rather . . . complicated relationship. But, Rose, if I do tell you, there's no going back. The world is going to look different to you for the rest of your life, and you won't like it."

"I'm not so crazy about the world right now, anyway," she said without any humor whatsoever.

"A little more than a year ago," the man began, "Mal's brother disappeared."

"Wait," Rose's small voice escalated in surprise. "Mal has a brother?"

The man took this question in, his calculating eyes floating to Mal and back to her.

"Yes. His brother, Tommy, and his brother's wife, Annie, they aren't around here anymore. They've gone far away from here."

"He's never mentioned them. Does he ever speak to them anymore?"

"I know he sends them money when he can. But it's . . . He doesn't speak to them. He can't. They . . . they don't know who he is."

Rose blinked three times, as if a tiny insect had flown at her eyes.

"Let me start at the beginning," the man said, beginning to pace around the couch. "Mal's brother disappeared. Mal went looking for him but stumbled onto a much larger situation. The last place Tommy was seen was in a building. Mal went into that building and found several impossible things. Among them was a room filled with doors that led to other locations, other buildings, all over the city, all over the world. Are you all right, Rose? Let me get you something to drink. This is just the beginning."

She nodded minutely, and he went to a mirrored bar behind a wall panel and returned with a bottle of water, which he passed to her and she held numbly, her hand limp on the sofa.

"Mal was taken away. His knowledge of the doors made him a liability, and he was put in a prison of sorts. There he met several other people, myself among them. I worked for an organization, a cooperative that used a schema of human interaction called the Global Dynamic to study demographic trends and social currents that were hidden in statistics. We studied them, and, where no one else could, we acted on them. This is how I uncovered the same trail Mal had. And I, like Mal and these other people, was imprisoned for it.

"This was a most unusual prison, in the form of a forest and a mountain. But they had been cut off from the rest of the world by people's minds. By forgetting that the place existed, by letting go of it, people detached it from the world we know, made it one of the forgotten places. They're all over, these places, but we don't see them. They're behind the world, like old, dirty alleyways that no one walks through anymore. Some of them *are* alleyways, in fact. I know that Mal uses these places to get through the city. Being in that forest tripped something in Mal's head. He's trained himself to find these forgotten places, spot them. *Remember* them, I guess you'd say."

"What about you? Can you see them?"

"No. I'm . . . not like Mal."

The more she listened, the more Rose came to understand that. The more he spoke, the less his voice seemed to fit the mouth that was issuing it. She felt like she was watching a badly dubbed movie or watching a puppet speak the words of its master. This more than anything else made the story this man was telling disturbingly easy to believe.

"I'll get to that shortly," the man continued. "The four of us found a way out of the prison, and we attempted to find out what was happening to us. When we did, though, we learned that we had all been erased, forgotten like the prison we had escaped from. No one remembered any of us, not the people we worked with, not our friends, not even those closest to us, like our families. Essentially, we no longer existed. I imagine that's what Mal meant when he said he wasn't in this corporation's 'system.' At any rate, I knew of a person, a sort of living database, called the Librarian. This person sent us in the right direction, which turned out to be the building with the doors, the building Mal had started in."

The man turned away then and went to the window. His body remained stiff, at attention, as he looked out at the city through the tinted glass, the forest of gleaming spires surrounding them. The movement also seemed unnatural to Rose, like a body being controlled by remote. She looked down at Mal's quiet, bruised face. She would have touched it, as she did sometimes when he slept, if the man had not been there.

"This next part is difficult," he said from the window. "The building was not a building, really. It was part of our enemy, part of the being that had done all this to us and was, in fact, exerting control over most of the people in the city, if not the country and the world."

"Corporations do that every day," Rose said, unintentionally dismissive of it. "Mal talks about it sometimes. When he talks."

"Yes, that's true. The corporations were doing this thing's work. They were, in some sense, just a part of it. The thing was in people's minds, riding them, controlling the way they saw and thought and felt. That's how we were erased."

"What are you talking about?" Even frustrated, Rose's voice hardly went above a whisper. "What was this thing?"

"It was an idea, Rose." The man turned back from the window and put his sharp eyes into her. "An idea that had evolved into a living thing because it had grown so powerful in people's minds. The idea of hopelessness. It grew and it thrived, and it was going to eat us all alive, everyone that ever lived, so that there wouldn't be people anymore, just machines made of flesh that carried this thing around in their skulls."

The eyes searched her, looking for disbelief, panic. But it wasn't there. Of everything he had said so far, this Rose had the easiest time believing. She knew the touch of the thing he was describing, had felt it eating her own mind — had, in fact, never known a time without it.

"The four of us confronted it." The man walked over, stood above her again. "But there was a disagreement about how to deal with it. I wanted the thing destroyed as soon as possible, but Mal and the others, they needed their loved ones back. Mal and I fought."

It was almost enough to make Rose laugh, this polished, pristine sculpture of a man trying to topple the blunt, stony Mal. She had little question of how that fight had ended.

"Mal beat me," he said without chagrin. "And he went on to confront the thing. But during our fight, a window was smashed. Remember, now, that the building we were in was not really a building at all, but a metaphor, the inside of this thing, the mind of this living idea. Realizing I couldn't accomplish what I set out to, I came up with a hasty theory and acted on it. I threw myself out the window. As I said, I wasn't jumping from a real window. I was jumping from the inside of this thing to the outside of it. And outside was a boundless neurological interface, a tissue that connects all the human minds in the world. This mindscape — or, more accurately, 'neuropleth' because it interacts with the entire nervous system, *everyone's* nervous systems—is what the Idea traveled through. It was through the neuropleth that the Idea could enter people and control them."

Rose was staring up at him, for the first time as though he were mad.

"That's where I am. Right now." As if to bear her out, his eyes became unfocused, looking at something unspeakably vast inside him. "This isn't my body. My body is gone forever. Throwing myself into the neuropleth converted my body into pure neurological impulses, pure consciousness. I can move from person to person, like swimming from one pool to another through the earth between them."

Or, Rose thought, *like a ghost, haunting houses, driving out their proper occupants.*

"Like the living idea you were fighting," she said, not sure he would even hear her. But his eyes snapped back into focus, and he stared down at her, not with anger but with mild confusion.

"No. Not like that," he said easily. "My consciousness can only enter certain sorts of minds; minds that are . . . how to put it? Unguarded, you might say; *open* minds. Once I'm in, I can move the body, speak through it as I am now, with Alan Silven. But once my consciousness leaves, I alter their memories, but nothing more. Like with Mr. Silven, here. I can't very well leave him the memory of all this. I create different memories of the time that he's missed and leave him with those."

He looked down at her, guilelessly expecting that she would have no doubts, no suspicions of his intentions. Momentous though it was, Rose had fixed on something else.

"What about the other two people?" Rose asked. "You said four of you confronted the thing." There was something there that Remak had passed over too quickly. She sensed in it the bonds that tied Mal to something else, that kept him eternally just out of her embrace.

"There was a man, a teacher, named Mike. He was the one who finally defeated the creature with his own sacrifice."

"How do you defeat an idea?" she asked.

"You prove it wrong," Remak answered, the most obvious thing in the world. "That's what Mike did, right at its heart."

"Destroyed it?"

"I think so," he allowed. "Yes. Made it vastly less than it was, at any rate. And Mike died for it. The building we were in, it was here, where we're standing now. That specific structure is gone now, crumbled away when Mike beat the thing. This place" — his hands opened around them — "is just a building. That's why I ride Silven sometimes, to check in, make sure."

"We don't seem to be so much better off," Rose said.

"I beg your pardon."

"With the Idea gone," Rose explained, quiet but resolute. "You weakened it, you said, but the people I see every day, they don't seem so much better."

"The Idea helped to dig us a deep hole," Remak said, his head dropping in thought. "The problem is that no one seems terribly interested in looking around and seeing that hole closing in around them. They would rather look back at themselves, focus on their own concerns, through the screens of their cells or the programs on the HDs."

Rose nodded. She didn't really need anyone to explain to her how the world sucked.

"You only mentioned three people." Rose drove the conversation back on the path Remak had again steered them away from. "Who was the fourth person?"

"A girl. Laura." His voice and face didn't change at all. There was no telling if she meant anything unusual to this man. "She had it worst in many ways. She had the most secure life, the happiest. She lost the most of all of us."

Laura. The enemy that had wrapped its tentacles around Mal's heart and kept Rose from touching it now had a name. *Laura.*

"What happened to her?" Her hand had again found Mal's, her fingers touching his rough knuckles.

"She got her life back," Remak said. "And she's safe."

"How did she—"

"What's happening?" Remak asked, his attention suddenly fixed on Mal.

"Nightmares," Rose explained. She had already felt Mal's slack grip tighten in twitches and jerks. "They won't leave him alone."

"Well," Remak said distantly, "Mal has certainly earned his nightmares."

Mal stirred. She took her hand back carefully, watched his dark eyes come slowly open.

Remak looked down at the boy, the same cool mathematics working in his head but also something else. Sympathy? Gratitude?

"You need a doctor, Mal," he said. "And we need to talk."

The doctor arrived with a severe face and a business suit over his slim frame. He referred to the young CEO casually as "Alan" and let no evidence whatsoever onto his patrician features as to what he must have thought about the two uncouth-looking kids lounging in the office. Rose had never imagined a doctor looking like this, and certainly not a doctor who came to *you* when you called him. Her experience with doctors topped out with the diagnosis app on her cell.

The doctor studied the lacerations on Mal's head, gently probed the bandages on his torso, opened his lips and reached in with a gloved finger, looked into his eyes with a small intense light that made Mal flinch, then took Remak aside and spoke quietly to him. He returned to Mal with a preparation, in hypodermic form, from a small leather pouch he carried in his briefcase. Without protest, Mal allowed the needle to slip into his arm, and for the second time in two hours, Rose watched Mal receive an injection of God only knew what from a total stranger.

The doctor peered into Mal's eyes with a dimmed flashlight, then rose to his knees and deposited a small packet of pills on the chrome and glass coffee table before the sofa. He nodded once at Mal and Rose, then shook hands with Remak and departed.

"You have three cracked ribs that have been adequately wrapped," Remak told Mal when they were alone again, "and a concussion that seems to be improving rather than worsening. The doctor gave you some stimulants to keep you on your feet for the time being. You have a tooth cracked off at the base, and the gum is infected." He motioned to the pills on the coffee table. "That's for the infection. Everything else is just bumps and bruises."

Rose took in each beat of the diagnosis as though the blows were landing on her own body. Mal's eyes wandered lazily around the room.

"He also noted that he'd never seen so much scar tissue on a person," Remak concluded after a pause. "So it was the Old Man who did this to you, wasn't it?"

Mal's eyes didn't fix on anything in particular. Rose was staring at him now, too.

"Wasn't it?" Remak pressed.

Mal's eyes snapped back to him, his face finding its stony default.

"Yes."

Remak nodded, rearranging his equation.

Rose had heard of the Old Man. Everyone had. He was a rumor. *The* rumor. The corporate bogeyman that made cities rise and fall, a composite of every fat cat who ever sat in a corner office with a nice view and adjusted the fortunes of the world according to his private agenda.

"Why does he want you, Mal?" Remak asked in a tired drone. Clearly, he was familiar with the process of trying to extract information from Mal.

Rose watched Mal go through the nearly imperceptible

hoops of figuring out whether or not the information really, *truly* needed to be divulged.

"He doesn't want me," Mal finally said. "He wants you."

Remak, preternaturally collected until now, reeled as if the floor beneath him had become liquid.

"*What?* How? How does the Old Man even know about me?"

Mal looked up at Remak from beneath his brow, silent. The answer was implicit in the question; even Rose could see that. If the Old Man was real, then his resources were beyond conception. Eventually, he knew everything. That was his nature.

"This is too dire, Mal. It changes everything," Remak said. "If he knows about me, does he know about the neuropleth? If he could gain access to the neuropleth . . . I need you to go back in Mal," Remak said it flatly, "to find out what he's planning."

"You go," Mal said, creaking himself up to a standing position.

"I've tried," Remak said. "My consciousness, it can't even get close to him. I keep scraping up against their inner circle, but their minds are too guarded. I can't enter anyone: his bodyguards, his assistant, this Kliest woman; certainly not the Old Man himself." When Mal didn't respond after a moment, Remak came down hard on his last words. "Do you understand how dangerous that is?"

Dangerous because you can't control them, Rose didn't say.

Remak straightened from his beseeching posture.

"All right, Mal," he said, the urgency gone from his tone, and the quiet confidence having rushed in to fill the space. "Our arrangement was made perfectly clear: One day you'd have to do something for me, no questions asked. I'm calling it in."

Mal's body tensed, his fists closed tightly, then he let go.

"They put a geolocator in me," Mal said. "They know where I am all the time."

"They know you came here?"

"I went other places first, confused the trail. This place won't stand out. But they will see me coming if I try to get close to them."

"We can fix that," Remak said, relaxing into a problem of logistics, an operation he clearly thrived on. "We just need to find its frequency. We duplicate the signal, then if we can get yours offline, even for just a second, we can replace it."

"I can get it offline," Mal said, and only then did Rose completely realize that the argument was over, and a shifting of allegiances had magically and invisibly occurred while she was watching.

"But Mal . . ." she said, and when they both looked at her, she flinched, cleared her throat, and started again. "But Mal isn't in any shape to fight." Despite the doctor's recent visit, that fact seemed to have eluded them both. Wasn't that just men all over? The strength of their bodies was their strength as human beings. Even Remak, who had no actual body anymore, was trapped by this pattern of thought.

Remak looked back at Mal appraisingly, and Rose already knew him well enough to know that he was judging not by how much more Mal could take for his own health, but how much more he could take before he became a liability to the operation.

"I'll help however I can," Remak said. "I can't get to the Old Man, but I can help get you in unnoticed."

Mal nodded, predictably ignoring Rose's plea as though it had never even been spoken. She wondered, *Would Laura have ever been so unceremoniously ignored?*

"This is it, Remak. This is the one I owe you. Do what you need to," he said, and then looked at Rose. "And I'll do what I need to."

Silven's limo, appallingly out of place, pulled to a curb in the shadow of two rotting apartment buildings. The policy of the mayor's office was to camouflage such symbols of municipal failure by maintaining solid, plain façades and leaving the insides to molder. Here, however, they were far enough on the outskirts of the "civilized" city that the well-heeled citizen and the average tourist would never see it. There was little purpose in draining resources to fix up these hulks, unless, of course, you cared about the people suffering inside them. A few sets of shadowed, cautious eyes shot over and collected the details of the three figures stepping from the limo.

"Hold your position," Remak said so that his cellens pickup would convey it to a man named Gerald Fisher, an employee of a Silven subsidiary who had been pressed into service as a decoy. A geolocator that transmitted on the same frequency as Mal's had been shot into Gerald Fisher so that his movements would appear to be Mal's. All that remained was to remove the transmission coming from Mal.

Mal's eyes scanned the sidewalk, the buildings, the seams in between them, and seemed to find something Rose couldn't see. Whatever the doctor had given him was doing something. Mal's eyes were focusing more sharply, and the squint of pain had disappeared. It was helping him now, but what would it do in the long run? Did Remak care? Did Mal? He led her and Remak over to the place where the wall of one grimy apartment building met that of the other.

Remak's eyes were scanning the area from behind cel-lenses, even as his jaw worked, subvocalizing orders. Mal looked up at him, and he nodded.

"Go."

Mal brusquely took Rose's hand.

"Take the route we discussed," Remak directed the de-coy, who was positioned just around the far corner, never having laid eyes on any of them. He didn't even know who he was speaking to on the cell, only that his orders had come from very high up. "Start now," Remak ordered. "Now." He nodded again at Mal, and Rose was pulled toward the junc-ture of the two buildings, too fast. She winced as her face was about to crack into concrete.

But instead, her body moved forward, unimpeded. She opened her eyes to find that, guided by Mal, she was stand-ing at the edge of . . . a park. Wildly, her eyes whipped back to Mal before she could even take in its details. The park, easily hundreds of square feet in size, had without any doubt whatsoever not been there between the two apartment buildings a moment before. Or, she realized as her brain be-gan to put things in order, it *had* been there all along. She had just forgotten to notice it. It was not the experience of suddenly seeing something that had been hidden, but more of suddenly remembering to look.

She looked behind her, but Remak and his limo were

gone. Now there was only more park, identical to the one she was standing in. Sounds from the real world — cars, people — became distended, warped into a mushy drone that echoed across the expanse of cracking concrete, rang off the rusting curves and arrays of metal meant to bring joy to daring children. Benches hunkered at the sides, peeling paint with no pigment.

Even beyond its forlorn desperation, the place was wrong, faded. The shadows themselves felt pale and grainy, as though Rose were watching them through a screen that was losing its clarity. The dingy light of a colorless sky fell down on them like dust.

"This is one of the forgotten places," she said.

Mal nodded. "They can't trace me here. No one can find me here. Or you. The Idea we fought, it made these places happen, it took the forgotten places in our minds and pushed them out of the world. It wanted to carve off pieces of our existence, to make the world grow smaller around us."

She looked at the walls of the apartment buildings vaulting up on either side, the windows lining up in neat rows. What did the people inside see when they looked out their windows? Or did they even know they had those windows anymore?

"It's so big," Rose said. "And it just went away from people's minds?"

"The size doesn't matter," Mal said. "There's a housing project up in the Bronx, seven buildings, thousands of apartments, thousands of yards surrounding them. They were abandoned, and now they're forgotten. And the world is that much smaller."

"Seven buildings," Rose echoed. "But what was this park? How could an entire city just forget a park in the middle of where they live?"

Mal chose a spot on the fading walls, sparing himself the painful view.

"A woman was attacked here one night, beaten, stabbed, raped while she bled to death. She screamed for help, screamed until she died."

"Why didn't the police come?" Rose's voice was almost lost in her fear of the answer.

"No one called them," Mal said. "Thirty-eight people saw what happened out their windows, thirty-eight people heard her dying. No one came. No one called."

"How do you know all this?"

"It was all over newsblogs and the HD."

"I never heard about it."

Mal would still not look at the place.

"You just forgot," he said. "Everyone did."

"How? How could people forget something like that?"

"Some things we forget because they fade from memory. Other things we make ourselves forget, because we're scared of them. Or ashamed." Finally, he looked down at her again. "I'm sorry, but I need you to stay here until I'm back. So I know that you're safe."

She searched his eyes when he said it, but couldn't find what she was looking for.

"How do I get out?"

"It takes a long time to learn that. If you walk off one edge"— he pointed at the space behind them where there should have been a street but there was only more park— "you just walk in at the other." He pointed at the far side of the park, where the egress revealed—again—more park where there should have been a street. It was distant, but, squinting, Rose could swear she actually saw the figures of Mal and herself standing there.

"I'll come back and get you," Mal concluded.

"But what if you can't, Mal?"

Mal looked at the fading walls around them.

"Watch me leave. You'll see the street. You'll lose it again, but remember where it is. You can make yourself see it eventually. Don't use your eyes. Just *remember* to see it."

"What about Remak?" she asked. "Can he get me?"

"No. His energy can't reach in here. The neuropleth he travels in doesn't exist in this place. That's why it's forgotten."

The last word echoed through the terrible space and died with unnatural abruptness, as though the air itself were too tired to carry the sound. She was desperate not to be alone here.

"What did Remak mean when he said you had to do something for him? What is he holding over you?"

She looked at him through the shafts of inert light, cutting through the limbs of the single skeletal tree. Her eyes were pleading, and all he could do was turn away.

"What about your brother, Mal?" she asked, gambling for anything she could get from him. "Remak said you had a brother named Tommy. Don't you owe me at least that?"

"Tommy lives away from here, out in the country," Mal answered, without turning back to her, still trying to keep this part of his life hidden, even as he said it. "Tommy and Annie, his wife. I send them money, when I can."

"Why aren't you with them, Mal?"

"They don't remember me."

"You could try to fix that, couldn't you?"

"Remembering me," Mal's voice came, but because she couldn't see his face, it felt almost disembodied, "wouldn't make their lives any better."

"What about Laura?" she asked, shocking even herself by bringing it out between them. "Does she remember you?"

JESSE KARP

He was so still that when he finally spoke, she started.

"Watch me go," he said. He took two steps toward the opening, then stopped and turned around. "You don't deserve this, Rose. I'm sorry. But I need you to be safe, and this is the best I can do."

She let the words fill her heart, then nodded, not trusting her voice to hold steady.

"I'll be back as soon as I can," he said, then turned away and walked out to a sidewalk that she suddenly remembered was there. She blinked, and it was gone, leaving the concrete and rusting metal, the flaking benches and impenetrable, forgotten walls.

Rose knew about being alone. Until Mal had come to her, she barely ever spoke but to answer questions at work, and yet being with Mal sometimes made the isolation resound even more powerfully. Loneliness was no stranger to Rose. But this was a sort of solitude she had never imagined.

AARON

THE BOY GLARED AT LAURA with a smoldering superiority that she could not hope to match, but she glared back
for all she was worth. They stood there, glaring in the
open field, until an agonized snuffling broke them from
their death match and Dunphy teetered up onto his knees,
rising over the line of grass, both hands clutching his
nose.

Laura was the first to break away and look at Dunphy.
A big red splotch was plastered across the center of his face,
visible around the hands that presumably kept the remain-

der of his lifeblood from pouring out. She turned back on the boy.

"You'd better get him to a hospital," she said.

The boy slowly let his eyes creep away from his target, as though she had live ammunition trained on him.

"Excellent," he said. "Well done, Mr. Dunphy. Worth every penny."

Laura shot him a look of astonishment, then went over to Dunphy, took him by an arm, and lent her strength to his huge body, pulling him up to his feet. He tottered for a moment, collected his balance, then looked to her for his next move. She slowly walked him, one foot at a time, through the tall grass, back toward the cars.

"Sorry, Laura, sorry," he mewled pathetically over and over again as they went. It came out garbled and mushy. Laura just barely managed to hold herself back from apologizing for the shocking assault. He had, after all, come at her first, and she hadn't even been aware what she was capable of.

Halfway to the car, she craned her head over her shoulder.

"Coming?" she called to the lone figure, following their progress from his unmoving position in the field.

Unhurriedly, he caught up with them by the time they

got to the car. Even so, Laura had to get Dunphy's keys, open his door, and set him in the back seat by herself. His torso and legs folded around his damaged crotch sent waves of queasiness through Laura's gut.

She turned to the boy and held out the keys.

"What do you expect me to do with those?" he said.

"Drive him to the hospital."

"I'm fourteen. I can't drive a car." He said it like she was an unmitigated fool for having suggested it.

"Oh my living Christ," she said, turning back and struggling Dunphy into the back seat of her own car. Sweating and out of breath, she leaned on the roof and looked at the boy. "What's your name?"

"I'm not going to tell you my name." Obviously.

"Just tell me your first name. Make up a goddamned name for all I care, or I'll make one up for you." Years of babysitting the neighbors' three boys had taught Laura how to be tough with punks.

"Eleanor Roosevelt," he said, unapologetically.

"Fine. Listen, Eleanor—"

"You can call me Mrs. Roosevelt."

"Seriously? Right. Okay. Mrs. Roosevelt, get into the car next to Dunphy. We're going to drop him off, and then we have a lot to talk about."

"I'd say so," he said, and much to Laura's surprise, he got right into the car without another word.

But for Dunphy's intermittent moans and garbled attempts at semi-lucid communication, no one spoke. Laura cruised just above the speed limit back toward town. She'd never been pulled over here, but now was surely not the time for it. She'd never been to the hospital around here, either, but her mother had demanded that she know where it was before she even got to campus.

She weaved through sparse late afternoon traffic, turned onto Columbia Street, and eventually pulled to a stop across from the emergency room. She killed the engine and twisted her body around so she was facing the back seat as best she could.

"All right, Dunphy. Can you make it in there by yourself?"

He looked out with already blue and swelling eyes at the big glass doors across the street, as though it were some impossible expanse of desert.

"Go," said the boy, unceremoniously. "Would you just *go*, already?"

With monotonous exertion, Dunphy pushed out the door, labored out, and moved in slow motion across the street.

"It would really cap things off nicely," the boy said, unable to pull his eyes from Dunphy's mesmerizing performance, "if he were hit by a car right now."

"So difficult to find good help these days," Laura said, meaning for it to be cutting, but finding that, like everything else, it bounced off his nimbus of superiority. It did, however, get the boy to turn back to her with bored eyes that bespoke how tedious this was all going to be. On the seat next to him and the door Dunphy had just used, bloody handprints blazed a smeared trail.

"Let's cut right to the business of this business," the boy said, the words tumbling out with no awkward phrasing or enunciation, as natural as if Laura's seventy-year-old English professor were saying them. "I will pay you an eye-widening amount to tell me where the Librarian is."

"I don't know who this Librarian is you're talking about, but if I did, you can believe me when I say that I would tell you whatever I could just to get you out of my life."

He made his shoulders slump in melodramatic disappointment.

"Must it be this way? *Must* it? I already know you have the information I want."

"Okay," she said, in a starting-fresh tone of voice. "Let's go from here: How do you know I have this information?"

"I heard you talking about it."

"When was I talking about it?"

"June of last year."

"June of——" She blinked herself to a stop. "Just how long have you been following me?"

"I have not been 'following' you," he said, offended by the idea. "I've been surveilling you. And not long enough. Your conversation of June of last year was what made me notice you to begin with. It took some time to find you after that. Your records over the last year were a tricky business to decipher."

That he was deciphering her records, *surveilling* her, clearly should have been setting off all sorts of warning bells. But now they were getting somewhere, somewhere that maybe even could help Laura.

"What did I say, exactly? When? To who?"

"To whom," he corrected.

"Seriously? Weren't you the one who didn't want to waste time?"

"This isn't a waste of time? Do you need me to prove what I know by describing every moment of your life over a nine-month period before you just accept my offer and give me what I want?"

"Let's suppose something for the time being," she said without a trace of condescension, a trait that came naturally to her and that more than one doctor and professor had told her would prove valuable in the career she sought to pursue. "Let's suppose that all the assumptions you've made about me aren't true. You've collected data, but it's obviously incomplete, because you still need information from me. So there are some areas that you've had to fill in with theory. Is that fair to say?"

He looked at her, his eyebrow cocking skeptically, but he nodded, prepared to play along for the time being.

"Okay," she went on. "If you grant all that, then I'm ready to make a deal. Let's pursue a path to the answers you want, by giving me the answers I want. It doesn't cost you anything to answer my questions, right? When we get to your information, I'll give you everything I know about it, and you don't even have to pay me a cent."

He stared at her, his lips twisting in a decision: Could she possibly be as guileless as she seemed? Clearly, he was not used to or comfortable dealing with people who had nothing to hide. Ultimately, though, her logic was unassailable. Even if he wasn't assured of getting the information he wanted, answering her questions cost him nothing.

"Yes, fine," he said with only an echo of grudge.

"So what did I say June of last year, where was I, and to *whom* was I speaking?"

"Shall I just show you? That would be easier."

Laura's heart beat a little faster.

"Yes," she said, the word nearly catching in her throat.

"I'm feeding it to your cell right now."

She reached down to get it, realized it was still in her room, collecting dust in the shadows under her bed.

"I, uh, don't have it with me," she said, already knowing the reaction she would get.

"You don't have your cell with you," he said, letting it hang there between them, drenched in disdain.

She searched the side of his head for his cellpatch, which she was sure he had. It took her a moment, though. It was smaller, no more than a quarter inch in diameter, and flesh colored as well, nearly invisible.

"You must have cellenses to go with that thing. Can I see it through those?"

"The lenses are fused to my irises."

"What?" She squinted at his eyes, saw nothing unusual. "I thought the contact lens version wasn't even available yet."

"It's not. To people like you."

Who the hell was this kid?

"I suppose," he said, "the hospital has a paycell somewhere."

• • •

They stood in the cold, medicinal hallway, huddled around the small screen of a paycell, and Laura watched herself doing things she'd never done, in a place she'd never been. On the screen, she was in a public station of some kind, all white and chrome. The camera was focused tightly on her, so it was impossible to make out exactly where she was, but the sound of crowds bubbled in the background, even announcements on a PA system crackled indistinguishably.

She saw her face, but it was tense, unfamiliar. It was carrying something with it she didn't know or understand. Though that Laura was no older than she was now, obviously, she felt almost as though she were looking at an adult version of herself. There was another figure, close to her. A big figure, a boy, with dark, close-cut hair and broad shoulders. For an instant, she assumed it was Josh. But then, even from the back, the face not visible from the angle they were watching, there was something that was clearly not Josh about him. He stood, rock-like in his stillness, attending the stranger Laura with him on the screen. But even so, there was an unmistakable strength in him that Josh simply lacked, a sense of stubborn immovability in the tension of his shoulders, the angle of his head.

Laura's body tingled. How could she possibly make those assumptions about someone she had never met simply from the back? Ridiculous.

"Then maybe what we need to do," the Laura on the screen said, the sound of her voice obviously enhanced, since she appeared to be whispering, "is go back to the Librarian."

The male she was speaking to said something, and she strained to hear it, catch even the sound of his voice. But it was a one-word response and swallowed by the ambient noise.

"I know we could find him again," the screen Laura said in the paycell. "I know he would speak to us."

There was a pause as the two figures stared at each other. Then they both saw something at the same time and moved away, off the screen, which flickered gray and went to static.

Laura looked up at the boy next to her as though coming out of a daze.

"Who was that I was with?"

He shook his head.

"Unidentifiable. He never turned to the camera. I assumed it was your boyfriend, Josh."

"No. No, that wasn't Josh."

He was looking at her queerly now, starting to be convinced by her confusion. Quite despite himself, no doubt.

"Where was that taken?" Laura looked at him, not bothering to mask her desperation anymore.

"Moynihan Station, in New York. June of last year, as I said."

"New York. I haven't been to New York since I was, like, fifteen."

He didn't bother with a response. The evidence spoke for itself.

"How did you get that?" Laura pushed on.

"I was —" He caught himself, looking up and down the hospital hallway, dropping his voice precipitously. "I was scanning for mention of the word *Librarian* in certain contexts, in certain locations. This was the only one I turned up of any use."

"Wait," Laura shook herself from her own immediate dilemma for an instant. "You were scanning every camera in New York City?"

"Not every one, of course," he said, clearly exasperated at the idea. "Like I said, in certain areas."

"How do you do something like that?"

"I wrote a word- and tone-recognition program, context algorithms, patched into city networks with it." He waved it away as if it were nothing. "Believe me, that was not the hard part. I was scanning for more than a year before my software picked this up. Unfortunately, surveillance cameras in places as large as Moynihan Station are strategically placed. That was all I got. The hard part was finding you. I ran your face through all sorts of identification apps.

Your likeness was on record; you were in certain systems." He recited her parents' names, her address in Stony Brook, her friends' names, her high school GPA, either from obsessive memory or because it was scrolling across the lenses grafted to his eyes. "But the records were static, ignored, as though they were made-up entries for a person who didn't really exist. When I sent out inquiries, no one even knew who Laura Westlake was. You're going to have to explain to me exactly how you accomplished that."

But looking at her suddenly trembling chin, her swimming eyes, it was plain that she would be explaining nothing of the sort.

"Until," he continued mercifully, though his tone was still quiet and hard, "suddenly, you did exist. Your records began to update normally. People knew who you were, interacted with you. Four months ago. Now, here we are." He looked at her expectantly now. He had provided everything he could. It was her turn.

The questions sped around her in such a violent whirlwind, she didn't even know how to reach her hand in and pluck one out. So she went in another direction.

"All right, Mrs. Roosevelt, who are you really?" she asked. "How do you do all this? And what do you want with the Librarian?"

His expression fell into deep distaste. A scowl looked disturbingly natural on his young face. But given all that, he was clearly beyond arguing now.

"Fine," he said, acid anger burning his words. "But not here."

They were in her car again, sitting beside another field, not far from the first one. He had insisted on an open area with nothing and no one in sight.

"You know," he said, when they had finally found a spot that satisfied him, "you might consider a cellpatch. It would save a great deal of time and concern for security."

Is that where we are now? Laura wondered. *Is it really such a burden to have to simply speak now?*

"My name," he said, his eyes sliding back and forth at the open fields around them, "is Aaron Argaven." His eyes fell on her. They were scarcely two feet from her own now, and she couldn't help but study their flat, gray surface for hints of the machinery that infested them. But they were clean, almost flawless, like the eyes of a little baby. He was studying her back, as though by uttering his name he had offered a revelation of great enormity. "Argaven," he repeated it.

"Okay," she said, trying to accommodate his expectations.

"You don't know the name?"

"Uh, I guess it sounds sort of familiar."

"'I guess it sounds sort of familiar,'" he actually mimicked her in a mock, singsong voice. The last time she could remember that happening she had been in the school playground in pigtails with a jump rope hanging from her tiny hand. "As in Alan Argaven." He stopped again and the silence stretched out. Still nothing. "The cofounder of Intellitech."

"Oh," she said. "Right." She had, of course, heard the name before. Who hadn't? But there was, in her defense, a lot on her mind.

"Yes, he was only the CEO of the most influential social technology development company on the planet."

"I get the point. Could you move along, please?"

He expelled a gust of air and shook his head before continuing.

"I take it, then, that you're not familiar with the recent decline of Intellitech's fortunes?"

"No, sorry."

"I won't bother you with the statistics of Intellitech's record on research and development in multiple areas of social data collection and tech development that revolutionized everything from medicine to communication. I mean, revolutionized on an unprecedented level. Like the global and unified integration of cell technology. The algorithms for the collection and analysis of data that modern surveillance and intelligence communities use to keep the country safe. I won't bother you with all that. Except to say that, even with that track record, with its stock at a fifteen-year high, and with no indication of decline from any external source whatsoever, everything crashed. Intellitech was on the verge of bankruptcy in a matter of five months."

Of course she knew that. Its implications on a variety of levels were still being discussed in many of her classes. But the *why*s were subsumed by the *what-now*s, and the hurried theoretical explanations given by professors were admittedly not of much interest to Laura, anyway.

"Why? What happened?"

"Hello?" he said sharply. "That's the damn point." His anger was back in full flourish; whatever softness he'd acquired from watching Laura's emotions teeter wildly was swept away. Little wonder, Laura realized. He was not talking about the collapse of a company. He was talking about the destruction of his family. "No one knows why. There are all sorts of theories: market instability, improper budgetary oversight, conspiracies of every sort ranging from a union of threatened foreign cartels to pure fantasies like the whim of the Old Man. But it's all unfounded conjecture. Anyone in a position to really know, all the people in power positions at the company at the time, are silent. They can't be made to talk, or they're not around to talk. Which means one thing, obviously."

Laura nodded, trying to give the sense that she found it obvious as well, despite having no figment of a guess what he was talking about.

"An internal matter." He threw it at her as he would the most rudimentary lesson to a dim child. "Something happened within the structure of the company, and it was so huge, it blew everything apart."

"Could it have been that huge, and no one knows anything about it?"

"Are you joking? What sort of world do you live in? Corporations are turning the fate of the world on a dime every day. Even you must have a sense that that's happening. But you don't know how, exactly. No one does. That's the essence of modern life. Decisions made behind closed doors shape modern existence."

Yes, Laura knew that to be true instinctively. And while it was theoretically chilling, sickening, it was so elemental a fact of life that it failed to stir any actual ire.

"Well," she said, "wouldn't your father know about it?" And her stomach dropped out. His father. She remembered it now. "I'm sorry," she said quickly, her eyes stinging with sympathy for him. Aaron's eyes, however, remained implacable.

"I don't want your sorrow. I want answers."

"I know. I'm trying."

"Are you? Do you know what trying is? When the company collapsed, my father ranted for months, until, finally, he was a pathetic wreck, locked in his room, gibbering in the dark. Until he didn't even have the strength or courage to go on with that anymore. So 'trying,' as you put it, is piecing together his babbling nonsense after he was gone and using it to hunt down his ghosts. I pieced it together. I constructed my programs; I cut into the systems I needed. How much help do you think I had with all that? Was anyone else in my family able? Were any of my father's associates willing to even speak to me? What do you think?"

He was raging now. His face was red, and his breath was coming short.

"Well, it took a year, but I found you. I enrolled myself in this liberal cesspool of a college just to get close to you. *That's* trying. And guess what? Now that I'm here, I still . . . have . . . *nothing!*"

She stared at him, the car filled with his short gasps. She was pressed against the door behind her, watching him.

A year just to find her. He was writing programs, *inventing* them from the sound of it, before that. Had he been twelve when he did that? Eleven? And officially enrolled in college, one that was apparently well beneath him, at fourteen? Putting aside that his IQ was clearly off the charts, he had spent two years of his childhood devoted to determining why his father had killed himself? Laura suddenly found it impossible to hate him. Pity him, yes. Fear him, surely. But her anger for him had evaporated.

"All right, Aaron. All right. Tell me, how does the Librarian figure into this?"

He looked up, his chest still laboring, although now it looked as though his energy was devoted to holding back tears. He was just too exhausted to resist her anymore.

"Of the many things my father let loose in his last few days, the one that preoccupied him the most was this Librarian. From what I could figure, the Librarian had once worked for him, was an employee of Intellitech a long time ago. But he developed a social algorithm called the Global Dynamic, a kind of a theory of human interaction that could predict business and cultural developments on a massive scale. It had the potential to revolutionize economics, the entire political-industrial landscape. He had developed it, but he wouldn't share it." Aaron shook his head in frustration. "Something like that. This is all from my father's disjointed ramblings. Intellitech's records of this Librarian, his exact position, the time he was employed, even his name, were all expunged. But from what I reconstructed of my father's logic, what happened to Intellitech at the end is pent up with this Librarian's theory and whatever it let loose."

Laura could see what the Librarian meant to Aaron, both a traumatized boy and a terrifyingly competent adult. In examining his pain, Laura's own whirlwind had quieted somewhat. Enough, at any rate, to see what the Librarian could mean for her.

"Aaron," she said, her voice soft and calm. "Something's happened to me. I'm missing a part of myself. Not just the memory of that conversation you have recorded, but that entire part of my life. Something took it out of me and put something else in its place. I remember finishing high school, saying goodbye to my friends, spending a summer with my parents before coming to college; things that, according to you, couldn't have happened. And you're right. They couldn't have. They didn't. I know it." She looked out at the open field around them, found it suddenly shadowed by something enormous, something that was hovering over her entire life that she was only now beginning to see. "I don't remember this Librarian, but I think he must know what happened to me, as well as to your family. We're going to go together, and we're going to find him."

"And," Aaron said in that voice that made his youth seem to disappear and animated his voice with something dangerous, "we're going to make him tell us the truth."

LAZARUS

MAL SET HIS CHIN ON his hand and watched the city pass through the darkened window of Remak's—Alan Silven's—limo. The city outside was a thing of gleaming silver and glass. Mal had seen it change around him, from the gray, lifeless place that had bred hopelessness into a living, breathing enemy. Even so, he could hardly believe it was the same city.

The crowds milled, bursting with a harried energy they lacked when their heads had been infected with that Idea. But the energy was all directed back at themselves, used for their own betterment. They were so focused on themselves that the city had wrapped itself in silver, hiding the rusted innards of a tortured and decrepit machine. It was all surface now, because that was as far as people were willing to look.

As if to offer evidence of its own guilt, the city streets opened up before the limousine as it entered the eastern edge of the island: Lazarus Heights. The dome — once a carapace of gray metal, the wire exo-frame making it appear as a hideous bug crawling over the city streets — was now reflecting the gleaming city around it, its surface a mirrored silver. Spearing up at five points along the eastern edge of the dome were the spikes of the Lazarus Towers, which were connected to one another by networks of walkways, enclosed bridges that were the highways of the city's upper echelon of corporate go-getters. Only the top tier of society, the most influential, the powers that ran the city from behind façades of cash and oil and technology, could afford a place in these exclusive buildings. An average citizen could not enter the towers, not even approach their doorways, without the gaze of the Metropolitan Counterterrorism Task Force's luminous green goggles falling on them forbiddingly.

Meanwhile, below the spires, people teemed around the dome, tourists lining up for blocks to get in, to see from behind the protective screens the ruined debris that had left a mark on the city. They swallowed the awed lumps in their throats, blinked back tears at what the city had faced, never doubting that it had recovered. How, after all, could a city that gleamed in the rising sun ever have forgotten its own humanity?

In the distance, beyond the towers, the hazy rainbow swell of colors glowed from the East River, both poisoned and beautified by the deadly chemicals that had infected its depths.

"I need to know what the Old Man wants," Remak said, as the limo pulled up a side street, out of sight of the dome and the towers. "If he knows about the neuropleth, how he plans to use it. Only with that information can I work to stop him."

Mal turned his somber eyes on the clean, polished face whose own eyes were so keen with intellectual hunger. Not for the first time, Mal thought that Remak's obsession was most of all that of a scientist, desperate for the facts to tally his theories.

"The last time I was there," Mal said, "they were carrying me in. I don't know what kind of security they have."

"MCT on the outside," Remak said. Of course, he had this cataloged and ready to go for God only knew how long. "Inside it's a standard level-twelve tech array: cameras, sonics, cycling digital chip scans, thermographics. Internal security is handled by a private firm: Lazarus Services; exclusively ex-military and ex-intelligence personnel. But above, at the top of the central tower, it's the Old Man's private suites. Just him, Kliest, and the two bodyguards. He won't allow anyone else in proximity — doesn't even allow them to carry guns around him." Remak spoke like he was briefing a black-ops specialist, not a battered teenager pressed into service and in way over his head. "You'll enter through the garage facing the water. Get to the elevators and go up as high as you can. I'll be assisting: I can jump from guard to guard, control them and the security systems. I'll get you up as high as possible, get you to the staircase or elevator that will take you closest to the top.

"This is enemy territory, Mal. I don't have anyone else to ask. By the time you're within sight of the tower entrance, I'll be out of Silven and into the guards, ready to assist you. It's enemy territory, but you're not alone, Mal. You're not alone."

Mal had always been on his own, and he knew it. Nothing was changing now. Remak reached Silven's well-manicured hand out in an awkward show of camaraderie.

Before it found Mal's shoulder, Mal's hand snapped out and grabbed the wrist hard enough to make the eyes wince.

"We're not friends, Remak," he said in a low, even voice. "You're holding Laura over me, so I'm doing what you asked. That's all." He let go of the wrist but held the calculating gaze for a moment longer. Then he opened the door and stepped out into enemy territory.

The stimulant the doctor had put into him was making the searing flashes of lightning in his head recede to distant cracks of thunder. So, seeing more or less straight, he walked down the block and turned the corner, where the spires of the Lazarus Towers cut the skyline like a razor. They had done the impossible: they had co-opted the skyline from the dome, drawing the eye away from what had once been the city's defining reality.

Mal was aware that even at this distance he was already on the spires' security cameras, maybe not noted by a specific guard just yet, but limping there on their screens, recorded for future review when necessary.

He spotted himself, warped and elongated in the liquid surface of the dome. He avoided Lazarus Heights for many reasons. His mother had lived near here once, with his stepfather, before the neighborhood grew beyond their means and swept them away with the other undesirables. They were not on friendly visiting terms, but circumstances had demanded he show up at their door once upon a time. Back then the dome was a creeping insect, its gray surface an implacable menace, hateful and terrified messages scrawled across its surface, the rot festering at the center of New York's heart.

He gladly left it at his back and came around the towers and turned so that the luminous rainbow of the East River swelled before him, painting Brooklyn with a weird swirling haze, as it squatted low across the water, in the eternal shadow of its regal brother. During construction of the dome's new shell and the Lazarus Towers, something had spilled into the river. Not oil, not waste, exactly, but some space-age chemical used to strengthen metals and weatherize porous concrete. Remak said that the molecules of the chemical had bonded with the water and that the river was not, technically speaking, water anymore. It was a new element that created a brilliant surface glow when the sun struck it at certain times of day, but was also, slowly, eroding the edges of the island of Manhattan itself, eating away at the very ground people lived on. That was what Remak had said, based on materials that had passed across Silven's desk. But there was never any mention of it in newsblogs, on the HD. To the world of people hungry for a new sight, a new experience, it was simply more visual stimulation.

Mal turned in disgust from the river that was not really a river anymore. He walked in the shadow of the towers until he was across from the tallest of them, the impossibly high central tower, the tip of its spire a pointed attack on the heavens themselves.

Probing the warm pulp of his missing tooth to painfully sharpen his focus, Mal spotted the ramp that sloped down from the street, into the bowels of the tower. As he stood and watched, a single car entered, cruising slowly in, the gunmetal garage door sliding open for it and closing behind it like the spiked gates of a medieval castle.

Mal scanned the expanse of street; these were loading docks, maintenance entrances, and a riverside path. Tourists crowded about the railing along the river, gazing down at its hypnotic surface, breathing in fumes that might very well burn out their lungs or give their children cancer. But their attention was all turned away from Mal. Besides them, there were only a few passing cars in the distance. He ran across the street, the asphalt sending small shock waves through his ribs and lacerated flesh.

Along the ramp entrance, there was a slim walkway down the slope that ended in a flat metal door with no handle. A camera with a blinking red light was perched above it. Mal stopped himself at the top of this path waiting for . . . something. A signal.

It took him a full minute to notice that the blinking red light had suddenly gone steady. He went down to the door, and as he reached it, there was an internal click and the door slid inward, permitting entrance. He was done pausing now. All he could do was leave it to Remak to facilitate his passage.

He slipped in, and the door shut behind him with a dull clang, cutting off the outside and putting him into a world of fluorescent half-light and a cavernous expanse perhaps one-eighth filled with sleek, expensive cars and long, ostentatious limos. He crossed the space, holding to the shadowed columns, his feet sounding with agonizingly sharp echoes across the empty space. The ding of an opening elevator door called his attention, and when he saw no one disembark, he knew it had been summoned just for him.

He crossed the last dim space, feeling as though he had entered some mythological underworld, a Hades that his father had once recounted to him in a story of long-dead heroes.

He stepped into the elevator, the suddenly sharp lights pressing dully into his drug-protected brain. The car went so far up and so fast that it compressed Mal's chest and skull, and he had to grasp the rails with his powerful hands so tightly that his knuckles whitened, bringing the chaos of crosshatched scars into high relief. Then it began to slow, leaving his stomach uncomfortably low, and finally it stopped.

The doors opened, and Mal immediately swung his body back in and pressed up against the wall. It had opened on a small landing with a flight of stairs going up. At the foot of the stairs, a suited figure stood guard.

How could the guard not have seen him, though, with the security lenses giving him a full 180-degree sweep of the space and a thermographic enhancement that would penetrate the wall Mal was hiding behind?

"Mal," a voice said quietly from around the corner.

Mal leaned slowly around the corner.

The guard maintained his position, suited, cellenses turning him into a human automaton. He had one hand resting calmly on a weapon, small and black and sleek like a wasp, slung over his shoulders. What Mal had missed in his first, brief glance was the second guard, slumped unconscious on the floor.

"I disabled the pertinent security equipment, too," the standing guard said with Remak's formal tone. "I'll move from guard to guard and help you however I can, but I can't go any higher than this. I don't know how long it will take them to notice the security equipment, but going faster is better."

Mal came across the landing, notable in that there was no stairway going down. He looked into the guard's face, and Remak returned his gaze neutrally.

Mal gripped the banister and began hauling himself upward and past another landing. The Old Man would not be anywhere but at the very top, the space closest to God Himself. Mal stopped on the third landing. There was another flight up, but a sign in black digital letters labeled it as ROOF ACCESS. He looked at the featureless door here with the camera above, its red light steady. As he watched, the door slit open with a whispered *whoosh* of sealed air. Mal heard nothing from beyond and so gripped the edge of the door with his fingertips and slowly slid it open.

The narrow hall was thick with a plush carpet that swallowed the sound of Mal's limping feet. A gentle hum pervaded this place, and it was the only sound he heard, so he followed that down the hallway, which curved gently, conforming to the curve of the spire at the tower's top. The eyes of ancient faces glared at him from out of marble busts. He passed framed paintings, windows that looked out onto pointillist parks, abstract figures, a wavering man on a bridge holding his head as he screamed.

The hum led him to the very end of the hallway, a set of double doors, which he remembered, even from the last time he was here. His fingers came up and rested against the wood. He could feel the heat even through the surface and remembered its hot prickle on his skin, facing the shriveled, cracking thing in the shadows, the Medusa. It was there now — he swore he could hear it breathing beneath the hum of the heaters.

Sound split through Mal's reverie. It wasn't loud, but the hum was so regular, the place so quiet, it shuddered his thoughts like an earthquake: the sharp drone of a voice from back up the hall, Kliest's voice. He came away from the door gladly.

Where were Roarke and Castillo? Off on a mission? Or sitting here behind one of these other doors, waiting?

Kliest's voice emanated from two doors back, her office. He stopped at it, leaned his head closer.

"Am I not making myself clear?" The acid tone scalded even through the door. "You simply don't offer any official statement."

"I understand perfectly," came another voice. It had a boxed quality, as though it was not in the room, but coming through a wall-mounted cellscreen. Nevertheless, its deep, articulate tone was familiar. Mal was sure he had heard it before, many times. "But the sort of shakeup you're talking about, it demands a response. Both in words and in action."

"Your cabinet has weathered natural disasters, military atrocities, and financial crises, Mr. Bramson," Kliest said, "and you've managed to hold back from any definitive action on those occasions."

Bramson? Mal recognized the voice instantly, then. Kliest was speaking to the president of the United States. Not simply speaking to him: berating him.

"This kind of action, in a city that size, even with the full MCT deployed, it's unprecedented," the president continued, his voice holding as strong as it always had issuing forth from newsblogs and HDs. "If, God forbid, this should slip from your control—"

"Things"—Kliest's voice was a razor held to the throat—"do not slip from our control."

"No," the president allowed after a pause, "of course not. Nevertheless, the American people will need to be reassured."

"And you, Mr. Bramson," Kliest finished the narrative with her own twist, "will remain silent."

"I cannot in good conscience—"

"Save it for your campaign," she cut him off. "You are planning on campaigning again? And being reelected?"

The room—and the hallway Mal stood in—flooded with uncomfortable silence.

"Yes," the president's strong voice returned. "But, Ms. Kliest, I'll have you know that I'm working toward a time when—"

"Until that time comes, keep your mouth closed and your head nodding." There was a thump, as of Kliest's hand hitting the cellscreen switch harder than she needed to. She disgorged a deep sigh. "The power-mad can be kept on a leash with one show of strength. Idealists need to be threatened over and over again."

"You knew he was an idealist when we installed this

cabinet." A third voice, liquid smooth and speaking in perfectly refined and enunciated English, also came in via cellscreen. "That's how we sold him, after all."

"Yes, yes. Government is so . . . superfluous. On to the other project," she said, making a new start of it. "Where do we stand, Mr. Alhazred?"

"As you know, the Metropolitan Counterterrorism Task Force holds steady at pacification-level yellow. A move directly to red would normally require a clear and direct threat to the urban environment."

"That won't do."

"Yes," the slick voice said, having already predicted this response. "You will need the MCT primed and ready to move into full urban pacification with almost no notice. Therefore a heightened state of readiness is necessary. Therefore certain pressures need to be applied to the governor. Therefore I have mobilized corporate interests to this end. I am just waiting on your word, ma'am."

"The word is given, Mr. Alhazred."

"I'll see to it immediately. If I may ask," Alhazred said carefully, "are you intending on being in the city when we initiate?"

"Your concern is duly noted, Mr. Alhazred, but we're quite untouchable up here. Quite untouchable."

Mal yanked his head back as someone's fist hammered

into the wood paneling he left behind, splintering it with one long crack running above and beneath the point of impact. Mal spun, and before he even defined his enemy visually, he put an uppercut into a hard gut and shot a right cross that cracked into a cheek and sent the figure reeling backwards.

Castillo toppled into a niche behind, upsetting the heavy sculpture within. From an open doorway just to the side, diagonally across from the one Mal had been listening at, Roarke glided out toward him.

He was large—half a head taller than Mal, even—but his feet and his body moved with synaptic quickness, and he went under Mal's hook and blasted rigid knuckles into Mal's taped ribs with horrific accuracy. Mal felt the shock wave as the cracks expanded, the rough edges pushing into soft tissue, sending an electric buzz through his nerves.

Roarke moved back into a defense, expecting that his blow would have put Mal out of it. Mal feinted, doubling over in pain, but then snapped back up and lashed out with a jab.

Roarke's performance-enhanced body had a matchless perception and speed, and he caught Mal by the wrist before the blow made contact. He began to twist it around, moving it into a lock, even as his other hand fended off a series of blows from Mal's free arm.

Never had Mal felt so physically helpless. He had lost fights before, of course, but never been so hugely outmatched, never been made to feel so much like a child at the mercy of a cruel adult.

Mal lurched forward, trying to smash in Roarke's jaw with the hard plane of his own forehead. Roarke avoided the head butt by pulling back, but in doing so loosened his grip and shifted his weight backwards. Mal shoved forward hard. The move sent him into Roarke, and Roarke into the recovering Castillo, and all three of them toppling to the ground. Mal leaped up, the hallway spinning around him again. From the jumble, a hand whipped out and caught his ankle, only to have its wrist stomped. It released, and, bouncing from wall to wall trying to keep steady, Mal raced back down the hallway. He heard another door open from behind.

"What the hell is—" Kliest cut herself short, obviously having caught sight of Mal's departing figure. "Don't be a fool, Mal," she yelled over the sound of feet beating down the hall after him. "This is our building."

He made it to the stairway door, shut it behind him knowing that, though it locked from outside, it would not from within. There were two private floors below him, but he had no idea what they looked like, what sort of exits they offered. Then there was the rest of the tower below, men

JESSE KARP

in neat suits with angry little machine guns. Remak could control two of them, three perhaps. Could he control five, twenty, a hundred? He could not, however, control Castillo or Roarke at all. Mal, as ever, was alone.

He shot upward, past the sign that read ROOF ACCESS. Below, the door shuddered. Remak had it locked so that even from within it couldn't be opened. Perhaps Mal was not as utterly alone as he'd thought.

As Mal saw the roof access door pop open in invitation, he heard the door below come open as well.

"Something locked this door." Roarke's voice echoed upward as he spoke to Castillo. "And I can't get through to security for some reason. You need to use your override code." The voice was coming closer, as Roarke moved up the stairs.

Mal made it to the final landing and cast a glance below him. Roarke rounded the corner, and with the clarity of rushing adrenaline, Mal could see the detail of his lips twitching in subvocalized communication, ordering Castillo elsewhere, in preparation.

Mal threw the door open, burst onto the roof. He found himself in a forest of small encasements, low housing units, metallic arrays wired to one another and down into the building. The edges of the roof were gated off by a high wall of tightly knit metallic links, and no sound at all was coming up from the streets, so far below they may as well have been a different universe entirely. The sky opened above him like a bright promise.

The door behind him hissed shut and sealed itself closed. Mal raced between the various apparatus and up to the fence, jamming his fingers through the links and hoisting himself up. His muscles stretched and pulled, tightening over the cracked ribs. Mal coughed hard, spraying the fence before him with blood, but didn't stop climbing.

He heard the door open, not like it was smashed, but with its signature hiss, as though Roarke had employed a security override. Mal pulled hard, levering his legs over the fence, feeling something stretch to its limit within him. His feet came down on a six-inch ledge of concrete that looked over yawning space.

He had come over on the south side of the spire, facing across toward the second tallest tower, its expanse of roof some three stories below and fifty feet distant. Windows ran down that building's north face, separating around the covered walkway that joined that building to this one many stories below. Far, far down beneath, a distance that made Mal's labored breath choke in his throat, was the insect crawl of people and cars, grouping like colonies around the dome to the west and the glowing river to the east. The whole city, spread before him, was trapped between the sky and the distant asphalt.

Mal pulled his face away from the view, pressed it against the metal links that his fingers were clutching with a death grip. Mal's life had been such that fear seldom crept into him. There was so little left for him, so little to hang his hope on, to look forward to. He wasn't afraid to lose anything, because there was nothing left to lose. He battled life just because he wasn't willing to give up the fight. But here, the immediate threat of a shattered body was so sudden, so total, his heart was racing, blood shivering through his veins like frozen needles.

"Mal, stay where you are." Roarke's voice was shockingly intimate, just on the other side of the links, right in his ear, the man's breath tickling his cheek. "I'll pull you back over."

His eyes focused tightly on the links in front of him, Mal lowered his body, fingers gripped in the links, foot finding purchase on the small concrete lip that arched over the highest window just a few feet below the ledge he stood on. Then his hands came down and found the ledge, and his feet slid down across the hardened plastic of the window and came to the lip at the window's bottom. Mal's eyes never left the surface directly in front of him, his face pressing against the nicks and bumps of the concrete as though it were a lover.

"You're a walking zero, Mal," Roarke's voice called from behind the fence, even and professional as always. "A walking zero."

Mal moved, hand to top of this window, foot to top of the next window, then hand to bottom of window and foot to the bottom of the next window, climbing down the building as if it were a gargantuan ladder. The wind rushed him, blustering around him like an enemy, tugging, shifting at unexpected moments. It gave Mal strength, infused his muscles with energy. An enemy was exactly what Mal needed.

Fight me, Wind. Fight me.

His hands moved; his feet moved. He pressed his body as close to the building as he could, making himself too small and flat a target for the wind to grab hold of. There were times, though, suspended between one window and the next, that his body couldn't lie flat, that he had to search with his limbs for the next hold, and the wind grabbed at him; his muscles tightened in anger, and he growled until he found the next place with a shaky foot, a sweat-slicked hand.

Like before. Like climbing down from that mountain in the Idea's impossible prison. Climbing down the harsh,

JESSE KARP

rocky surface. But not alone that time. With others. With Laura.

An impact shuddered against the window that Mal pressed his face against. Castillo stood there, behind the tinted plastic. Thank God the surface was made to withstand extraordinary pressures. Castillo's fist crashed against it, but it held. Nevertheless, Mal felt the vibration of it, the shock of Castillo's angry face lurching through his heart. The adrenaline racing, the blood flowing, it was working the doctor's stimulants right out of Mal's system. Beneath the strain of holding his weight aloft, he could feel the tears and the bruises getting the better of him again. He could feel the pain in his ribs spreading through his torso, his entire body like burning acid. If his vision weren't locked on the space just before his nose, it would be swimming, he knew. He could feel the thunder in his head, cracking against his skull from within.

Fight me, Castillo. Fight me. He looked down, away from the burly man's angry, screaming face.

Beneath him, the building stretched down and down forever, vertigo or his concussion whipping the view from side to nauseating side. But a story down and one line of windows to Mal's left was the top of the covered walkway that joined the buildings.

Mal looked back up at Castillo. He thought to smile but could not pull his lips from the rigor of strain they were in. Mal put his tongue on that jagged tooth and bit down, felt blood course from the tongue and the infected wound beneath, tasted iron and pus, the pain giving a single instant of crystal focus. He used it to shift, reach to his left, find the next window over, and grip it hard enough to—in his mind—crack the concrete beneath his fingers.

Castillo threw his body against the window. His frustration was so intense that he had not thought to use his security override to open the window. Yet.

Mal was at the next window, in line over the walkway. The trembling in his arms was uncontrollable now. The wind snatched at him, whipping his hood, the cuffs of his pants against his flesh so hard they felt like lashes. He looked between his feet at the roof of the walkway fifteen feet below, and he let go.

For a single moment both chokingly terrifying and heart-racingly beautiful, Mal flew free, the wind raging in his ears, tears streaming from his eyes.

"*Laura!*" He screamed it at the wind, his voice swept off into—

He came down on the roof of the walkway on his feet and his forearms, felt his ankle fracture, sending a blade of pain up his leg, felt his cracked ribs break loose, their jag-

JESSE KARP

ged edges slicing into his lungs. Immediately, his throat was clogged with fluid, which he retched out in great red and yellow gobs. It cleared, but he could not catch his breath, could not take a full gulp of air. He held there on his elbows and knees, hacking, coughing, expelling fluid from his nose and his mouth, involuntary tears from his eyes, the wind racing around him, still trying to tug him that extra foot that would put him over the edge.

Minutes passed before he could even raise his head up with an effort. There, straight before him, was Castillo, at the window directly above the walkway. The tinted surface slid up neatly, and Castillo pulled back, shocked for an instant by the strength of the wind. But then his eyes found Mal again, and he began climbing from the window. If his enemy would do it, he would do it, too.

Mal looked beneath him, at the surface of the walkway's roof. It was the same tinted plastic as the windows, held in by a framework of metal. He gathered what was left of himself into his fist and plunged it down in the center of a square pane of the plastic.

Castillo made his way out, uncertainly onto the walkway, throwing himself back and clutching at the wall as the wind encompassed him. Mal pounded down, again and again, leaving bloody knuckle prints on the surface.

Castillo went down to his hands and knees, began

crawling across the ten feet to his prey, his feral gaze never wavering.

Mal felt something crack, was hopeful until he realized it was two of his knuckles splintering apart, separating the scarred skin covering them and sending rivers of blood onto the plastic. Mal growled, switched hands, and pounded down hard, the mallet of his fist landing as though on the end of a pile driver.

Castillo was five feet away, almost close enough to reach out and make a grab, when the plastic buckled at its edges. Both the plastic and the metal were too strong to crack under mere human flesh and bone, but the area joining them revealed itself as the weak link. Mal punched once more, and the panel of plastic fell inward, with Mal toppling in afterward.

Mal came down on his shoulders, rolled to his back, and sat up with a stab inside his chest like someone was working a knife in him. People in the walkway had stopped, fascinated by the drama seen through the clear roof. Now they pulled away in horror as the drama shattered the social agreement by becoming real.

Mal came to his feet and lumbered forward as Castillo appeared in the gap overhead, shuffling his body to lower his feet through first. Mal made it to the end of the walkway and entered the building he had just been climbing, as he heard Castillo drop, curse.

"Where is goddamned security? Somebody go to the nearest security booth and *get them over here!*"

Mal was in a climate-controlled outer hallway. He hobbled, pressed against a wall to carry his weight, hurrying toward the nearest corner. He turned it, and there stood a neat-uniformed guard with a badge that identified him as TALBY and a small, black weapon clutched in his hand. The blank face of the guard swiveled toward Mal.

"Christ, where the hell were you guys?" Castillo scolded, running up. The automaton regarded Castillo and then raised the gun . . . at him. "What the fu—"

Castillo threw his body backwards, crashing through a nearby door before the weapon could be fired.

The guard, Talby, whose neurological impulses had been commandeered by Remak, took Mal by the arm and half dragged him ten steps to the next bend. They came to a set of elevators, one door held open and waiting. Talby's body deposited Mal into it, and the door closed on the dead, implacable face of the security guard that Remak inhabited.

Mal held himself up on the rail, knowing if he let himself down, his body wouldn't find the power to stand again. The car drove down. The light of the elevator was spearing through his eyes now, like scalpels cutting into the gray twists of his brain. He could feel the pressure of his descent inside him, where his blood was pouring into his punctured lungs, stopping his breath. He was going to suffocate.

The door slid open onto the nearly empty parking lot again. Mal dragged himself out, throwing himself from surface to surface to keep himself up. The door hissed open for him. He limped agonizingly back out toward the alien glow of the river. People's backs were to him; cars passed by, uninterested. Couldn't Remak take one of the drivers, get Mal away from here? Or would that cost him his ability to put a chokehold on the building's security?

Mal made it to the corner, began crossing the street toward a line of expensive apartments and stores.

Through the thudding in his ears, the sound of his own body breaking down, he heard the clatter of running feet, turned.

Castillo and Roarke were charging toward him from half a block away.

He rushed to the other side of the street, tripped on the edge of the sidewalk, then collapsed to the ground, snapping another rib as he went down. Blood spilled from his mouth like vomit. Every molecule of air he drew in was a shuddering effort through his body. He scanned the buildings over him with dying eyes, squinting against the painful light.

Figures, pairs of figures, hurried by, not seeing him for their inward focus, the urgency of their own lives available to them through their cells, their cellenses. A woman accused her son of lying at the top of her lungs as though she were in her own living room. Not seeing Mal and not *wanting* to see him, both. The clattering of feet stopped nearby.

"Unbelievable," Castillo said to his partner in relieved good humor. "You know, if the Old Man let us carry guns, this would have been over before it started." When his partner didn't respond, Castillo pushed nervously on. "And what the hell is happening with security?"

There. Beneath a metal ramp that led to an upscale tobacco shop, Mal saw what he needed. He started crawling away from them.

"Where you going?" Castillo asked as the sharp edge of a heel cracked down on Mal's spine, separating something, making one of his legs ring with a blessed numbness.

"What are you doing, Mal?" Roarke said, the professional flatness slipping from his voice. "You want to die on the street? Stop fighting and let us take you inside. It'll go fast, easy. Nothing's going to stop it at this point."

Mal pulled himself toward his goal, his cracked, bleeding fingers scraping along the concrete of the sidewalk.

"Have you ever seen anything like this?" Roarke said.

"Kid's a fighter," Castillo had to allow.

Mal pulled himself into the opening beneath the ramp, just enough to remove him from their view for an instant.

"Whoa, okay," Castillo said, hurrying over.

Mal's fingers found the rusty edges of the forgotten grating, pulled it open, dropped himself into the dark hole.

"*What the fuck?*" Castillo nearly screamed it out of shock. "Where is he? There's nowhere to go in here."

Roarke's response was lost as the sound of their voices stretched out and warped, blended with the faraway sounds of the remembered world.

Beat you, Mal thought as he tumbled down. *I beat you.*

He fell into a pool of muck, its brown hue scoured pale. The pool of muck had formed because, while people had forgotten this place, the rain had not, seeping in through the grate and creating puddles that never evaporated.

The darkness in here, like the color of the muck, had paled, the shadows lightening to such a degree that even with his failing eyesight, Mal could see the subway tracks that extended indefinitely both to the north and the south.

The muck felt only cool, its moisture, its wetness having retreated into a mere suggestion, a tingle. Blood soaked into his sweatshirt — pouring from his nose, bubbling from his mouth — and swirled into the faded liquid, stirring it with intense color briefly, before that color, too, was swept apart and faded away.

He bit into his tongue with the jags of his cracked tooth to focus himself, but he couldn't even feel that tiny pain anymore. His life was pain, the world was pain, and it was receding.

Roarke had been right. Nothing could stop this now. But just because he was going to die, didn't mean he was going to stop fighting.

He came up to his knees, swayed, felt things inside himself giving way. He clutched the metal of the track to keep himself steady.

Dying in a forgotten tunnel, Mal pulled himself through the faded shadows.

MOM

LAURA ROOTED UNDER THE BED, plumbing the shadows for her cell. Once retrieved, she brought it to the desk and began unfolding the screen to full size. Aaron surveyed the operation like a scientist observing a rat move through its maze.

"Okay," she said, turning to invite him, but he was already coming forward, and when she turned back to the screen, she saw that it was already filling with gigabytes of tightly packed data.

"There," he said, once the screen was filled. "This is every piece of information I've collected over the last two years that has possible ties to the Librarian." He had the expectant expression of a little boy awaiting a cookie.

Laura bent and put her face closer to the screen. The first thing her eyes fell upon was a paragraph about the uncovering of a small cement room underneath a government office building in Sacramento, California. Maintenance workers had come upon it after a water main break that caused a flood in the building's basement. The cement room was not on any blueprints of the building, but when the metal door was pried open, it turned out to be filled with hard copies of bills about to be passed, about to be vetoed, about to be voted on, even drafts of bills by legislators who had not even submitted them yet, every one of them related to corporate finance, land purchases, tax shelters, and subsidies. The commercial future of the state of California, collected into one damp little cement cube.

The paragraph following concerned an airplane bound from Chicago to Texas that had to set down for an emergency landing in Nebraska due to engine trouble. According to standard airline procedure, every passenger was checked off against the passenger manifesto as they deplaned and again as they were received by airline personnel. A single passenger, listed as Charles Alan Beaumont, never departed the plane, nor had any sign of him turned up on the plane, nor did security cameras pick him up in the area of the plane, nor did security cameras in Chicago, in fact, pick him up entering the plane. All of this despite a full flight with no irregularities noted among the gate crew. Someone had manufactured a passenger and booked him on the flight, though he did not exist to claim his seat, which was taken by a mother and her two children visiting cousins in Texas.

Paragraph after paragraph of this stuff unfolded before Laura as she scrolled down: bookstore employees opening up in the morning to find their entire American History section vanished without a trace; an entire building's worth of law-enforcement computers in Delaware spontaneously devoting themselves to a search for a missing shipment of surveillance equipment in Idaho; the twenty-two-person team of corporate lawyers defending their clients from a multibillion-dollar civil suit all resigning their positions without warning or explanation, leaving the company that employed them ruined by the payout it ultimately had to face. It went on and on, stories, graphs, flow charts, from one end of the country to the other, occasionally veering out into Canada, Mexico, Western Europe, Asia. Long before the progress bar showed that Laura had reached the one-quarter mark, she straightened up and faced this bizarre boy.

"What do you expect me to do with all this?" she asked him.

"You're the one who knows the Librarian. He's in there

somewhere," Aaron gestured with a sharp cut of his hand at the screen. "Find him."

"You've—" She turned back to the impossible tangle of information and then back to him, nearly sputtering. "You've got to be kidding. I told you I don't remember anything about this. Not really. How am I supposed to pull that mess of stuff apart?"

His eyes smoldered at her.

"You're just supposed to," he said quietly but with a hard chord in his tone that spoke to Laura more of desperation than anger. He had finally found what he was looking for after all this time, and he needed to unburden himself, to give the backbreaking responsibility over to someone else, just for a moment, just for a breath.

"All right," she said. "All right. Well . . . I've never been to most of the places in there. Lose all the stuff that didn't happen in or around New York State."

"An hour ago, you didn't remember being in New York City," he said bitterly. "And you just got through telling me that you don't really remember anything we're talking about. You might have met the Librarian in Australia for all you know."

"Listen, you said you wanted my help. This is me helping. We narrow it down; at least that's a place to start. What have you got to lose?"

He turned away from her, walked over, and sat on the bed.

"Well?" she said.

"It's done," he snapped, like a child told to do his chores one too many times.

She turned back to the screen, and the size of the document had decreased drastically. She scrolled down and found somewhere between fifteen and twenty items.

"Okay, put these in order of distance from Vassar, nearest to farthest, and we'll work from there."

"Now?"

"Right."

"The two of us are going to get into the car and go from one place to the next? Together?"

"Yes." She felt like a babysitter again, having to reassure her charge for the tenth time that he would get to watch HD after he finished his homework. "That's the whole idea. I assume you won't have any trouble getting into the records here, putting me on mental health leave or something that will salvage some of my parents' money."

"No, no trouble."

He watched her start picking through the detritus on her desk and eventually come up with a pen and a notepad.

"What are you doing?" he asked.

"Leaving my roommate a note. I don't plan on seeing her for a while." *Or ever again.*

"On *paper?* What, do you live in the last century? Are you a grandmother?"

Kari, she wrote, *You're going to have the room to yourself for a while. Everything's okay, but I had to head back home. E-mail if you want, and enjoy the extra space!*

Writing it made Laura think of the class she was missing right now — Intro to Diagnostic Psychology — and the entire schedule that, in her head, had already become the responsibility of another Laura.

She signed the note and laid it on her roommate's pillow.

"Okay," she said, taking in the details of her room a final time and sucking in a gust of its air. "Let's go."

Aaron stood up and headed toward the door, but she didn't follow.

"Wait," she said. "Sorry. There's one more thing."

He rolled his eyes and assumed an impatient posture. She stood, watching him, as he crossed his arms on his chest and began tapping his fingers in a show of annoyance.

"Picking up social cues isn't really your strong suit, is it?" she said.

"What?" He stood up at attention, like a baseball player

who's afraid the fly ball just flew right over his head and he didn't notice it. "What do you mean?"

"Could you excuse me, please?" She made it as clear as possible.

"Fine. Be quick about it," he said, and let himself out of the room.

With Aaron gone, the feeling of loss filled the room again, became palpable.

She turned to the unfolded cell screen and keyed the number for home. Her mother's face flickered onto the screen, underlined by a scrolling ad for room fresheners.

"Hi, honey," she said brightly. "How are you do— What's wrong?"

"I've got some news, Mom, and I don't think you're going to love it."

"Oh no. It's about Josh, isn't it? I'm so sorry."

"No, it's not about Josh. I mean, things aren't great there, either, but that's not why I'm calling."

"What happened? Did he do something?"

"No, Mom. Stop talking about Josh. He was never real, anyway."

On the far side of the screen, her mother's face washed with confusion.

"What does that mean, Laura?"

Laura's shoulders slumped, and she took another deep breath.

"Honestly, Mom, I have no idea. I'm leaving school." It sounded so harsh in her ears that she fumbled for a lie and added awkwardly, "for a while."

Her mother's brow collected between her eyes.

"You're . . ." The silence stretched out so long that Laura thought the connection had gone bad and there was a frozen frame of her mother stuck on the screen. A new ad extolled the virtue of an all-natural tension-relieving vitamin supplement. "Leaving school," her mother finally managed to say it.

"For a while."

"What's going on, Laura?" Claire Westlake's voice had acquired a vein of panicky concern. "Are you all right?"

"I'm not all right, as a matter of fact, and it's because of school and because of Josh and because I'm not—" She wrestled the thought, her mind forcing a word out of her mouth she couldn't predict. "Me."

"Laura"—her mother reined her voice back in, playing the steadying angle now—"everything is going to be okay, honey, I promise you. I'd be happy to come to you, take you to dinner. Or why don't you take a week off and come see us. Your father would love that."

"I am taking a week off, Mom. I'm going to take a whole bunch of them off."

"You're being flippant now, Laura, and that's just not fair. This is a huge bombshell to drop. Help me understand it."

"I can't help you. I don't understand it myself."

"Then you need to stay until you do. Running away isn't the answer."

"School *is* running away. Leaving school is me *not* running away anymore."

"You're going to have to explain better than that, Laura."

Laura's elbows went down on the table, and she leaned forward, confronting the screen.

"I'm not a child," she said through a hard jaw.

"You *are* a child, Laura. You're on the verge, you're almost an adult, but we still owe you more taking care of, more being looked after."

Laura's head slumped down between her shoulders, and she felt her eyes burning hot.

"Mommy," she said, letting the tears out—she had never been any good at holding them back. "Mommy." She brought her face back up and let her mother see her pleading face. "There's something wrong with me. There has been since I got here. You must have fought it so hard in your own head. You must have prayed it wasn't so. But this isn't me. I went off course somewhere, and you know I did."

Her mother was looking back, biting one edge of her lip. She was crying, too.

"You can't help me," Laura said. "No one can help until I know what's wrong. Leaving school is the first thing that's felt right since . . . since I can even remember."

"Just as you want to pull away, Laura, I want to hold you closer." Her mother managed a weak smile. "Where are you going to go?"

"I'm going to drive for a while, just around New York."

"You're going to drive around by yourself?"

"No," she said. She could give her mother this; at least she could give her this. "A friend is coming with me; Traci."

"Laura," her mother's fingers were flexing, instinctively wanting to reach out and touch her daughter's face through a screen that wouldn't permit it. "Come home."

"Soon, Mom. I promise." She wiped her tears with a forearm, made a brave go at a smile. "I promise."

Claire studied her daughter—the *image* of her daughter, Laura reminded herself—through the screen. Her jaw was trembling.

"Being a mother is like having your heart outside your body, Laura. Can you understand that?"

The sense of loss she had been feeling welled up in Laura, and she nodded, unable to speak.

"You call me, Laura. Every night."

"I will, Mom. I'm not going to drop off the edge of the earth. I'm just taking a drive."

"Okay. You find Laura and bring her back to us."

They looked at each other while an ad for Kleenex scrolled below.

"Laura. I was wrong. You're not a child."

"I love you, Mom."

"I love you."

Laura managed to hold herself together until the screen went dark, but then tears came like a tidal flow, racking her body so badly that she had to grab on to the edge of the desk until her knuckles were white. She gasped in, unable to catch her breath, fluid streaming from her eyes and nose, her torso spasming as if in an epileptic fit.

She was dimly aware of the door starting to open. Aaron appeared, caught totally unprepared, and instantly closed himself out once again.

She put her hands over her face to plug the dam, and tears crept through her fingers, dropping onto the desk before the unfolded cell, the totem of technology before which they all prayed now.

She took in gulps of air, let them out slowly.

Not quite finished yet, she managed to stand up and re-fold the cell. As she weighed it in her hand, the tears tapered away and her ragged breathing filled the room. She took the object by its edge and winged it under the bed again, once more consigning it to darkness.

She used the balls of her hands to scrub away the last of the tears, then marched out of her room to find her future.

PART II

THE BEAST

ROARKE ADOPTED HIS ACCUSTOMED SOLDIER'S bearing before the door of Arielle Kliest and knocked.

"Come," Kliest said from within, and he pushed through and shut the door silently behind him, taking a spot directly before her desk, looking down at her cool, sharp features. "And so?"

"Nothing, ma'am," he stated as tersely as he would have brought news of resounding success. Judgment was the purview of those in charge. He merely reported facts. "The locator signal was coming from a man named Gerald

Fisher. He's been subjected to a standard interrogation array. There's no indication that he knows Mal."

"If Mr. Fisher's geolocator was functioning as a cloak, now that we've taken it out of the equation, why hasn't Mal's come back online?"

"Tech has no explanation, ma'am. As you recall, it went offline briefly after we put it in the first time. Some kind of a manufacturing flaw?"

"Not likely," Kliest said, her voice softer than Roarke would have expected at the news. "And the girl's apartment?"

"Rose Santoro's apartment is still empty."

"And," she ventured carefully, "no sign of Mal himself?"

"No, ma'am. The space Mal disappeared in . . ." For the first time, a crack appeared in the granite of Roarke's face, an aperture to the moist, shaking spaces of the inexplicable. "There's nothing there. It was a short ramp leading up to a tobacco store. Eight feet long, three feet up at its highest point, barely enough space to fit him. There was no exit from it that was not visible to us at the time. I simply don't have an explanation. I'm sorry, Ms. Kliest."

She nodded, her eyes unfocused before her.

"I'll have a security team sent down to pick over it carefully," she said absently, perhaps not even to him.

"Yes, ma'am. If I may, I'm not sure I'd fully trust a security team at this point. To say that they dropped the ball on this one would be putting it mildly. Mr. Castillo reports that one of them actually pulled a gun on him to assist in Mal's escape."

"Yes," she said, bringing her formidable attention back on to him. "We have that on camera. He climbed down the building," she said in the same breath, and it took Roarke an instant to register that she was no longer talking about the guard but instead about Mal. "He *climbed down* the building. *Injured,* no less."

"I could fill in details, ma'am, but that's about the size of it. I will say, Ms. Kliest, that if Mr. Castillo and I were permitted to carry firearms——"

"Guns are never permitted in the Old Man's vicinity, as you well know," she said, tossing the issue aside. "Does it impress you"——her eyes sharpened, studying his reaction with interest——"that Mal managed to escape in such a physically depleted state?"

"No, ma'am."

"No? I'd have thought you would admire such a high degree of commitment."

"To be quite frank, ma'am, it made me sick. He's a child, and he nearly murdered himself to get clear of us."

She nodded, offering no indication of her own feelings

on the subject. Instead, her expression flattened, and she rose from her seat.

"I'm going to need you to join me for the report. He may have some questions."

"Questions for me, ma'am?" Roarke attempted to pack his sense of unease behind the dispassion of his countenance.

"Does he frighten you, Mr. Roarke?" It was not a taunt. There was a vein of sympathy in the question, and something more, even; a show of warmth.

"It's irregular, ma'am." He almost let it stand, but her eyes seemed to be inviting him. "I don't fully understand what he . . . is."

She gathered in Roarke's rigorously self-imposed dispassion.

"Do you know what separates us from the animals, Mr. Roarke?"

"I'm sorry, ma'am?"

"The crucial step we took up the evolutionary ladder that the lower life forms did not," she said. "What was it?"

"Tool use, ma'am."

"Exactly so." She seemed genuinely delighted with him. "Tool use, the ability to manipulate the environment to our own advantage. He" — her head inclined ever so slightly toward the room at the end of the hall — "understands this at a level you and I never could. *Everything* is a tool to him.

Every institution we've created, every body that governs us, every emotion we feel, every belief we have. To him, they are a lever by which he can shift the balance of the world. He's human, Mr. Roarke, like us, but more evolved; far, far smarter. He has always understood more deeply than others how to use tools."

"How?"

She shook her head.

"He tells me what to do," she said, "and I do it. I know he is interested in Mal, because Mal can help him ascertain the whereabouts of a man named Jon Remak. Remak has access to something the Old Man wants access to, as well. A new and powerful tool, I'm sure. What is the tool?" She shook her head with finality. "He doesn't share, *ever*. Would you share your tools with an animal? No, you'd expect something quite different from your inferiors." She studied him, ascertaining whether he gathered the implications. "I will tell you this, though."

She took another step toward him, and her hand fell onto his. He had often thought of her as an automaton, able to summon or dismiss emotion as the efficient execution of her duties required. But her eyes found his and offered something, an invitation to something deeper. Her hand was warm and soft, and he found, to his surprise, that he liked it there.

"Fear is one of his most useful tools," she said, her breath tinged with mint. "Make sure there's none of it in you when you're speaking to him, because he will use it. It's like offering him a doorway into your head."

Roarke gathered the fear and forced it, squealing, into an invincible steel box, which he slid into the recesses of his consciousness. Twenty years of military service and five years of work with that monster Castillo had trained him for at least that much.

He gave her a single, sincerely dispassionate nod. Her hand lingered just an instant longer, then she stiffened, turned, and led him out of her office and down toward the end of the hall.

A beast lived inside Lee Castillo. Sometimes he imagined it as a great, snorting bull bucking at the stem of his brain. Years in the marines had taught him the advantages of staying collected, patient. That same time had also taught him the value of being able to unleash the very worst he was capable of on instant command. The thing had always been in him, but the marines had taught him to direct it. If the beast was in charge, after all, Castillo would never have been able to so calmly approach the Lazarus Services Security office on the thirty-fifth floor. He would never have been able to hold a smile on his face while he asked the man at the desk where security guard Brett Talby was stationed at the moment.

"He's in briefing, Mr. Castillo," the man said. "That's down the hall, first door on the right."

Castillo did, however, let the beast spring out — just a flash of its horns, a blur of heaving body — to kick open the door of the briefing room. Desks and a podium were set around the room. Cellscreens were set up along the walls. Five startled faces shot up toward Castillo as he entered and picked out the particular face he was looking for.

The beast held staunchly at bay — for the moment — he stood over Brett Talby and put one thick slab of hand down on the man's uniformed shoulder.

"You recognize me, right, Brett?" Castillo asked.

"Of course, Mr. Castillo," Talby replied, his eyes nervously darting to the others in the room, who were all riveted to the scene but had made no move to Talby's defense.

"Of course," Castillo said. "I'm wondering, Brett, how it is that if you recognize me, you felt like it was a good idea to pull a gun on me."

A murmur of confusion rose from the bystanders. Talby's thick, serious face was overcome with bewilderment.

"I don't understand, Mr. Castillo," he said. "I never — "

"Yeah," Castillo said. "A gun. You helped that kid to

the elevator and held me back by pointing a gun at me. We've got it all on security cams."

"Security cams?" Talby was starting to realize he had cause to panic. "That's not—"

His words were cut off by Castillo's hands, which had suddenly snapped around Talby's throat. The room stirred, and Castillo looked up, giving them a glimpse of the beast. The room held its position, everyone but Talby, whose hands grasped and clawed at Castillo's wrists and whose feet kicked and pushed frantically.

Looking down into Talby's face, Castillo was admirably holding tightly to the creature inside him. By sheer luck Talby's flailing foot caught the outside of Castillo's knee, where a piece of shrapnel had lodged many years ago. It was no bother to him for the most part, but hit it hard enough at just the right angle and a jag of pain crackled up Castillo's body and lit the beast.

Castillo teetered, caught his balance, and yanked Talby from his seat by the neck. He threw him to the ground with the force of a pile driver. Talby squirmed there, a tiny animal trapped. Castillo lifted his foot up, the beast already supplying an image of what Talby's face would look like after Castillo had finished.

"What's that?" Castillo asked, his vision suddenly clearing of red, his foot still held in the air over Talby. One of the cellscreens on the wall showed a map of the city, and on it a dot lit up, chirping a familiar tone that had reached past the beast and pulled Castillo's attention back out. He set his foot down, the leg still aching from the shot to the old wound, and looked around the room at the other faces.

"What's that?" he asked again, quietly.

"Uh," one of the security guards piped up, "that's the feed from Ms. Kliest's office, some project she's been working on."

Castillo walked over, examined it more carefully, then nodded slowly. He pulled a cell from his pocket, keyed it.

"Roarke," he said to the voicemail screen. "Where the hell are you? I'm coming up. Mal just came back online."

He stepped over Talby and walked out of the briefing room. Talby might not have gotten quite what was coming to him, but Castillo had been able to pick up on what really mattered, and now they had Mal again.

That was the benefit of being able to control the beast inside.

THE STONES

LAURA WOKE UP, FACES SKITTERING out of her waking
mind and back into the dark of her suspect memory.

This was the third motel room she'd awakened in in
as many days, the whole lot of them blurring together with
their stiff, starched sheets and their almost-clean carpets,
their ancient HDs, and the sad views of their own parking
lots. From town to town they'd gone, once stopping to check
out a vast, echoing, and abandoned warehouse that, a year
ago, had one day been filled to the prefab walls with cutting-
edge uplink equipment and the next day utterly empty; an-

other day stopping to speak with a highway patrolman who, two and a half years ago, stopped a speeding car only to find that neither the driver nor the car had any record in any data bank the officer had access to. What did the officer remember about this two and a half years on? Exactly, to the word, what had been written in his report. It was all she could do to drag Aaron away from that one, raging and spitting, before they had both been hauled into county lockup.

They extended their search, moving from location to location, Aaron becoming more and more sullen with each stop that yielded nothing; his face darkening, his responses getting shorter and harsher.

She pulled herself up in the bed this morning, wanting to scour it all from her head with a hot shower. She stripped off the T-shirt she had slept in and stepped under the water, as hot as she could stand it.

She stood under the burning water until she could look at the day ahead of her without a haze clogging her vision. She stepped out into the steaming bathroom and started drying her black, black hair, staring in the fogged mirror. Her blue eyes were bright enough that they were practically the only thing she could make out in the humid reflection.

Naked, with the towel wrapped around her head, she stood trapped in reverie. She was waiting for a revelation, driving from one spot to the next, waiting to recognize something, for a memory to burst free from the murk in her brain and shudder her body with its power, and until then all she could do was hold her smile and keep pushing Aaron. Nothing here? On to the next. And the next. And the next. And who was there for her? Who kept pushing her?

With a small surge of anger, she spun to the door and whipped it open, prepared to storm out and snatch up her underwear with hard-edged fortitude. But when the door opened, a figure was coming quickly to its feet and stumbling back, and Laura screeched and then, again much to her surprise, instead of leaping back and throwing the door closed, she jumped forward with her fists balled up and her knees bent.

"I didn't—" Aaron said. "I wasn't—" For an instant, the little boy inside him was apparent on his face, a child caught in the hot spotlight of guilt. But he quickly recovered himself, flattening his features and standing up with rigid dignity.

Laura pulled the towel from her hair and swathed herself in it, glaring in astonishment.

"You were looking at me from under the door," she said.

"No," he said. "I was trying to determine who you were."

"Are you kidding me? This is *my* room. Who the hell else would I be?"

"I knocked and no one answered, so, given the situation we're in, I let myself in. When I heard noise in the bathroom, it seemed prudent to make sure it wasn't an intruder before I announced myself."

Laura studied the boy with the acne and the nervous fingers.

"You," she said, "are completely full of shit. How did you even get in here?" She pictured him, staring down with a contemptuous smile at the cellock holding her door closed. "Forget it. Get out."

"Laura, it's very important that you believe me. I think trust is of paramount —"

"Shut it. Get out. See if you can figure out a way to see through the wall while I get dressed, why don't you?" She put a firm hand on his shoulder and steered him out and shut the door in his scowling face.

They drove from the motel in silence, but for Aaron's calling directions out in monosyllables. *At least,* she thought, *the embarrassment shut him up.* There was no grumbling, no complaining, no masked pleas for assurance. *Is the next one going to be it? Are we going to find something soon?*

"I want to make it clear," he broke into the hypnotic

hum of the road around them, "that I was not spying on you in the shower. You must admit it's not unlikely that if we're on the right track, someone might be following us."

"You know," she said, not taking her eyes from the road, "you are digging yourself a deeper and deeper hole. The mature thing to do at this point would just be to admit what you did and take it like a man."

That was low, and she knew it, giving him trouble on the basis of his age, which he worked so hard to camouflage. Sure enough, his face reddened, and he started sputtering a diatribe about being on his own for long enough to know exactly what the hell the "mature" thing to do was and if there were anything to admit, he would have done it.

The green and white of a passing sign snatched her attention. POPE SPRINGS — 2 MILES.

"Pope Springs," she said quietly.

"What?" Aaron was brought up short, still in the middle of his ridiculous, teetering defense. "Yes. That's our next stop. A few miles on the other side of it, actually."

"What happened there?"

He paused, collecting the information.

"A house on top of a hill burned down there a little more than a year ago. An anonymous buyer had spent a great deal of money appointing it with all sorts of electronics, but then never moved in. According to the data I have, the place was empty at the time it burned down, though it was reported by the local fire department that when they arrived, a number of people were already on hand, milling about, watching the place burn."

Laura made no comment.

"Why are you asking?" Aaron prodded. "Do you remember something about this?"

Did she? Not really. Actually, it seemed like less to go on than Aaron's usual, with just the anonymous owner filling it with tech gear to flag it. In truth, all she had really done was notice the sign.

"No," she said. "Just wondering."

"Are you sure, Laura? Because—"

"Aaron. It's nothing."

They came into Pope Springs and found it to be nearly indistinguishable from the other dwindling little towns they'd passed through over the last few days. The lonely cell and wireless store seemed to be the only functioning business on the desolate main street, which had a different name than the main street in the last town and the one before that, but the paint on the forlorn houses was peeling in the same way; the rust on the cars, the absence of visible inhabitants, all the same, another little town that was giving up on itself. Laura brought them through it and up the hill on the other side.

"Here," Aaron directed. She pulled off the side of the road, and they got out.

The empty spot still resonated with the absence of a house that so clearly belonged there. The grassy plain formed a nearly perfect circle, with a patch of light forest growing along a gently sloping hill back down toward town. Set back toward the far end of the lot was a slight rise, the solid foundation of what was once a house, but now, over it, a flat bed of hard gray stones were packed down to bury the ruins of what had once stood. The field, to Laura's eyes, was haunted by the house, which was no longer there, a view yearning for completion.

"Well," Aaron said, coming up beside her at the edge of the grass, "do you recognize it?"

She took the space in with eyes desperate for something to nourish her memory.

"No."

No point lying about it just to keep Aaron's spirits up. She did have the feeling about the house, but that was just her sense of the place, not her memory of it. There was something else, though, something stirring in her belly.

"Is there a record of ownership?" she asked, just to head off his seething response.

"The electronic trail is like a dark alleyway leading back

JESSE KARP

on itself. It's owned by a limited liability corporation that is a subsidiary of a real estate development fund owned by another LLC, which is, in turn, owned by the first LLC." Aaron shook his head in simultaneous frustration and admiration. "That's one of the reasons I had it flagged in the first place. For all the good it does us," he ended bitterly, turning back to the car, so he could slam the door hard and stew about this waste of time for the rest of the day.

But Laura kept looking at the empty space, at nothing. The feeling she woke up with, of having lost something crucial to her, of something she needed deeply having gone from the world, was swelling in her as she looked at this lot. She didn't recognize this place in the normal way, but it connected to something in her. Maybe that was the best she was going to get.

"Wait," she said. "I've got a feeling about this place."

"A feeling?" Aaron had stopped himself behind her. "What does that mean?"

"If only there was some way to get beneath the rocks, maybe we could find something in the ruins."

"It's possible to get beneath the rocks, Laura, but I'm not going to waste time and resources on a drawn-out operation just because some overwrought girl woke up on the wrong side of the bed."

"This spot is making me feel something that none of the others did. Maybe that's the best we're going to do, Mike. So instead of thinking up new ways to—"

"Okay." Aaron was nodding his head slowly and looking at her carefully, like she had misapplied makeup into a gross smear across her face. "I'll get it started."

"What? Why did you change your mind so quickly?"

"You just called me 'Mike.'"

"What? Who's Mike?"

"I don't know, and I'm betting you don't know, either."

"I don't," Laura said shakily.

"So, something is happening in your brain. The brain doesn't store memories in one place. There are different kinds of memory, and you don't have a visual one of this place for some reason, but you may have an emotional one. That will have to do for now."

He walked out toward the bed of stones, subvocalizing on his cellpatch with God only knew who, leaving Laura alone.

"Mike," she said softly, trying it out on her tongue. "Mike."

In less than thirty minutes, a red pickup pulled up behind Laura's car. A door with the words SLATE CONTRACTING stenciled in fading white letters opened, and a man stepped out. Thick with undefined muscle through his torso and limbs and a crew cut of ash-gray hair, he stood and took in the two figures waiting for him. Unsure of whom to address, the boy who was clearly far too young or the girl who was clearly far too much of a girl, he held his spot until Aaron addressed him.

"Mr. Slate," he said, offering his hand, which disappeared, after an uncertain moment, into Slate's rough paw. "I'm Aaron Argaven. We spoke on the cell."

"That was you. Okay. What are we looking at?"

"As I said, I want those rocks cleared."

"Yeah," Slate said. "I put those down myself. You know there's nothing under there but charred wood. House burned down 'bout a year and a half ago."

"One year, four months, actually. I want it cleared. By tomorrow."

"By *tomorrow?*" Slate's eyes nearly bugged out of his head. "That's not going to be possible. I'd have to call in both my crews to do something like this in twenty-four hours, and we'd have to work around the clock, which we don't do. Plus, I've got people on another job right now. We wouldn't even be able to start until next week. Then there's the matter of permits from the town."

"What's your standard fee?"

"I don't know. I'd have to look it over. I could write you up an estimate by tomorrow."

"Go look it over, Mr. Slate. Decide on a fee, then multiply it by ten, and have the job done by tomorrow."

Slate looked up at Laura for some measure of sanity, which she couldn't supply. Aaron's manner was somewhat short but completely professional. If it hadn't been coming from a fourteen-year-old, there was no doubt Slate would be jumping for joy.

"You think maybe I should speak to your father or someone?" Slate suggested casually.

"Is money only good if it comes from somebody's parent?"

"Nooo." Slate drew the syllable out. "But that's a steep offer you're making, and I, ah, haven't seen any money."

"Right. Give me a quote, and the money will be in your account by the time you make it back to your office to gather your men and equipment. If it isn't, you needn't bother returning, and you've lost nothing but an hour from your day."

Slate examined the offer hard but could not seem to find a flaw in it.

"Twenty thousand," he said flat, not even bothering to look at the stones, let alone go over and examine them.

"Done," Aaron said without skipping a beat.

"You understand that's——"

"Two hundred thousand dollars. Yes. It will be in the account you give me by the time you're back at your office."

Working hard to hide both doubt and excitement, Slate gave over the account number and got back into his pickup.

"You seem to have made a real impression on him one way or another," Laura said as the pickup disappeared down the hill.

"No point trying to be inconspicuous. Slate's going to tell everyone he knows about this, anyway. The work would attract plenty of attention by itself, I'm sure."

"Right," she said, her head swimming at the amount. "I guess you'd better transfer the money. Easy come, easy go." Laura had never suffered for money. Her father had worked at the same architectural firm since she was born and managed to support the family alone. Paying for college had been their greatest expenditure, and Laura was treating *that* with such respect, wasn't she? But tossing off two hundred thousand dollars like that gave her a sense of the sort of consequence-free world Aaron must be used to. Consequence-free, until his father killed himself.

"Already transferred," Aaron said.

"Thanks to the handy little wire in your brain, huh?"

"'Wire.'" He smiled condescendingly. "Right. Something like that."

Laura looked at the flesh-colored bump at his temple.

"Is it true those things give you brain cancer?" she asked.

"Yes."

"What?" Her eyes widened in shock, expecting the standard denial.

"In about forty percent of test cases, brain cancer did result. They're first generation, you know. There's plenty left to work out."

"But, then, what about the ozone satellites? They're not responsible for it?"

"There are no ozone satellites, Laura," he said, becoming bored with the conversation. "They're PR, pure spin."

"What's replenishing the ozone layer, then?"

"Wishful thinking."

"But . . ." She worked her jaw, trying to find words sufficient to this horror. "If the cellpatch causes brain cancer, why are you wearing it?"

"This one is a third-generation prototype, actually. Proper shielding and less than a quarter the electromagnetic output. I'd never take a risk like that."

Laura stared at him but couldn't help think of Josh, of all the kids on campus strolling about with those things drilled into their heads.

• • •

Slate's crew finished just after lunchtime the next day. As the dusty, exhausted figures filed back to their trucks, still surmising to each other about the mysterious circumstances of their extraordinary good fortune, Aaron hurried right to the edge of the exposed pit. Laura was slower to come over, hesitating at the idea that there might be something that would pull the plug from the dam of her memory and let it all come flooding painfully back. Or, worse, that there would be nothing of the sort.

Slate had not been deceiving them. There was nothing in that shadowy pit but ash and torn chunks of wood and metal that still smelled of smoke. Not in the least discouraged, Aaron lowered himself down and, balancing precariously, started picking through the charcoal remains.

Laura let herself down eventually, as well, though she had no idea what she was looking for or how to do it. There was so much of it, where did you even begin? She watched Aaron dig around for hours with a spade and a claw he had bought off one of Slate's workmen. He was being meticulous about it, moving from what appeared to be one carefully calculated spot to another, though to Laura, she couldn't distinguish what made one position any different from another. The one time she inquired, she received only a frustrated grunt in response.

The wind had acquired a chilly edge and the shadows

stretched long across the field when Aaron threw the shovel down with a resounding metallic echo. He seemed to be holding something in his hand, though with the sun disappearing beyond the horizon, the sunken space they were in was nearly plunged into shadow, and she couldn't be sure.

"Did you find something the fire didn't ruin?" she asked, her voice coming out rough and tight. She realized she hadn't spoken a word in several hours.

"This wasn't a fire," Aaron informed her, walking carefully closer. "Something was detonated in this place."

"How would you know that?"

"Just look at all the shrapnel. It's jagged, not melted. But also because I found what I was looking for." He held out the object in his hand for her to squint down at. A small square fit neatly in his palm. It was charred over most of its surface, but a dull metallic glint caught a bit of dying sunlight.

"What is it?"

"A digital core. What's left of one would be more accurate. These things are the best-protected part of any large digital system. Everything the system does or did is stored on these, and they are, consequently, very hard to destroy. No fire would reach one of these. This was blown free from its system." He looked back up at her. "By an explosion.

One that must have been specifically calculated to damage or destroy it. Someone was looking to cover their trail."

"Did they?" Excitement was boiling behind Laura's eyes.

"If this was a year and a half ago, yes. But technological progress is measured in days. A year and four months is like a millennium of technological evolution. It had enough left in it that I could sponge it up with my lenses. Plenty is lost, I'm sure, but some of the information will be intact. If information came into or out of the system along wireless routes, those pathways should still be here. There should be enough to pick up a trail."

Aaron was preternaturally calm. She had never seen him like this. But he was all cerebral push, always looking for information to lock on to and extrapolate from, and now, after years, he finally had it.

Laura, though, was quickly losing her sense of calm. This was the first scratch she'd gotten for the tickle in her brain. At the end of this trail that Aaron was talking about was someone who would answer the question "What happened to Laura Westlake?" The problem was she didn't know if she could bear the answer.

THE NEUROPLETH

TIME WAS LOST TO ROSE in this forgotten park. The sounds of the outside world had become a garbled sludge in the hollow air, though she imagined she could pick out from beneath them the sound of distant, ancient screams. These would be the screams of the woman who had been beaten and stabbed here, her pleas for help, her screams of pain trapped in an echo and dying away like the park itself.

There was no sense of seconds ticking by. Perhaps she had been here for only a day, or maybe it had been a week or a month. She wasn't hungry; the place seemed to have emptied her out of urge, desire, even need. The only emotion she could manage to summon was an edgy panic at the idea of being trapped here, unable even to starve to death, as the park faded out of the world forever, taking her with it.

She wasn't tired either, exactly. But she must have slept at times, her consciousness lost in a swirl of oblivion. Or had she? Could she even differentiate between awareness and oblivion anymore?

It was from within one of these stretches of oblivion that she started awake. A sound cut through the space and into her stupor like a razor slashing flesh. For an instant, she thought it was the screams of the woman who had died here, returning in full force to exact revenge on the only human accessible: Rose. But it was not a scream—it was a metallic shriek of rusted metal scraping against itself. Her eyes flashed back and forth, looking for the cause of the sound.

At the far side of the park, behind one of the benches, a grating had come open. Her head quaked with the impossibility of it. She had not even known there was a grating there, its metal paled and blending with the neutral contours of the concrete around it. What could be down there, beneath a forgotten park? What could possibly be coming out of it? Was there a creature, some forgotten monstrosity that lurked through these places that Mal never even knew about?

Hands came up from the hole and anchored themselves

on the ground, straining to pull the rest behind. A head appeared, a torso, legs. The body pulled itself from the grating achingly, stopped, gasping for air on the dull pavement. It was covered in blood, and, even in the viscous light, the blood was so bright compared to the world around it that it burned Rose's eyes.

"Mal," she said, squinting at the red explosion of life covering the figure. *"Mal!"* She lurched forward, unaccustomed energy animating her limbs. She sprinted over, rounded the bench, knelt beside him.

His cargo pants and hooded sweatshirt were soaked through with blood in large patches. His face was warped with lumps and discolorations. His dark hair was matted with more blood.

"Oh God, Mal. How did you get here?"

"Forgotten subway tunnel," he said, blood trickling from his lips as he did. "East Side line, never finished, abandoned, and forgotten. It runs straight beneath Lazarus Towers and the park. That's why I put you here."

She could not have cared less about the geographical explanation. She had meant to understand how he had gotten here in the state he was in, his body ruined, life ebbing away. Trapped in a middle ground between relief at his return and a futile desperation to help him, she gently wrapped her arms around him and lowered her head to his chest. He didn't have the strength to stiffen as he had in the past when she tried to embrace him. She could hear his heart thudding weakly, feel the bones beneath his flesh cracked out of alignment.

"It's not fair, Mal." Tears ran down her face and mingled with Mal's blood. "I can't do this. This isn't . . ." She could barely form the words through the sudden violence of her sobbing. "This isn't how it's supposed to work." *He* was supposed to protect her, be the strength for her. She managed their life, the apartment, the food, the clothes. Mal was supposed to be the strength.

"We have to get out." Mal's voice was so weak that, at first, she had thought it her own wishful thinking. "Call Remak."

Remak. Yes. Sense stirred in her head. She had been in here too long. They had to call Remak.

She felt him moving beneath her, and she came away from him, her clothes stained crimson. He was trying to pull himself up, but his arms trembled and his teeth gritted at the effort. She came to her feet and used her own arms to help steady him. His weight nearly pulled her down, but he came up, and, using her as a crutch, they moved together to the edge of the park.

One instant she was staring at the prison of concrete and rusted metal, and then Mal brought them forward, and the memory of the street, the buildings, the people flooded her head. She remembered that the world existed.

It was a world she had never had an acute fondness for, but it now looked joyous to her in its smallest detail: the people rushing by intentionally heedless, the sky offering rays of genuine sunlight, the walls of the buildings that met behind her, showing no access to a park at all. Even in her head, the park was fading, already not like a memory of her own but like a memory of someone else's only vaguely related to her.

"Remak," Mal said, the burden of his weight on her growing greater.

Her cell was already out, and with unsteady fingers she keyed the private, direct line Remak had given her for Alan Silven. She could only hope that Remak was "in" Silven when she called.

"Hello?" Silven's voice and features held an edge of uncertainty, as though he couldn't figure out what a number he didn't recognize was doing coming through his private line, what a face he didn't know was doing staring back at him.

"It's Rose," she said, her voice teetering on the edge of panic.

"I'm sorry," said Silven, "I don't know any . . . Rose." The tone of the voice suddenly and distinctly changed on the last word, and the uncertainty vanished from his face.

"Mr. Remak?"

"Yes, it's me," Remak said. "Is Mal all right?"

"He's . . . he's . . ." She chased the words down her own throat, unable to commit to one.

"Where are you, Rose?" Remak asked. "Turn on your geolocator app."

Her fingers fumbled to key it in. An ad for car rental services scrolled merrily across the bottom of the screen.

"You're right where I left you," Remak said, regarding the locator on his end. "Is Mal there?"

"Yes," she said. "He's right—"

"Pardon me, who is this?" Silven's face showed polite confusion, and his tone had changed once again. "I believe you've got the wrong number."

Rose stared at the face on the screen, looking for Remak's eyes and not finding them.

"I'm . . ." She barely managed to choke that much out. Had Remak left him on purpose? Why was he leaving her alone?

"How did you get this number, exactly?" Silven asked, his face growing harsher as he collected details through the screen. "What's your name?"

"Hang up, Rose," a man standing next to her said. He was short and overweight and had long hair tied in a ponytail. But his eyes, those were unmistakable.

"Mr. Remak," she said.

"I'm here," the man said, and moved around to take some of Mal's weight. Rose keyed the phone off on Silven's confused expression. "Bring him through the building on the left. The man I'm in now lives right there. We'll use his apartment."

They struggled Mal through the door, then down a short, dark, foul-smelling hallway to the first door, which Remak pushed open. By the time they rested Mal's body on a bed with old, torn sheets, he was no longer moving.

Remak leaned over, examining him carefully, lifting clothes away from bloody wounds with chubby fingers.

"He's dying," Remak said, clutching Rose's heart in her chest. He looked up at her, the eternally incongruous eyes sharp in the soft, fleshy face. "Did he tell you what happened? Did he say what he learned?"

"You can't let him die," Rose said, her ears deaf, her eyes blind to anything else. "You *can't*."

"Rose, listen. This situation is bigger than Mal, bigger than me, bigger than all of us. Did Mal say anything about what he learned?"

"*No!*" she screamed, her voice rising louder than it ever had in her memory, driven by the terror of Mal's stillness.

Remak's eyes lingered on her briefly, searching for the truth beneath the emotion, then went back to Mal.

JESSE KARP

"I can save him," he said heavily, as though it was not a relief, but only greater hardship. "I can save him."

"Do it. Please. What are you waiting for?"

"It comes with a price, Rose."

"I'll pay it."

"It's not for you to pay. When I went into the neuro-pleth, my body was converted into neurological impulses. Essentially, I'm made of an energy that can enter other bodies through their nervous systems. This energy is what my life is made of — do you understand that at all? I can use that energy to kick-start Mal's metabolism, to knit his bones, seal his organs, mend his flesh. The energy will become Mal's life."

"Do it," she said, repeating the only words that made sense to her anymore.

"Rose." His voice fell on her like a hammer. "That energy is *me*. Once it's been spent to heal Mal, there won't be a Jon Remak anymore."

"You made this happen to him," she said, desperation igniting her words. It was hard, so hard, to feel something for Jon Remak when she was not even facing the same man she had met in Silven's office. How easy it was to tell a disembodied idea of a man to give himself up. "And . . ." She stumbled over the outrageous demand she had made, trying to mitigate it without withdrawing it. "And you can't stop the Old Man yourself. Mal is the only one who can do it. The only one."

His eyes slid from Rose, found Mal. With his head bowed, he considered the boy.

"Yes," he finally said. "I know." He knelt down and rested one hand on Mal's head and one hand on his chest and closed his eyes.

Rose's heart hammered. She stared at Mal, waiting to see the tears of his flesh close, the bruises on his face disappear. A minute passed.

Remak's head came up, his eyes opened.

"What happened?" Rose demanded. "Why isn't he healing?"

"He's almost gone, his mind is shutting down," Remak said without looking at her.

"But if you heal his body—"

"Is that what you want, Rose, an intact body with no mind? I have to fix his mind first; I have to pull it back."

"How?"

"I need to go in and find something that will make him fight his way back. Mal is an unyielding fighter, but he has to *want* to fight. Only then can I heal his body."

"You're going into Mal's mind?"

"Yes, I have to."

"Take me," Rose said.

Remak looked up at her.

"Take me with you," she said again, doing her best to keep the need from filling her voice. "I'm the only person Mal has. I can help bring him back."

"Rose, I've never—"

"But you *could*."

"I don't know. Theoretically, if we had neural sync . . ."

She could see something shining in him, fascinated by the idea.

"Then what?" she prompted.

"I can move through the neuropleth from brain to brain on my own, but if I'm going to take you into the neuropleth with me, then our nervous systems have to be in sync."

"Okay," she agreed, needing nothing more but the hope of it.

"For neural sync, we'll need to make physical contact," he said. "And once you've synced, you'll have a door to the neuropleth in your head forever. Are you ready for that, Rose?"

She twitched a nod. Her body was spasming with fear and anticipation.

"Sit down," he said, and she sat on the floor with her back against the cracked plaster of the wall.

The man Remak was occupying sat beside her, rested one hand on Mal's bare skin, and took her hand with the other. His eyes closed, and the room was left with only the sound of Mal's shallow, ragged breathing.

"I'm ready," she said, her eyes searching for something she knew had no form, no solidity. "I'm—"

A bolt of lightning cracked through her, starting from the hand Remak was holding and lashing up her spine, across every nerve in her body, and turning her brain into a searing current of electricity. She was no longer in a room, no longer in a body. She was a synaptic flash, pulsing along a highway that branched infinitely, connecting into a limitless panorama of human brains that throbbed with their own bursts of electrical life.

This is the neuropleth. Remak's voice filled her consciousness. *Your body still exists, unlike mine, but by coming here with me, you now have a doorway to the neuropleth in your brain. Mal will have the same doorway when he awakens. I suggest neither of you ever open it. You might be able to touch other minds through it, but if you ever try to inhabit another body as I do, your own body will be converted into neurological impulses. You will become like me.*

She took it in, felt the pulsing minds connected to her by this neurological tether.

Tell me you understand, Rose.

I do, she said without words. *Mal and I will have these*

doorways. If we ever try to inhabit another body, we'll become like you.

You have to make Mal understand it, too, he said.

I will.

Then, gently, she was pulled along the pathway, the sensation of Remak's presence guiding her. The brains, coursing with electrical fire, rushed past her.

This, Remak said, *is Mal.* It crackled with hard gray light, like burning iron. But the iron light of the mind was dim and growing dimmer as they watched.

The spark of Remak leaped out and joined the synaptic buzz of Mal's brain, and Rose was drawn along. Together, they entered Mal.

THE TOWN

"I NEED TO ASK YOU something," Laura said, her eyes on the flat road stretching out endlessly before her.

"I told you, I *wasn't* looking at you in the shower." Aaron's voice was modulated into a plaintive whine. "I thought you were in trouble. I was trying—"

"*Fine,* what*ever*. That's not even what I'm talking about."

"Okay. So what, then?" His tone instantly shifted to that of impatient condescension. He was a master of disguising defensiveness by being patronizing. They had been driving for another day now, without even the occasional respite of stopping to investigate one of Aaron's sites. Laura had become intimately acquainted with his defense strategies, though for her part, she often incited them by calling upon the bathroom incident. She found herself falling into that dangerous babysitter/child dynamic of playful aggression to relieve the pressure of hanging around this little punk. She had to remind herself that he was, in many ways, still a child and that he was not benefiting from someone keeping him on the defensive. This was a boy who desperately needed to feel superior, in control, at all times.

"You said that those cellpatches do cause brain cancer," she said, loosening her fingers on the steering wheel and trying to flex her knotted shoulders.

"There's a statistical correlation, yes. But like I said, mine is several generations ahead of the current model."

"Yes, that's exactly what I want to ask you about. You're brushing the whole thing off because it's not going to affect you . . . as far as you know, anyway."

"Do you think I'd be using one of these if I wasn't —"

"Again, not where I'm going."

"Well, then," he said, "maybe it would help if you get there."

"What about everyone else? What about all the other

people who are going to die because they let someone drill machinery into their brains without knowing the facts?"

"What about them?"

Her shoulders were tighter than ever and her knuckles were stark white against the steering wheel.

"You're in a position to help them. Why don't you?"

"What in the name of God are you talking about? I didn't sync them with cellpatches; they made their own choices. That's the way human existence works. The people who are weaker for whatever reason—including inadequate knowledge—die out. It leaves the stronger ones."

"The stronger ones have a responsibility, Aaron, to help the weaker ones." She was certain this would appeal to his sense of superiority.

"Not to help them," he said. "To lead them."

"What do you mean?"

"Society produces unusual individuals of greater ability. Other people try to tear them down—out of jealousy, generally speaking. But the superior man must take a position of leadership."

"And just how are you leading all these people who are going to be wasting away in hospital beds inside the next few years?"

"I'm not talking about leading people, *per se*. I'm talking about leading society in general, guiding it upward. Read some Nietzsche, and get back to me when you know what you're talking about, Laura." He turned away from her and gazed at the fields of grass tediously streaming by.

She choked down the astonished shriek of rage boiling up from her stomach. Honestly, she couldn't remember anyone who could throw her so easily into a fury. *Remember,* she told herself, *remember why this boy is here.*

"Did your father read Nietzsche, Aaron?"

"Yes," he said, his eyes not leaving the world outside the window. She pictured him sitting at home, listening to his father lay out the philosophy of the world to him: the strong and the weak, those who led and those who followed.

"Your father chose a side, Aaron," she said. "Or it was chosen for him by his situation, by the power he had and the company he made. He chose to honor profit over service. Don't let his memory choose your side for you."

"Don't talk about my father."

Laura sighed.

"Don't come running to me when the revolution comes for you," she said, thinking the argument finished.

"Revolution?" Aaron said incredulously, spinning on her and clearly fired up for a whole new argument. "A revolution is no longer possible. Our society, the one you're so concerned about, is no longer capable of standing up and making their voices heard, because all they have to do now is sit down and log on."

"You just made my point."

He looked at her with clear disdain for that idea.

"Corporations," she said, "like Intellitech, have lulled everyone into subservience through technology. By giving everyone a voice through it, they've taken all our voices away. They push it and push it and push it on us. Now, with cellenses, everyone can be talking every second of the day. With six billion voices going all at once, how can anyone hear anything worthwhile?"

"Are you suggesting some kind of antiprogress philosophy to me, Laura? To *me*, of all the people in the world?"

"I'm just saying that maybe we're not meant to become so intimate with technology like this. Maybe it's not natural for us to be so dependent and so entangled with technology, and that it's blinding us."

"Not natural." He played around with the word on his tongue, obviously searching for its flaw. "Well, Laura, it's not 'natural' for us be outside when the sun isn't up. It isn't 'natural' for us to buy our food instead of hunting and foraging for it. It isn't 'natural' for us to live in gigantic structures made of concrete or even to be able to preserve a record of our thoughts by *writing it down*. So, tell me, are we better off putting a chokehold on our own evolutionary capacity to create tools and grow, or are we supposed to stagnate?"

"I'm not saying we should be static. Just that . . . I don't know." It was true, these things were occurring to Laura practically as she was saying them. She hadn't spent her life dwelling on them. But by the same token, they seemed to spring into her head fully formed, as though shot forward from some deep, dusty recess of her mind. "Just that we might be going too fast. You said yourself that a year was like a millennium when it came to technological development. That's so much faster than it ever was before. We were ready for writing when it came along, right? I mean, we couldn't have grown without it. Now we're hurrying to grow ourselves just for the sake of the growth. I just think we're getting more clever, but we're not getting any smarter or any wiser."

"That's quite a little speech, Laura. Do you know what we're doing here? I mean, do you understand what is happening right now?"

"You're patronizing me like you're my grandfather?"

"My cellpatch and the lenses they're synced to are interpreting the wavelength we got off the digital core back near Pope Springs, and they're picking it out of the air around us, differentiating it from a thousand other signals that are nearly indistinguishable. Essentially, I'm *seeing* an interplay of energy that's invisible to the human eye." Though his words were carefully paced and spoken in the low, heavy tone of the helplessly self-important, those eyes he was talking about were alive with the fervor of the fanatic. "It's gotten us across four states and to within — what? — probably about six hours of our target now. Our target being somebody who's been manipulating data and God knows how much of your precious human interaction for years without anyone knowing about it. We're doing that because we've developed tools that enable us to overcome our weaknesses and make ourselves strong. Tell me, please, how by any remotely intelligent stretch of the imagination, that's a bad thing?"

She turned away from him and back to the road. He had mastered this magical technology that let him glimpse the ethereal, but he couldn't even drive a car, wasn't interested in the least. For some reason, Laura found herself fighting back tears.

"Turn off here," Aaron said, indicating a small road that broke off the highway, through grassy fields.

She was going to ask him how he knew the small road would get them to town, but realized he was consulting the GPS on his cellens. Laura's head was still mired in the idea that you needed to be holding something in your hand and looking at it to see it. Hopelessly obsolete at eighteen years old. Was that the new way of things?

The road acquired a gentle curve over the course of three miles or so and finally opened up into a main street, and the calm façade of a quiet and friendly town met them. They passed rows of one- and two-story houses, neatly painted, with clean lawns and cozy porches.

"Where to?" she asked. "Do you want—"

"Just keep driving," he responded sharply. His face was lit with the furious concentration she was sure only the freakishly smart ever truly acquired. "I'm having trouble reading this. There's so much data flowing through here, it's like a hailstorm."

Laura looked again at the tranquil town around her. The chaos he was recounting was hard to imagine, like a still graveyard, haunted by a swirl of invisible spirits.

"I can barely tell one thing from another," he said, almost breathless. "It's all flowing up that way, out of town."

"So do you want me to—"

"Just keep driving!" he snapped back at her, and retreated into his data.

The signs outside the few businesses announced the town's name as Woodhaven in tidy, dignified lettering, and she cruised along Haven Drive, perusing the town: a restaurant with darkened windows, a pharmacy with a wood façade that looked like something out of the nineteenth century, a tiny library—how quaintly welcoming—that abutted the tasteful town hall, a Woodhaven flag fluttering humbly between them. Off the town green was a grocer and general store, the only business here that showed any traffic whatsoever. Cars were parked sporadically along the curb, and Laura saw three or four people walking slowly along, not paying her any undue attention. Laura's car was the only one moving on the road. There was a bookstore with posters of "the latest" bestsellers about six months out of date, and another restaurant that bragged it was an ICE CREAM PARLOR AND SODA FOUNTAIN! and then a swell of more residences and the town gave way again to highway.

"Stop!" Aaron said with a sudden vehemence that made Laura jump.

"What? What's wrong? I thought you said the data was all flowing out of town this way."

"Go back into town and park."

Laura didn't even slow down.

"I am not your chauffeur, Aaron. We're doing this *together*. If you want me to do something, you *ask* me to—"

"*Please* go back into town and park," he said with more vitriol than he had barked the order a moment before.

Laura kept driving. She could feel him tensing, practically vibrating, as though every inch they drove was irrevocable and sending them into the heart of darkness.

"Tell me what's going on," she said softly.

"How will it help you to know, Laura? Will you even understand what I'm saying?"

"Make me understand. Or get out and walk."

"Turn the car around, and I'll tell you."

She kept driving. With children, you had to put your foot down somewhere.

"There's a massive flow of information concentrated all around here," he spoke quickly, like his life depended on it. "Along the wavelength from the digital core I found. It's impossible to see any other data through it, and there's *a lot* of data flowing through the air in this country. But the concentration here is all flowing up this way, out of town, like there's going to be a house along the way, and it's all going to lead there."

"So what's the problem? Why aren't we going there?"

"Aren't you *listening* to me?" He nearly screamed it. "The flow is making all the other data invisible. Anything could be flowing into or out of that town, and I have no way to see it. The massive stream going out of town is working like a cloak for everything that's *in* the town. Do you *understand?*"

By way of answer, she slowed the car and turned it around and cruised back toward Woodhaven. It seemed to relax him minutely.

"If we're going to look at the town, then turn off your dataflow thingy," she said.

"No possible way."

"You just said it's not doing you any good now. Turn it off and actually *look* at the town. Maybe you'll learn something from that."

"Fine. I did."

"Really do it. Or I'm turning the car back around." She tapped the brake.

He glared at her, but before he spoke, she saw a tension leave his body, his brow unknit.

"Fine," he said.

She pulled the car up to the sidewalk in front of the pharmacy, and they got out. She stretched and shook the kinks from her legs. Aaron turned in place, taking it in as if for the first time. A stout woman with a bag of groceries smiled at them as she passed by.

"Seems perfectly lovely," Laura commented, watching the woman go on her way.

"Are you kidding me?" Aaron said. "This is the most bizarre place I've ever been in."

Laura's eyes flickered back and forth, looking for what she had missed.

"What are you talking about?" she asked.

"There wasn't a single dish antenna outside the houses coming into town, no apparatus for satellite HD or wireless service. There's a bookstore but nowhere to buy or service a cell. A *bookstore?* Come *on*."

Laura looked around again and confirmed what Aaron was saying. Without another word, she walked around Aaron and into the pharmacy. Like the town itself, the rows of products in here were neatly lined along tidy shelves and, though the space was small, there was a warm feeling to it washing off the old wooden walls and the faded Christmas posters hanging on them.

Aaron came in a moment later, hesitating like he was entering a torture chamber, and caught up with her as she approached the counter in back.

"Good afternoon," said an old man with tufts of white hair like clouds and a sprightly, almost mischievous face. "No school today?"

"No classes." Laura smiled back. "We were wondering if you could help us."

"Of course," the man said. "What can I do for you?"

"Where is there a school around here, exactly?" Aaron,

perennially missing his social cues, interrupted what had been shaping up to be a pleasant conversation.

"Comstock, two towns over," the man answered politely.

"Two towns over." Aaron was consulting his cellenses. Laura had picked up the facial ticks by now. "That's forty miles from here. Your kids travel forty miles to and from school every morning?"

"That's where the school is." The man smiled back, as though it were the most normal thing in the world.

"Is there a place to stay in town?" Laura asked quickly, before Aaron could come back with something else.

"Nope." The man shook his head. "Nothing like that around here. There's a motel up Route 4 a little ways. But don't leave without stopping into the ice cream parlor. You never had such a good root beer float. You kids will love it."

Laura nodded, the smile never leaving her face.

"Thanks very much," she said.

"Pleasure," the man said, nodding once more and turning back to his work as they departed.

"Us kids do love root beer floats," Laura said once they were outside. She found it impossible to imagine Aaron eating ice cream, though she had to admit she could go for some herself.

JESSE KARP

"So does that convince you?" Aaron said as they walked across the street toward the town green.

"What, that the nearest school is far away? Who knows how those things work? This is a small town. There probably aren't enough kids here to—"

"There's no hotels. That motel he said was 'a little ways' is twenty-five miles from here. This is exactly the sort of town that should do business with people weekending from the city."

Laura had to allow that this was true. She and her parents used to take long weekends to a town much like this every Thanksgiving and every summer.

"But there's no place to stay in it?" Aaron was pressing on. "Every town like this we've passed through for the last three states has a place to stay in it or near it, and this one doesn't."

They were in the town square now, along a little path between the grass, flanked by welcoming trees and comfortable benches. Everything about this town seemed to offer welcome. On the surface.

"Well," she said with a sigh, "I'm not sure whether you've convinced me or pulled me into your weird delusional paranoia, but if you're looking for a librarian, I know where to start."

"Where?" he asked, his body lurching with excitement. But Laura had already walked past him, along the path leading out of the green. His eyes followed her course and saw it would end at a small building across the street.

The library.

THE MEMORY

REMAK AND ROSE CRACKLED THROUGH the metallic light of Mal's brain, and suddenly the light collapsed into a foggy darkness. The fog swirled and moved — no, it wasn't fog precisely, and it didn't exactly swirl. It would be more accurate to say it skittered and shifted, like a swarm of black insects. As the darkness coursed around them, an image beyond became partially visible: a small room, its ceiling so low that Rose felt an urge to crouch, though she had no actual body here. There were no doors, but through a window, there was a brief glance of a city, its black sky pouring down sheets of rain, buildings whose pinpricks of light made weeping faces.

The darkness shifted again, offered hurried impressions: Mal sweating, struggling at bonds that held him to a chair; a man in a suit, his face bizarrely incomplete, almost a sketch of a face—eyes, nose, mouth—that had no real character. Was this true, or just an effect of the murky fog? The suit, similarly, seemed only the shape and size of a suit, but with no real specificity, not even a distinct color.

We don't want to be here, Remak said. *This is Mal's nightmare.*

More skittering fog opening brief apertures: the man in the suit's fingers, long—too long—and hideously flexible, probing Mal's face.

Rose felt a sense of pressure: Remak guiding her elsewhere.

Riveted, she watched: sharp fingertips forced themselves into Mal's nostrils, his eyes. Mal gave an animal snarl, and the snarl receded, as if moving away down a tunnel, as Rose was pulled back, away from the nightmare, deeper down into Mal . . .

Mal, six years old, sat on the floor, looking up at another boy. He was slightly older, maybe eight, but he had the same black hair, the same dark eyes looking out of a moody face.

Is that his brother? Rose asked. *Is that Tommy?*

Yes, I think so. These are Mal's real memories now. But look around. They're dim, fading.

Remak was right. As Mal's mind slowly ebbed away, the memories were thinning, viewed as if through a dark fog.

Tommy was hammering a nail into the wall—almost dropping the hammer twice—hanging a newly framed image: a roughly drawn picture of himself in a boxing ring, knocking his opponent off his feet, rocketing him through the air. Tommy turned away from the picture, looked down at Mal.

"Good?" he asked.

Mal nodded. *Good.* If Tommy could knock opponents out of the ring, then Mal could, too, someday. If their father could be proud of Tommy, then he could be proud of Mal, too. Maybe, with Tommy's help, Mal could draw a picture, too. And, if Tommy said it was good enough, they could hang it beneath his. *If* Tommy thought it was good enough.

Rose felt the emotions sweep through her as if they were her own. Was this what it was like for Remak, living through other people's minds?

"What are you doing?" a shrill voice cut through Mal's pride. Their mother appeared in the doorway, her eyes ruthless, her expression filled with sharp edges.

Tommy looked at the picture he had just put up, knew what was about to happen. So did Mal.

Their mother came over, tore the framed picture from the wall, glared down at it, and threw it hard at the floor. Glass splintered outward.

She looked at the two of them. This was a place they often found themselves: balanced precariously on their mother's next actions.

"What happened?" Their father—Mal writ large, with shaggy gray hair, exhausted eyes—spoke in a tired voice, having just come home to the sound of anger. He saw the frame he had given them the money for, the picture shredded by sharp glass. His eyes came up again.

Mal listened to his mother tearing into his father, like a boxer herself, a vicious, dirty opponent, but one who used words instead of fists. His mother's face was hot with rage fueled by the contents of a bottle discarded on the kitchen counter. His father stood, took the punches, sagged under them like a fighter on the ropes, but gave nothing back.

His father turned away from her briefly, glanced from beneath his lowered brow at Mal. Exhausted, heartbroken, his eyes struggled to give something to Mal. *Just take it,* was all they could come up with. *You're strong enough to take it. You're strong enough to take anything.*

JESSE KARP

"Don't look at him," Mal's mother raged. "He's nothing."

Again, the words receded as Rose was pulled away, pulled onto the next . . .

Mal's mother, stumbling back into the house, using one hand to steady herself on the wall and the other to bring a tall bottle half full of sloshing golden liquid to her slurring lips. Mal, eleven years old, looked somberly over the cover of his book at his mother's return. And naturally, she saw the eyes, as she was meant to.

She began screaming at him about respect and how he goddamn well better not be looking at her, lying in wait every night for her return so he could judge her. Then, her voice got quiet, and that was when Mal knew that trouble, real trouble, was coming. He rose from the chair, intending to retreat to his room.

"Don't you dare walk out on me." Her voice was hardly louder than the hiss of a snake. The bottle of liquor shot from her hand and blasted apart on the wall inches from Mal's face. Had she meant to hit him with it or merely scare him? He never knew. But a shard of glass caught him across the bridge of the nose, deep enough so that the mark would never leave.

Rose knew that scar, had touched it tenderly with

the tip of a curious finger while Mal slept. She had never dreamed that this is where it had come from. She had gotten Remak to take her in here because she could help bring Mal back. But seeing this struck her with the hateful realization that she barely knew Mal at all.

This can't be helping Mal, she said.

No, Remak said. *But this is the path that Mal has opened, and sometimes we have to follow the route we're offered . . .*

"This is home now, Mal," his father said, sitting in an unfamiliar chair in an unfamiliar room.

"What do you mean?"

"We're not going back to your ma. That's gonna get you killed." He touched his boy's nose gently. Max had bandaged it himself, from the kit he kept in the bathroom. "You and me both."

"But what about Tommy?" Mal asked, knowing he could survive this if Tommy were here, too.

"I'm sorry, Mal. Tommy is . . . I don't know how I can explain this to you. Tommy is your mother's. I can't do a thing about that. It's always been that way. You were mine, and she gave you hell just like she gave me. And Tommy was hers. I can't make you understand any better than that."

Mal didn't understand at all. He had never seen his father give up on anything—*anything.* Why should the first thing he ever gave up on be his own son?

JESSE KARP

Rose was overcome with a sense of loss for Tommy, a boy she had never met, never even known of before a few days ago.

This is too hard, Rose said, her words tangled with emotion. *I feel everything the way Mal did.*

You're touching his mind, Rose, and we're following a path of pain, Remak told her. *We have to move through it. If that's what Mal has given us, that's what he needs us to do . . .*

Six people stood in a small clearing in a pale, fading forest. Rose didn't recognize any of them. Mal was much as she knew him now, no more than a year or two younger. The conversation between the six people was fraught with suspicion and contention, but Mal was looking to another boy with a sense of deference Rose would never have attributed to him.

The other boy had a tight dark blond cap of slicked-back hair. Dark blue ice-chip eyes and razor-blade lines — high cheekbones, aquiline nose, sharp chin — made his young face dangerous. Beneath lacquered skin, his slim body was ridged with tight cords of muscle.

Who is that? Rose asked.

Nikolai Brath, Remak said. He was, if Rose sensed properly, disturbed to be seeing this. *He was Mal's best friend.*

Mal has never mentioned him, she said.

I'm not surprised, Remak said, his voice haunted.

Each of the six in the clearing was disclosing whether or not they had told anyone where they were.

"No," said a slim, hard-looking girl with jittery eyes. "I didn't have a chance."

Brath, his eyes suddenly dull with lack of interest, pulled a gun from behind his back and shot the girl in the head.

"Jesus!" someone shouted.

"Oh my God!" another voice cried.

Mal hadn't been hit by the bullet, but his head split apart. What was Brath doing? Brath turned the automatic on another girl. Mal wanted to move, *needed* to move, to protect her, but his arms and legs were actually paralyzed from the shock.

Betrayal. Rose felt it as sharply as Mal had. *His life was filled with it.*

And this is the one that hurt him the most, I think, Remak said, as the scene around them shifted again . . .

Mal was in an office, walls, ceiling, desk, chair, devoid of character; simply shapes. In one wall was an elevator, and the door opened to a bottomless shaft, above which two figures were suspended in the air, unconscious. Rose recognized one as Tommy, though he was full-grown now and no longer the boy she had last seen. The other was a pretty girl with short blond hair; Tommy's girlfriend Annie, Rose assumed.

Between Mal and the suspended figures was a man in a suit, the one from Mal's nightmare.

"So, here is what you wanted," said Man in Suit. "Your brother. I am going to let him die shortly, as you can see. But he can be saved. They both can. All you have to do is cross the threshold, push them to the safety of the other side. They will be free, and they will, if their hearts are resilient, recover and perhaps even thrive. Go. Help them."

Mal stared at Man in Suit without moving.

"Yes. You will fall and die," Man in Suit said. "But they will live. Not only that, but you will prove by giving up your life that hope has a chance, that human existence can come to more than . . ." Man in Suit looked around him at the industrial emptiness.

Mal could see Tommy from here, hanging, hair a little too long, face trapped in a rigor of tension. And Mal could also see Tommy through a tunnel of years: a boy he used to box with around the living room; who used to steal his little brother's boxing gloves and give them back with a punch in the arm; with whom Mal used to hide, pressed close together beneath the covers as the sound of their mother's voice tearing into their father penetrated the walls. But when Mal left, he had never been able to find the strength to take his brother's hand and pull him out, too. Just like now.

"But sacrifice is not a fight, is it?" Man in Suit asked him. "No. It is a failure to fight. Truly, the ultimate surrender: death," Man in Suit said. "That is why you will not help him. You are fighting what everybody is fighting in the end. Your father fought it, and lost. And if you go in there, *you* lose the fight."

Man in Suit waited. The door to Tommy and Annie remained opened. Mal didn't move.

"I'm sorry, Tommy." They were the only pitiful words he could find. "I'm sorry."

He betrayed Tommy, Rose said, yearning for eyes from which to cry.

He believes he did, in any case, Remak said. *The pain of it nearly ruined him.*

Rose could feel it, the only pain so horrible, it had robbed Mal of his will to fight.

But by reaching the depths of Mal's pain, Remak said, *we can now find his reason to fight.*

Me, Rose said, *where am I? Where are his memories of me?*

Rose, Mal is running out of time. We have to find—

I can give him hope! Her emotion was so powerful, she

felt the electrical charge of herself light up for an intense instant. *I can.*

All right, Rose. Give him hope. Find yourself.

She sizzled along the pathways of his brain, moving farther into Mal . . .

Mal sat in Rose's apartment, bruised, aching from a fight. A roll of cash the fight had produced lay on the table near his blood-encrusted knuckles. In front of him, Rose herself sat up in the bed, shook sleep from her eyes. Watching the scene, Rose remembered the moment herself, waking up and finding Mal sitting in the room, waiting for her. The Rose in the memory studied Mal's face, looked past the bruises, tried out a tentative smile.

Only when Mal snapped to, saw the smile, did she realize that Mal had not really been looking at her at all.

Rose pulled away from that memory, found another . . .

Mal, sitting in the diner where she worked. She sat across from him, on her break. She spoke quietly to him about something she had seen in a park, that maybe they could go back to and see again. He listened to her, but his eyes were focused elsewhere, over her shoulder.

Rose turned away, moved to the next memory . . .

Late at night, in her apartment. His shirt was off, muscles etched in shadows. She came over to him, touched his bare shoulder. Without looking at her, he gently moved her hand away.

Rose felt helpless. Was this the life they had shared? No more than this? She searched for another . . .

Mal, standing in the forgotten park, no more than a day ago.

"What did Remak mean when he said you had to do something for him?" the memory Rose asked him. "What is he holding over you?"

Her eyes were pleading, and all Mal could do was turn away.

Rose yanked back from the memory.

He's always looking away, she said. *What is he looking for?*

His hope, Remak said. *I'm sorry, Rose. He's looking for his hope.*

What is it? Her voice was empty. She knew the answer already.

Here, Remak said, bringing her along once again toward a round face, vivid in Mal's mind. The face was framed by black hair tied in a ponytail, a Mets cap pulled low. Bright blue eyes shone out, lighting something up in Mal that Rose had never seen or felt. This was not a face Rose had ever encountered, but she knew whom it belonged to.

Like grabbing a handful of sunlight, the world was suddenly aglow with memories of Laura . . .

Laura, unconscious on the dry, sharp grass of the forgotten forest where Mal had first seen her. Mal's heart beat faster in his chest.

Laura, her face glistening with sweat, tight with effort as she gripped the hard surface of a rock mountain, reached one hand out for help. Mal reached back, unable to stop looking at her luminous blue eyes.

Laura, in bed, her head resting on his chest, the skin of her cheek warm as she listened to Mal's heart. Mal held his hands away from her, afraid that if he touched her, she would disappear, as all the good things, all the things worth holding on to, always had.

Laura, screaming at him with tears in her eyes, screaming at him to get up, to keep going, because she made a choice, a choice to be with him forever. Mal's mind saw her through a haze of despair, which slowly cleared as she stopped screaming and looked deeply into him and gently kissed his lips.

Laura, smiling sleepily back at a mirror, her black hair loose over her bare shoulders. Something deep and utterly unfamiliar consumed Mal: happiness.

Laura, running through a park, glancing over her shoulder, her eyes frantic with worry. Mal yelled to her, *Faster, Laura, run faster.*

Laura, looking up from breakfast, staring for a moment, her face breaking into laughter, a laughter that gathered so forcefully, it made her gasp for air as her face turned red. Mal, feeling the happiness again, becoming accustomed to it. But even then, small veins of fear and doubt running through it. How long could the happiness last, after all?

Laura, throwing a highly competent right cross, connecting with the face of a man in a gray suit and sending him stumbling backwards. Mal ran to her, grabbed her, tried to pull her to safety, though she struggled, kicked at the air as he lifted her up and hauled her away.

Laura, in pictures and home movies projected on an old, cracking wall, eating ice cream, dancing, swimming, looking up angrily from homework, the phantoms of her mother and father always there, offering support, comfort, acceptance. Mal turned to look at the real Laura, sitting beside him, to find her face awash in tears.

Rose was overcome with Mal's feelings, even as her own hatred of Laura — for the idea of what Laura was — redoubled in her.

We're done here, Remak said. *Mal's mind is awake, alive. All I need to do is heal his body.* His tone did not echo the personal implications. Rose was heedless of it, anyway.

You can alter memories, like with Silven and other people you inhabited, she said. *You said you could do that.*

Yes, if I have to, but it's not necessary. Look around you, Rose. Mal is fighting again.

There was no denying that. The memory of Laura blazed like it was made of the sun itself. Rose could feel the stirring of Mal's consciousness around her.

Take Laura away, Rose said. *Put me in her place.*

Rose, do you know what you're asking? I might as well erase the memories of his mother, of how he failed Tommy. Those things are who Mal is, just as surely as the scars on his face.

No, you've got to, Remak, she said, her voice echoing harshly in the vaulted recesses of Mal's mind. *The emotions, the memories will still be there. It will just be me instead of her. And Mal—*

I'm going to heal Mal now, Remak said. *He's going to live.*

Fighting Remak was not in her. But here was an opportunity to change things, to become part of Mal, share his strength. She could not fight Remak, but she didn't need him, either. The neural electricity of Rose became a knife and she plunged downward, straight toward Laura.

But she barely moved at all. Remak's dominant will held her fast.

Time for you to go, he said.

No! She used all the force of her mind to throw the word at him. But the sense of the word shifted, bent, until it wasn't a sense anymore but an actual sound.

"No!" Rose was screaming as her eyes came open in the room. As consciousness returned to her own body, she lurched with a sense of vertigo, as if she had been sleeping on a tumbling wave and suddenly come awake on a still bed. Next to her, the body Remak had been in was still and silent on the floor. Across from her, Mal's bloodied body lay on the bed. Standing over them were two large figures.

"Good timing, Rose," Castillo said, towering above her, huddled on the floor. "This way, I don't have to carry you."

Rose opened her mouth to scream again, but Castillo clamped his massive hand over her mouth even as his other wrapped around her arm and pulled her to her feet.

"You've been a hell of a lot of trouble," he said. "Good thing Mal's locator came back up, because if I had to go through all the trouble of tracking you two down again —"

"Enough," Roarke said, hoisting Mal from the bed in preparation to move him. "The Old Man is waiting."

THE LIBRARIAN

ALMOST TWO YEARS AGO, A shot rang through the upper floors of the penthouse triplex, enough to send micro-ripples over the surface of the pool that Aaron Argaven had been sitting near. He knew what the sound was, and when he made it to the closed door of his father's office, he couldn't bring himself to open it. Was he scared? Aaron had been living with fear for some time now. It had been born when Intellitech began to crumble, and it became the constant, jittery atmosphere in which he lived every day as his father went gibbering down the halls of their home. Everything was to blame: employees, stockholders, board members, even "the

Old Man." That name had been invoked in Aaron's presence before, a bogeyman for grownups, an urban ghost with an ethereal finger in everything, never mentioned in full seriousness, but never really dismissed either.

There would be no more of that. The shot was not the ignition of fear, but the end of it. The fear was gone now, incinerated by Aaron's sparking, super-heated anger at his father. The death of this fear had left behind a valuable legacy as well: a mission and the knowledge that since his father was the only person smarter and more powerful than he, the weight of that power had fallen to Aaron now that his father was gone.

Now, here, in this town, Aaron found a sense of disquiet again. It wasn't the Librarian that made him nervous—surely not; if anything about the Librarian scared him, it was the prospect of *not* finding him. No, it was the town itself that made him jittery. Laura, the silly twit, walked blithely through it, though it was stomach-churningly clear simply by looking around. Bookstores, smiling pharmacists, and ice cream shops instead of cell stores, data-cafés, and receivers in every house and building; there *were* no towns like this anymore. This was not a town—it was a disguise.

Which meant, in the end, that the Librarian *was* near. That was what, once again, burned away the fear: the anger that drove Aaron forward would soon be unleashed, and the debt owed for his father's death was about to be paid in full.

Laura walked—nearly skipped in her unconsciously jaunty stride—up to the glass double doors of the library. It was not lost on Aaron that the glass doors were an open invitation, a standing embrace: "Come see, we've nothing to hide." It was not lost on him, despite the fact that he had a hard time taking his eyes off Laura's bottom as she pulled one of those doors open and stepped inside.

Through the small foyer papered with the clumsy crayon scrawlings of little children, they entered the library proper. Aaron had, of course, been in libraries before. His school, every Intellitech office, even his family home, had a library: large, climate-controlled rooms filled with screens and keyboards to plug your cell into and rows of HDs whose channels you could key into on your cell and get audio and streaming facts about the images being broadcast. Sometimes, as in the Argaven home and some of the Intellitech offices—though not at school—there was a small section or single shelf or display case devoted to books. The books were always of some sentimental or historical note, the information in them having long ago been transcribed into more useful electronic form.

This so-called library was filled with books, shelves of them, row upon row of confusing, unaligned, irregularly sized bindings, the titles impossible to read at a distance, re-quiring you to enter the morbid, dusty forest of them. There was not a single cell interface or HD screen visible, not even at the single desk that stood off to their left, behind which was a figure regarding them.

The woman sitting behind the desk, with clear, ques-tioning eyes, her gray-streaked hair cut short to frame her pixyish face, looked up curiously. Surprise might have passed across her features, not expecting visitors in the middle of the day, teenagers who should have been in school. Or it might just have been a look of greeting. Aaron didn't excel at picking up and reading social cues. Laura had pegged that one, he had to admit.

"Hi," Laura said brightly. "We're, uh . . ." She glanced quickly at Aaron and then back. "Looking for someone?"

One could never be sure what sort of gobsmacking idi-ocy Laura would come up with. Nevertheless, Aaron had to allow, people seemed to respond to her. It was, at any rate, best to let her do the talking right now. Aaron did not feel equipped to speak to this woman—an antique nameplate identified her as Ms. Hubert—without bellowing in her face.

Ms. Hubert remained silent for a stretch—a peculiar response for someone in the service business—then nodded slowly and rose from her chair. She came out from behind the desk, revealing a neat gray suit that seemed to Aaron incongruous in the midst of such a calculatedly homey town. Her hand touched something beneath her work surface, and Aaron heard—felt—the nearly subsonic *snik* of the cellock activating on the outer doors.

"Follow me," Ms. Hubert said, turning her back to them and proceeding toward the shelves of books. Laura spun toward Aaron, her eyes tense with uncertainty. He patently ignored her, following with his glare the woman's receding back into the far reaches of the book-lined alley.

Clearly exasperated, Laura huffed, rolled her eyes, and went after the woman. Aaron held his place a moment longer, surveying the space again. No screens, no ports, but a cellock. This place was just another disguise. He went cautiously after them.

Passing between the towering rows of books was distinctly uncomfortable. They smelled of dust and the acid of the pages, and he felt the weight of the metal cases crushing down on him. This was age, inefficiency, the leaden mass of obsolescence. When Laura disappeared from view around the other side, he doubled his pace and came around the corner to see Ms. Hubert standing at a door in a shadowed corner. She reached into a pocket of her slacks, and, again,

Aaron felt the technology of a cellock—a whiff of the modern world—activate. Ms. Hubert opened the door, and she waited for them to catch up.

Aaron peered around Laura when he got there, looking through the door and down a flight of stone steps into darkness.

"Where in the name of living hell do you think you're taking us?" Aaron couldn't contain himself anymore.

"The cellar," the woman explained without urgency.

"There is no way—"

Laura went down the stairway. Just to show Aaron up, probably. Ms. Hubert's curious eyes fell on him. With a sour look, he followed Laura.

With the flick of an ancient switch, a dirty light bulb over the stairs flickered, struggling to produce a halo of sickly light. When they reached the cold, hard floor, they could see another light, isolated amidst groping fingers of darkness. The woman's heavy footsteps preceded her appearance. They held their ground as she walked between them without a glance and up to a wall that, only now that she had distinguished it by her position, could Aaron tell was actually a metal door, flat and plain and heavy. Laura started toward it, Aaron trailing her, but before they came within striking distance, Ms. Hubert spoke.

"You're going to have to sleep your cellpatch." Her

voice was barely more than a whisper, but it resounded like a sonic boom in this cold, dark, still place.

"Over my rotting corpse," Aaron responded without hesitation.

"This place kills live celltech."

"Don't worry—you've got nothing that could touch my codes."

"I assure you, we do," she said simply.

"I don't believe you."

She shrugged.

"I didn't invite you here," she said. "You came on your own. You can make your own decisions."

Again, it was Laura who ended the stalemate.

"I'm going in," she said, stepping forward.

She'd given no sign that she remembered any of this. She was working as she had up to this point on her instincts, which Aaron would have snorted at had those instincts not been on the mark every single step of the way.

"Wait," he said. "Just wait a second." He turned to Ms. Hubert. "Who are you?"

"A custodian."

"What's on the other side of that door?"

She looked at it, then back at him.

"Not what you want, probably."

"But," Laura said, cutting in, "what we need?"

"Probably."

Laura stepped up to the door without even sparing Aaron another glance.

Though it had no apparatus on its smooth, blank surface, a last cellock activated and the door opened, accompanied by the popping thrum of fluorescent lights coming to life. Illumination cut from the seams of the slightly open doorway, slicing into the gloom of the cellar. The woman swung the door open, nearly blinding Aaron. Laura stepped up and, silhouetted for an instant like a departing soul stepping into a heavenly blaze, crossed the threshold.

Fighting every instinct he had, his stomach queasy and his muscles twitching from the tension of it, he uncelled himself, shutting his tech down to the very last maintenance routine.

The steady hum of electricity that was a constant stimulation to his brain was gone, leaving him feeling naked and alone, more so than he could ever remember, even at the funeral of his father.

Stifling a desperate sound boiling in the pit of his stomach, he walked forward and passed into the light.

From outside, Ms. Hubert shut the two of them in with a whoosh of airtight seals.

The room was small and stark white from the Hoffman tiles that covered every inch of its surface. The tiles created a perfect null to wireless technology and electricity, provided the tile surface was contiguous. Consequent to the null effect, the tiles had to conduct electricity themselves, since no other power sources could function within. It was the largest Hoffman space Aaron had ever seen, though he had heard that the military was trying to construct a room of nearly this size for the president.

The only objects within were a white table and two chairs, most likely laminated in Hoffman coating, too. Aaron looked at Laura, waiting for a sign, some assurance that this was right, that she knew this place. Instead, she stared blankly at the white corners, also, apparently, waiting for a sign.

"Well?" Aaron demanded of her.

She spared him a glance, then pulled out a seat and sat down.

"Sit," she said.

"Why?"

"So I can't kick you in the 'nads, which is what I'm about to do."

He yanked the chair out angrily and put himself in it.

"Was this supposed to accomplish something?" he said acidly. "Was this supposed to — "

"Aaron," said a voice that must have been using the tiles themselves as the transmission medium. It would have to, since no external wavelength could penetrate them. The voice was also electronically modulated; a perfect, crystalline simulation of a real man. "I was so sorry to hear about your father."

The greeting jolted Aaron like a lightning bolt. Calling him by name as though this were not their first meeting and probing such a raw nerve—it was a potent strategy on the Librarian's part. How could someone who addressed you with such intimacy be your enemy?

"How dare you speak of my father," Aaron lashed out, leaning forward in his seat, channeling his aggression toward the empty space before him.

"I knew your father very well, a long time ago. Better than anyone, if familiarity with the data that describes a person could be considered knowing him."

"You're lying." Aaron's voice was growing more shrill. He was falling into this meticulously designed trap. But he knew it, he *knew,* and so he was still better; better than the trap, better than the man who set it. He felt Laura's hand cover his, the warmth positively shocking in the midst of this cold white place. He shook it away angrily, without regard to what she might be feeling here.

"I worked for your father." The cool metallic voice echoed from the tiled walls without urgency, without emotion. "I was Intellitech's archivist, its librarian, from the moment they incorporated. Every dollar spent on every project, every theory behind every line of research, the details of every life that made up the company, passed before me."

"Why did you hate him so much, then?" Aaron fired out into space, in hopes of wounding the ghost. "Why did you drive him to his own death?" Aaron's eyes were burning, but he would not cry in front of Laura. He would *not*.

"I'll tell you what drove him to his end, if you like," the voice said with painful detachment. "But you had better be sure you want to know."

"You think I don't understand what you're doing? Stripping me naked, locking me in here where I can't even see you. Trying to scare me with your portentous warning. I came here to settle accounts with you, and I'm going to do it."

"Aaron, you've come here with a score to settle, I see that, and you've dragged this poor girl into your campaign. You've brought your anger in here with you, and it colors everything you hear. This is not a trap. I am not your enemy. I'm warning you because I have no cure for the truth. Once I tell it to you, I can't ever make you unknow it. And I assure you, it will change a great deal more than your view of me. It is going to break the world apart for you, and you're going to have to piece it together the best you can."

"My world is already broken," Aaron said, feeling the burning lines of tears cut down his face. Laura's hand returned to his, and this time he let it stay. "Do your worst."

The chamber filled with the feedback of the speakers, an electronic hum that stood in for silence.

"You answer easily," the voice returned. "But you're not answering just for you."

"Tell us," Laura said, before the voice could address her specifically. Aaron felt her hand grip tighter as she said it. "The truth is why I'm here, too."

"In 1976," the voice offered without further delay, "a biologist named Dawkins at Oxford University —"

"I know what memes are," Aaron cut in angrily. "What's this got to do with my father?"

"If you want the truth, you'll have to take it as I give it." The electronically smoothed tones didn't chide, didn't cajole, and it robbed the figure on the other end of some sense of humanity. "What, then, are memes?"

"They're ideas, units of idea transmission, really," Aaron said. "It's theoretical, but supposedly they're something like viruses, living organisms that transmit from mind to mind instead of body to body, and that's how ideas grow, how we learn, anything from mathematics to a commercial jingle." Aaron glanced up at Laura, for presumably he was being forced through this performance for her benefit. But her face had the strangest expression. Because Aaron faltered when it came to the specifics of social cues, he could only guess, but she looked as though she was searching for something, a notion forgotten, a word on the tip of her tongue.

"Yes," the Librarian confirmed. "Imagine, if you would, what controlling the transmission of memes would amount to for a company whose primary agenda is profit. Suppose you could control which memes got to people, how powerfully, how often, when. Suppose you could, in essence, control what people thought. Can you think of a greater engine of commerce?"

"Are you saying that Intellitech tried to control what people think?" Aaron said. "What corporation doesn't? What *person* doesn't? Isn't that what you're trying to do right now?"

"By controlling what people see and hear, yes. By controlling what's outside a person's head, you try to influence what a person thinks. What I'm talking about here is the sacred privacy *within* a person's head and a living idea, a parasite that's born in your mind and controls you from within according to its own agenda."

"Controlled," Aaron said dubiously, "by Intellitech. That's what you're getting at, right?"

"No." The false voice echoed through the tiles. "That was what they wanted. But even the youngest child knows you can't control an idea. They engineered the most contagious, powerful idea they could, and it slipped through their fingers and into their heads, into everybody's heads. It nearly destroyed all of us. It *did* destroy some of us. Your father, to name just one."

The words hung in the room, heavy and inescapable, like the drowning waters of a black ocean.

"What was the idea?" Laura asked, her voice weak. She was fighting to speak from within some kind of internal brain seizure or something. Her face was contorted with effort; her hand had grown cold on Aaron's.

"It was the most powerful, contagious idea they could find, one that promoted a craving for relief, a relief that Intellitech fancied it could provide; at a cost, naturally. The idea was hopelessness, and, already such a powerful part of us, when it first awoke — first became self-aware — it had already basically won."

"So how are we still here?" Aaron demanded. "Why my father? Why haven't we *all* been incorporated?"

"Hopelessness affects people in different ways, according to their strengths and weaknesses. It got your father where he couldn't fight it. In truth, I didn't think anyone could fight it, except by hiding. But I was wrong. A small group of people fought it, and they won."

"So it's gone? That's what you're saying? This small group of people beat it, and now I can give up my search because the thing that killed my father is gone?"

"Gone?" The Librarian tried the word out. "It enlarged a quality in people that already existed. Just because the cause is destroyed, doesn't mean the human quality it exploited disappears. Let us say that the disease is gone, but many of the symptoms still remain."

"How do you know any of this?" Aaron found, as he often did, that when he was defenseless, his best course of action was to challenge, to attack. "Where are you coming up with all this?"

"I don't function by mere supposition, Aaron. My method is founded on a powerful tool. While still employed by your father, I developed a method of predicting sweeps of human development via seemingly small and unrelated information. An equation made of human interaction. Something you would appreciate, no?"

Aaron offered nothing in return.

"The Global Dynamic is a tool that allows unparalleled insight into human affairs. But like any tool, the hand that wields it determines its use. I tried to prevent this tool from being misused long ago, when I left Intellitech. However, someone eventually got his hands on it."

The quiet that fell on the room, filled with a sense of the Librarian's own trepidation, was distinctly uncomfortable.

"And that would be?" Aaron pressed, the ominous pause getting even to him.

"The Old Man." It echoed off the tiles like a death knell.

"Are you joking?" Aaron spat with dogmatic force. "The Old Man is a bogeyman, a concept used to explain why the world sucks. He's not real."

"That's his power, Aaron," the voice intoned coolly. "Misdirection, camouflage, invisibility. He manipulates government and corporate powers as though they were chess pieces and the world was his opponent. Imagine how simple it would be to beat an opponent that didn't even know he was playing. Security is invoked, and it becomes legal to monitor our cell conversations. A law is introduced, and people can't litigate against corporations anymore. We miss it because a new movie shatters box office records, and we all look the wrong way. When we turn back around, the world has changed."

Aaron's hands were balled into fists on the table. His voice was pitched high as he began. "The Old Man is—"

"The Old Man"—the voice took the conversation back smoothly—"has no original name, no date of birth I can find anywhere. It's impossible to be certain exactly who he is, or was. But I am familiar with references to a young scholar, a disciple of Carl Jung's teachings, most specifically his theory of the collective unconscious. A very long time ago, this scholar formulated a radical theory of his own about how people's minds are connected in hidden ways and how, by touching subtle levers, one person can shift the outlook of huge groups. It seems that this scholar made a test run of his theory by creating a movement among the students at a university in Europe. He used it to develop something of a cult and, finally, made his followers into a small political movement. This had a particularly hideous ending. The university folded; the followers were arrested as dissidents. All to test out this theory. The scholar himself was never found. He took his formulation and" — the voice let the statement hang in the electronic hum for an instant — "disappeared. There has never been another trace of him. Unless you believe as I do, that this was the Old Man."

"You're suggesting that, what, he weaponized psychoanalysis?" Aaron sneered.

"Aaron, are you familiar with the concept of cake mix?"

"Are you kidding me?" This was simply too much to tolerate. He looked at Laura for support, and, no surprise, she was staring emptily at the blank tiles.

"Cake mix. The flavored powder you buy in the baking aisle. Instant cake. You've heard of this?"

"*Yes,* I've heard of it."

"It was invented in the 1950s, a time-saving innovation for housewives. You poured the powder into a bowl, simply added oil, baked it, and you had a delicious cake ready for your family when they got home. The children loved you more; the husband appreciated your kitchen savvy. A complete failure. No one bought it. It was about to be relegated to the trash heap of failed commerce. But then they consulted a team of psychoanalysts. The housewives, it seemed, felt that they had, in effect, been equated with an appliance. The food they prepared for their families was the manifestation of their love, the meals a contribution to family itself. The psychoanalysts came up with a solution. Do you know what the solution was, Aaron?"

"Thrill me."

"Add an egg."

Aaron's expression went dead in the face of this revelation.

"Add an egg," the voice repeated. "The company removed the powered egg from the mix, leaving that step for the housewives to take care of. It was about perception. The housewives needed to *feel* as though they were doing something for their families. All the company had to do was include the direction to add an egg. They sell a great deal of cake mix these days. Commerce won. Our minds were manipulated by misdirection. Simple psychoanalysis, but if that kind of manipulation isn't a weapon, I don't know what is.

"The irony"—the Librarian drew the pause out, his reticence suggesting a sense of regret absent from his electronic voice—"is that I used this scholar's theory of human interconnection myself, in a way. I stripped it of its original intention, employed it as a means of observation and analysis rather than manipulation. That's how I developed the Global Dynamic algorithm. Because it is not concerned with guiding people, but rather seeing how people are naturally guided by social currents, the Global Dynamic has much wider application as a predictor. Nevertheless, you could say"—again the Librarian's voice slowed with old resentment—"that the Global Dynamic is a collaboration between the Old Man and myself. Like his original formulation, it's just another tool to him, just a means to a larger, more effective tool: the human mind."

"*Stop!*"

Aaron jolted in his seat. He had, for all intents and purposes, forgotten Laura was there until her scream tore the room in half.

"This is insane," she said desperately. "It's madness."

"Yes," the voice returned, unmoved. "It is madness. And it's going to get worse. The Old Man subscribes to the ultimate corporate philosophy: *total* consolidation under one executive power. Through the Global Dynamic, he's come to know just how interconnected everything is. He will use that, manipulate it, finesse it with the most effective tool he can find, and he *will* make it happen. These people who stopped the Idea before, Remak in particular, he wants them because he believes they have access to such a tool."

Aaron wanted, *needed,* his cellpatch back, craved the blanket of the dataflow so much that it made his stomach cramp. He looked at Laura and saw a blank face staring into the middle distance of white.

"Well, then . . ." Aaron fought to order the information properly in his head, to design the proper mathematical proof to solve this. "What you need to do is find the people who beat the Idea before. You need to find them."

"Yes, Aaron," the electronic voice agreed. "That's why I've told you all of this. That's why you were even let down here in the first place. You already have found one of those people. She's sitting right next to you."

THE NEGOTIATION

WHEN ROSE WAS SIX YEARS old, she was in her cousin's room and spotted a small statuette of a princess sitting on the windowsill. With the light beaming through it, it seemed cut from pure crystal, though when she took it up in her nervous fingers, it proved to be as light as the cheap plastic it was actually molded from. Chipped and dirty close up, it lost none of its luster or wonder in her young eyes, and she slipped it into her pocket before her cousin came back into the room. Her cousin, however, spotted the missing item immediately and accused Rose of the theft. Hauled out and berated loudly by her uncle while her own parents looked on, Rose handed the toy back and apologized through embarrassed tears. Seeing the object come out of her pocket, her uncle swept her off her feet and threw her down onto his knees so hard, she gasped for her lost breath. He tugged her pants from her bottom violently enough to tear the zipper apart. He spanked her with bitter, stinging strikes that went on and on. Through tear-blurred eyes, she watched her parents standing across the room, staring ineffectually at the door, the window, her uncle—anywhere but back at their daughter. Her act had made her so hideous, they couldn't even look at her. At home that night, her father sent his wife from the room and grabbed Rose by the wrist, screaming at her for embarrassing them like that. His rage was so great, his grip so tight, Rose went to bed with a fractured wrist.

When Rose was ten, she was awakened one night by voices. She listened at her door as a man her father worked with berated him harshly. She peeked through a crack and watched as the man carried out their HD and several other appliances. Rose's gangly, shark-faced father did not get the bat she knew he kept in the front closet, did not interpose himself between thief and front door, did not even open his mouth to speak. When the man had gone with their things, Rose's mother hissed angry accusations at her husband. *That* was when her father leaped into action. Only once before had he beaten her mother so badly that she'd been forced to the hospital. That time she'd had three broken fingers, which, she explained to the doctors, had been caught in a door. This time the diagnosis was a fractured nose and three broken ribs. Three days after her mother was admitted, her father refused to take Rose to the hospital for a visit. Rose cut out of school early and, terrified at navigating so far afield from familiar territory alone, found her way to the hospital. She made her way to her mother's bed only to find a strange woman occupying it. That night she found her father sitting limp on the sofa, staring at the cracked window in lieu of the missing HD.

"Mommy's not at the hospital anymore," she said to him.

"I know," he said. "I don't figure she'll be back."

Her eyes grew larger. She couldn't turn away.

Her father's eyes came away from her, went downward then, edgily wandered back.

"Get out of here," he snapped. "I can't look at you."

When Rose was fifteen, a man in a suit showed up at the door and handed her father a notice. They were being evicted. Not behind on their rent, nowhere near the end of their lease, her father was baffled. One night, while Rose was lying on the sofa, another tenant came to the door. When her father answered, the tenant explained that the corporation was converting the building, but they were supposed to honor the tenants' contracts, of course. The tenants were going to form a coalition, pool their money, fight this. Her father sent the tenant away.

He walked back into the living room and saw Rose staring at him, and his eyes became hot and manic.

"Stop looking at me," he hissed at her. She couldn't.

He grabbed a pillow and put his weight on her chest.

"Stop staring at me. I can't take the sight of your face anymore."

He pressed the pillow over her face, over her staring eyes. She reached up and touched his wrists, but let them fall limply away. He pressed down, until all she had left to breathe was darkness.

He tossed the pillow away, leaving her gasping.

Rose found work at a diner, a place her mother had worked at years before, where the owner remembered the child Rose had been, tagging along with her mother on odd days, receiving smiles from the sporadic, tired clientele, free lollipops from the other waitress. He hired Rose, and the other girl who worked there helped Rose find an apartment. Rose's father came into the diner regularly, expecting to be given his food for free. Rose paid the bill herself, never mentioning it. He never looked up at her face. One day her father didn't show up and not ever again after that. Without any effort, without having to take any kind of a stand, she was on her own.

Six months ago, Rose was working the night shift at the diner alone. The owner couldn't afford both girls at the same time any longer. She stood behind the grimy counter, looking out the window at the flickering dark, and started when someone spoke.

"You got something I want." The voice came from a stocky figure bundled in a thick jacket, a hood hiding his face in shadow. He had walked in and come very close while Rose was transfixed on the dim world on the other side of the glass. His voice was a sharp whisper, and his breath was hot and sour.

She backed up instinctively, though the counter remained between them.

"You got something I want," the shrouded figure repeated. "You understand what I'm telling you?"

Rose had no response, no words at all. Her body grew weak underneath his ravenous gaze.

"Leave," said another voice from behind the figure. The face in the shadowed hood turned to get a look at who was addressing him.

The person standing there was broad and tall in cargo

pants and a hooded sweatshirt. Under a crown of short dark hair, the lean face was that of a boy, but for the incongruous wash of scars and scrapes plastered across it. Honestly, the face looked like someone had held it too close to a sand-blaster, some of the cuts still red with blood, some of the welts a throbbing pink. Rose saw the hands hanging loose at the sides, the knuckles crisscrossed with old damage and red and raw with new damage. This boy had just come from a fight, was ready to step into the next without so much tension as to make his voice rise or his fists clench.

The stocky figure did not even turn back to Rose, but slid from between the counter and the boy and left. In that one word — "leave" — one single syllable, a possibility opened up to Rose that was as astonishing and unfamiliar as a great crystal tower bursting forth from the concrete of the sidewalk before her.

She brought the boy food, as much as he wanted, stood at the far end of the counter, unable to take her eyes off him, unable to come any closer. Two hours later, he hadn't left. She needed to close but couldn't imagine turning him away.

"Do you have anywhere to go?" she asked as steadily as she could from behind her mask of hair.

He looked at her with dark eyes that did not belong in a boy's face. Impossibly, the eyes held no judgment, no contempt, just comfort.

He shook his head.

That same boy sat next to her now, in the back of a limousine, watched over by Roarke's rigid gray eyes and Castillo's wandering, bestial gaze. Mal was not a savior anymore, but an unconscious body.

"Do you see this?" Castillo said to his partner, prodding him on the shoulder, pointing at Mal. Roarke's eyes turned minutely. He was a man of small, precise movements. It took him a moment to study the body. The windows in here had been darkened so that Rose couldn't see where they were going, but it left the inside muted and dim.

"His breathing is strong," Roarke said. "He should make it back. I'm surprised he's still alive at all."

"Yeah, but look." Castillo leaned in closer. "It's not just his breathing. I don't think I see any wounds."

"What are you talking about?" Roarke leaned forward, too. "There's blood all over him."

"Blood, yeah, but do you see any *wounds?*"

Roarke slid closer to Mal. He moved his hard hands over Mal's body, touching the various stains of blood, probing gently but thoroughly. Rather than becoming alarmed as he failed to find what he was looking for, his expression became emptier. His hands moved up to Mal's face, parted his lips, moved his fingers inside.

A moment later, without warning, he yanked his hand

out as though Mal had been playing possum and tried to bite his finger off.

"What?" Castillo demanded of his partner. "What is it?"

"His tooth," Roarke said. "I knocked a tooth out of him when we found him on the street."

"Yeah?"

"It's there," Roarke's empty expression had become positively ghostly.

"What do you mean?"

"It's there, in his mouth. It grew back."

Rather than coming in for a look himself, Castillo slid farther back on his seat. Roarke, however, turned those gray eyes on Rose.

Rose folded in on herself, like a plant wilting under intense heat.

"What is this?" Roarke asked her, indicating Mal's inexplicable condition with a stabbing hand.

Her head gave the smallest of shakes, her eyes locked on the floor so that she couldn't see if Roarke was still looking at her.

What this was, was that Remak had been successful. Mal was going to live. The joy over this was muted, not only by their current situation, but also by the implication of Remak's success. It meant that Remak himself was gone forever, sacrificed to give Mal his life back. With Remak gone and Mal unconscious, Rose was on her own, without strength or hope or even the ability to look back into someone's eyes.

The car rolled to a stop. Castillo hustled Rose roughly out of the car as Roarke managed Mal's body. They moved through what appeared to be a service entrance and then through a small but scrupulously tidy hallway that led into a larger, carpeted hallway lit with a peaceful amber light that made it feel as though the world were covered in warm honey. They moved Rose up to a large, wooden double door.

"Uh, this is where I get off," Castillo said with a sense of relief. Roarke paused in front of the door and gave Castillo a long, almost mournful look.

"Right," he said, and took Rose by her arm with the hand that was not keeping Mal's large frame perched on his shoulder. The hand clasped her bicep like an iron manacle. Castillo went down the hallway and through the door that led back to the car. Roarke took another moment, straightening his back and shifting something in his head, and then pushed through the doors.

The space beyond looked like the back room in some private club, its walls deep oaken brown, glass cabinets filled with liquor in crystal decanters. There was a long table made of ancient wood, and above it was a line of paintings of solemn old men glaring down. The chairs were rich brown and red velvet, as was the chaise near the center of the room onto which Roarke lowered Mal's form.

The room was bathed in a dim, red glow, and the temperature and thick humidity instantly made Rose's clothes cling to her body.

In this light, Rose squinted at the one inconsistent detail here. Against the far wall, almost lost to the low red illumination, was a wheelchair.

At first, Rose wasn't even certain that there was something in the wheelchair, so slight was the figure. But, suddenly, the wheelchair moved. The nearly inaudible whine of electronic controls attested to the presence of *something* in the seat.

It approached and, releasing Rose, Roarke stepped forward to meet it. Rose skittered back, pressing herself against the large chaise longue that Mal rested upon. Roarke's body was obscuring her view of the figure in the wheelchair. The large man spoke in short, clipped whispers, his back rigid.

A moment later, Roarke turned toward the exit and marched, like a soldier, out of the room. Near the door, he turned briefly and spared Rose a final look, before the door closed with a resounding echo.

Rose did not want to turn back, see what was waiting

there. She could already feel it examining her. Rose always spurned the attention of others, always felt inert and hollow when eyes fell on her. But this, this was as though she stood spotlighted before a stadium of thousands, the weight of the attention here crushing the breath from her chest.

"Where," said a voice that was the sound of dry air gently escaping a tomb, "is Jon Remak?"

"He's dead." She was happy to say it. Not because she wished Remak dead, but because she had the true answer, did not have to resist or try to trick this thing.

"That's why . . ." — the voice paused to take in air — "the boy lives."

"Yes." Rose nodded, her eyes riveted to the floor. "Yes, Remak healed him."

"Because Remak was not . . . human anymore. Because he had become . . . the power of pure mind . . . pure will."

The blessed relief of it: the thing didn't just believe the story; it already seemed to know it. All Rose had to do was nod.

"Because he had entered . . ."

It hung there until Rose had no choice but to finish it.

"Remak called it the neuropleth. How — how do you know all this?"

"I've lived . . . a long time. I've spent all of it . . . coming to know how human minds work. You understand more than an insect . . . because you are so far above it . . . you see more of its world . . . have a greater sense of the cause and effect that determine its life."

The room was silent then, and Rose would have been tempted to look up, had she not felt its terrible eyes still on her.

"I understand more than you," it explained, "because I am so far above you. My grasp of cause and effect . . . is over yours . . . as yours is over an insect's."

"Who are you?" The question vomited from her mouth in a wash of fear.

"Man created the narrative of religion . . . to give his life form and meaning. But in this era . . . that narrative has been replaced. Humanity has created a story of old men in hidden rooms . . . who play the world like a game. If this theology of conspiracy has replaced religion . . . and I am at the center of this new belief system . . . then who am I?"

Rose's eyes fluttered, the fear running up against the urge to see the face of the man who made such a claim. In the end, the fear won, as it always did.

"Then we're nothing to you," Rose said. "What do you want from us?"

"Remak entered the neuropleth . . . and was changed. But it is possible . . . to have access to the neuropleth without being changed . . . as he was. I want that access. I want to touch . . . every mind in the world."

"But you have so much power now . . ." Rose flailed helplessly at even the idea of such power. "What more do you need?"

"The future, girl. The future. Guiding people from the shadows . . . leaves too much power in the hands . . . of others. There is too much room . . . for mistakes . . . for waste. My will is far beyond . . . what Remak's was. I will be able to do things in the neuropleth . . . that he never could. I will be able to use the energy of the brains there . . . to power this body, make it strong again . . . stronger than anything. Strong forever. And I will be able to control those brains . . . make puppets of their bodies without losing my own, as Remak did. Then there will be one power . . . guiding an utterly consolidated workforce. All I want . . . is absolute control . . . for the rest of time."

Again the room fell silent as the thing accumulated the strength to go on.

"Remak has been in that boy," it said after a time, "and so . . . he is my last connection to the neuropleth. I will have what I want . . . if I have to peel his brain open . . . and take it."

Rose's arms clenched around her body. Remak had said that Mal would have a door to the neuropleth in his head, too. What would the Old Man do to Mal's brain in order to have it for himself? Rose couldn't stop this thing from getting what he wanted.

But to save Mal, she could give it to him herself.

"Wait," she said, struggling to find her voice. "Wait. I can . . . I can give you the neuropleth. I can."

There was no response, and after a moment she hurried on, snatching whatever chance she could.

"Remak took me into the neuropleth and left a doorway to it in my brain, too. I can give it to you."

"How?" asked the voice from the tomb.

"Physical contact," she said, repeating Remak's own explanation. "That's how he put it in me."

"Look at me."

"What?" Rose said. She had heard the voice, but this was what you said to the inconceivable.

"Look at me and . . . say it again."

Slowly, fighting a powerful force, Rose's eyes came up, struggled upon the Old Man.

It was small, shrunken, its dry head sitting atop a deflated torso, its arms and legs skeletal extensions. The dim red glow marked every irregularity in the face, engraving a thousand ancient fissures in shadow. Its eyes were lost in the darkness of the crevices, but Rose could feel them searing through the flesh of her face.

"Tell me . . . again."

"I can give you the neuropleth," she said, almost unable to make the words audible. "Right now."

"Yes." The voice had acquired a note of something it had surely not experienced for many years: awe. "Yes."

In coming to her feet, Rose braced her hand against the chaise behind her, and her flesh brushed against Mal's face. The sensation of it brought the world more sharply into perspective.

"Wait," she said. "Wait. If I do it, you have to let Mal and me go. You have to let us go."

The head creaked and swiveled minutely to take in a slightly different view of Rose.

"Negotiation," it said. "That is something I am . . . intimately familiar with. It is either that . . . or fight, after all. You could fight . . . you know. I am old and weak. You could . . . kill me easily. My man is outside the door. He wouldn't even know."

Rose stared at him, unsure whether this negotiation was going her way.

"But you . . . are a victim. Fighting is . . . a fiction to you . . . a story told to wonder at. Far easier . . . to trade on your victimhood . . . to get what you want . . . by making yourself more of a victim."

She shivered listening to him.

"Very good. I shall accommodate you. I promise that I . . . will not stop you or the boy from leaving. Now . . . do it."

Rose stood, unsure how to approach. Unsure if she was *able* to approach.

"Do it," the thing hissed.

She stepped closer, reaching out a tentative hand. It neared the hand resting on the arm of the wheelchair, and as it did, the gaunt fingers rose, fluttered through the air, and brushed her skin. A shiver ran up her arm, down her spine. Even in the sweating humidity of the place, the fingers were bone cold. It felt as though rot were crawling beneath Rose's flesh.

"Kiss me," the Old Man said.

She gaped at him, her face slack with disgust.

"That will be . . . our physical contact. I am the oppressor and . . . you are the victim. Without it, there is no contract. Kiss me."

Rose could not swallow. The air whistled dryly through her throat. His hand rested on her forearm, exerting the gentlest downward pressure, less than that of a sleeping baby.

She closed her eyes, her last sight that of the gray, cracking lips, seamed with dried saliva and yellow crust.

Mal, she thought. *Mal.*

She brought her face forward until the putrid breath,

the stench of his rotting insides, filled her nose. She gagged, and as she swallowed back bile, she felt the rasp of sharp, cracking skin on her lips. She almost pulled back, almost. But as soon as their lips touched, she felt his consciousness flash across, forcing its way in.

With only a small portion of her awareness, she felt his moist, flicking tongue enter her mouth, slide across her gums. But that was far, far from the worst of it. She also felt the slow crackle of the Old Man's synaptic electricity prickling like spider legs across the folds of her brain, searching, searching . . .

She felt the aperture to the neuropleth in her head open; she glimpsed the pathway of buzzing light branching endlessly to the effervescent brains.

Then a flash of electricity, the spider amputating something from her brain and scurrying away with it. Instantly, the view of the neuropleth was gone. The aperture hadn't simply closed — it had been burned out of her, stolen away forever by limitless greed, limitless hunger. Just as suddenly, the spider was gone.

The humid red world rushed back, and Rose tumbled to the floor, her mind aching with a sense of disconnection, of loneliness as she had never known in a lifetime full of loneliness.

"*Mmmmmm.*" It was a deep, orgasmic moan from the

depths of a primordial chasm. The Old Man's flaccid body twitched in a hundred different places. "Feel them," he said, the voice already growing more potent, the timbre deepening. *"Feel them."*

Rose tore her eyes from him, looked at Mal. Could she lift him, drag him out of here herself?

"No," said the voice, vibrant with strength, responding to her unspoken question. "No, you cannot."

THE TRUTH

"TELL ME, LAURA," THE ELECTRONIC voice inquired, and perhaps the merest touch of sentiment vibrated through the Hoffman tiles. Or perhaps Aaron was reading that into the exchange; the voice liked Laura better because she was sweet and vulnerable and Aaron was too smart. "What is your life like now?"

"What do you mean?"

"Over the last few months, what have you done in your life? Nothing more complicated than that."

Laura stiffened, straightened her posture as though she

were facing a verbal examination for a crucial grade. Her hands were trembling on her lap.

"I'm in college. I take classes. I see my friends. I date — I dated a boy. I speak to my parents sometimes."

"Is that so bad, Laura?" The question rang down like a judgment on her.

"Yes!" Her response was instant and harsh. "Yes. Because it's not *mine*. I know it isn't. It's like — " Aaron watched her face enter a rigor of strain. "It's like someone dropped me into a fake life, with a family and friends and a job, but none of them are real. But I have to keep up the charade, have to keep up this *performance,* because if I don't, if I run offstage, behind the curtain is horrible, horrible darkness."

"Then don't, Laura," the voice said, and now Aaron knew that it felt this, that there was a person behind this electronic camouflage who was pleading with Laura, pleading with her to just, God help her, hold on to the fake life she had. "Don't look behind the curtain."

"I have to. Otherwise I'm empty. There's only this fake person living a lie. There *is* no more *me*."

The room throbbed with a heavy silence. Aaron looked at Laura's trembling hands, and it struck him that now would be the time to offer his own hand, to let her hold it in that crushing grip again. That was what she needed right then: human contact. Aaron's hand fluttered but didn't take hers.

"There were four of you," the voice said. "Each of you was caught up against the Idea for different reasons, had each stumbled across it in the course of your daily lives. But unlike so many others, you four resisted it. It took everything from you—your lives, your friends, your families. It snatched you out of their heads as though you had never even existed. But each of you had something that allowed you to cling to hope, to fight. Ultimately, that was how you beat it. One of you knew about me, and you came to me for information."

"To Pope Springs," Aaron said, driven by his unflagging interest in proving himself right. "At the site of the fire."

"Yes. There. I told you what I could, and you went to confront it, as I already described."

"Who?" Laura asked. "Who were the others? What were their names?"

Silence.

"Please . . ." Laura's voice was choked with anger and grief, her expression caught between the two extremes, anguish and rage burning her face. "Please just *tell* me."

"Jon Remak. Mike Boothe."

Laura clutched her stomach, her shoulders folding forward to protect her from the names.

"Mal Jericho."

It was as if a jolt of electricity went through her, seizing her muscles and bunching them into painful knots.

Aaron's fingers moved across the cold space between the two of them and touched her shoulder as they would a most delicate piece of digital equipment, the fingers barely exerting pressure.

"Do you remember?" he asked softly.

"No!" Her eyes were on fire, gushing tears, and she glared up at him; he pulled his arm back as though it had been singed by her gaze. "No, I don't remember *anything!* The names are killing me, but I don't *know* them. Why can't I *remember* them?" she demanded of the empty room.

"I'm sorry, Laura," the electronic voice filled the room coolly. "I know you came here to find out what happened to you. For 'the truth,' as you put it. But this is an area where my information falters."

"You've got to know *something,*" Laura said, and Aaron judged it not a question but a plea to salvage her fracturing sanity.

"All right, Laura, all right. I'm prepared to make you a deal. I can see you've already set yourself on a course. I'll tell you what I can. Conjecture mostly. But as I do, you have to unmake up your mind. You have to examine what I say and, only *then,* decide on your course."

Aaron stared at her, unable to understand why she sat there, in trembling silence.

"Say 'yes,'" he whispered to her, like a stage manager prompting an actress who had forgotten her lines.

She didn't heed him, just sat, staring into the middle distance, quivering as if chilled to the bone.

"What?" Aaron hissed. "What's wrong?" But then he realized, even before the last angry syllable left his mouth. She was actually thinking about her answer. She was not simply working to get the information she needed. She was trying to figure out whether she could take that deal and then answer *honestly.*

"Yes." Her voice echoed in the room like a pronouncement from God. "I'll take that deal."

"Mike Boothe"—the voice proceeded without further preamble—"died in the confrontation with the Idea. It was, in fact, his sacrifice that ultimately defeated it. You and Mal emerged from the battle together. You . . . stayed together for a time. I wasn't keeping constant surveillance on you, but I did, of course, make a point to check in. From what I observed, you began to build a life, of sorts. But it was a troubled life, troubled by circumstance. Things kept . . . interfering, interrupting. Matters of settling your pasts: your parents, Mal's brother; there was great trouble, a great deal of guilt and suffering putting things in some semblance of order."

"Sounds like you were watching us plenty," Laura said, not without a cool resentment in the midst of her desperation that managed to impress Aaron.

"And then, of course, there was the Old Man." The voice carried on without noting Laura's rebuke. "He was in the process of learning about you. He sent out tentacles, kept probing and testing you both to see what you were capable of."

The narrative trailed off, and the electronic hum buzzed through the room long enough that Aaron was finally the one who could stand it no longer.

"*Then?*" He struck angrily into the emptiness.

"Then you were in college, Laura, back with your parents and your friends. And Mal was alone."

"How?" Aaron had taken the role of her proxy, since she was clearly too shaky to keep this goddamned torturous retelling moving along.

"Yes. This is where the conjecture begins. After your confrontation with the Idea, Jon Remak disappeared. From what I gathered, neither you nor Mal knew what had become of him. I know there was strife between him and the two of you, a differing of philosophies and strategies. I assumed he had died. But over the course of time, I have received both queries and information from an individual I believe to be Jon Remak, based not only on knowledge he had of how I work and intelligence he was able to turn up, but on purely factual elements: syntax, grammar, word choice, and tone.

"The thing of it is, that the inquiries and intelligence I received from what I thought was this single individual all came from wildly differing sources: CEOs of major corporations, directors of intelligence organizations, journalists with reputations for paranoid secrecy. And yet I would swear to the fact that every one of them was Jon Remak."

When silence fell again, Aaron had no immediate words. He was not even, strictly speaking, clear on just what the Librarian was suggesting.

"I believe," the voice continued, unbidden, "that Remak was somehow able to alter your brain topography and that of your friends and relatives in such a way that you could be returned to your proper life."

"Not my proper life," Laura said in a soft voice.

"Maybe. But now comes your end of the bargain, Laura. Consider this: it could be that you got that life back because your companions didn't want you with them any longer. If Remak did this, he did it for a reason. He was not a man who acted impulsively or without sound motives. What he did to you may have been motivated by factors beyond your ability to fathom now."

"It doesn't matter," she said, and Aaron watched her muscles bunching again; not reflexively this time, but rather to contain her anger. "It wasn't my choice."

"Are you sure?" the voice responded coolly.

"What?" Her voice was struck empty of that anger all of a sudden.

"How can you be sure, Laura, that you didn't ask for this? Who, in their right minds, wouldn't opt for a future filled with warmth and love and hope over a life of constant tension and danger?"

"But . . ." Laura's voice picked up its familiar tremble again, and Aaron's stomach turned at her feeble inability to control this emotional roller coaster. "But I never would have left Mal alone."

Aaron opened his mouth to respond, to remind her that Mal was no one she knew anymore. This Mal might have been a monster. He might have been cruel to Laura, might have beaten her every day.

"Maybe Mal isn't alone," the Librarian's voice echoed down before words reached Aaron's lips. "If Remak is alive, as I surmise. Perhaps others have been recruited. I've no doubt that they are fighting the Old Man right now. Maybe you're here, Laura, because you don't belong in the middle of a war, and you knew it."

Laura stood up with such speed and intent that Aaron thrust back on his own seat as though he were about to be attacked. She held her place, her body extended as if she were about to give the room the harshest reaming out in history. But her clenched jaw formed no words.

She spun around, marched to a wall, put her back to it, and slid to the floor, clutching her knees to her chest.

Aaron watched her a moment longer. When he was certain she wasn't about to burst back up again, he spoke.

"I think we're done here," he said.

When no response came back immediately, Aaron imagined an image of a man sitting in shadows, surrounded by screens showing this room, and the man in shadows staring at Laura like a precious creature, a child of his own, even.

"Yes," the voice returned, obliterating the image. "All right, then. I'll have Ms. Hubert come for you."

Aaron rose and went over to Laura's huddled figure. He stood over her, his hands at his sides, his eyes searching her warily.

"Where are they?" she asked, down to the floor. "Where are they now?"

"I don't know, Laura," the voice said. "And it surprises me. They were in New York the last time I knew of them, and I have no record of them trying to leave. I've tried to find them, but if Remak is alive, then he's working hard to hide them. It only makes sense. The Old Man would have access to many of the same resources I do. Don't go to them, Laura. Let something good have come of all this. Go back to the life you had, and make it your own. Make it a happy one."

Laura looked up, and maybe there was a response within her. But the room suddenly felt lifeless. The electronic hum popped and disappeared, and the room felt like a coffin now.

Aaron looked at Laura impatiently. Her eyes wandered aimlessly about the white.

There was a sudden hiss of air seals, and the door opened, letting a musty darkness into the pristine expanse.

Ms. Hubert examined them with her curious blue eyes, beneath the neat cut of her short salt-and-pepper hair.

"This way," she said, gesturing through the cellar, still dense with shadows.

They stepped through into another world—their world. Crossing the threshold, Aaron activated his cellpatch, and the information coursed into him, lighting the world up in the digital rainbow of data. It produced a nearly physical high in him, and he felt his muscles shudder, his extremities tingling. He was armed again.

"Did you get what you needed?" Ms. Hubert asked as they mounted the stairs.

Laura came to the top, out into the library proper, before she answered.

"Yes," she said. "I suppose so."

"I'm sorry," the woman said. "Truly sorry."

Aaron walked slowly through the town, his eyes sliding suspiciously from storefront to storefront, as they might if he were trying to move through a cave full of sleeping snakes. Did everyone here know they lived in the Librarian's town? Surely they all knew that the trappings of contemporary technology weren't welcome here and managed to function without it. But the polite pressing on of strangers, the smiles covering the vague misdirection of questions — were they all, in fact, serving the Librarian in some larger way, part of some vast operation of which Aaron had caught only the merest whiff?

There was Laura going on about how technology was digging the world a tomb, but the truth was it was people who lied to you, hid things from you, betrayed you, and abandoned you.

A woman sitting behind the counter of a bookshop "happened" to look up as Aaron passed and gave him a nod calculated to impart warmth, but looking beneath the surface, all Aaron could see was a knowing show of superiority. He slid his eyes away.

Eventually he came back to the town square, found Laura sitting just as he had left her, hunched with her arms wrapped around her knees, atop a rock with an old burnished plaque on it.

He approached from behind and stopped on the grass several paces away. Her position was nearly identical to the way she wrapped herself up in the corner of the room, lost and alone. Aaron surely knew from lost and alone. Well, alone, anyway. And who had pulled him from that? Frankly, he pulled himself from it, as he solved all problems in his life. But he did owe Laura something.

"When I asked for some time alone," Laura said without turning around, "I didn't exactly mean you should stand back there and stare at me."

"I wasn't staring at you."

"Right. Sorry. You definitely *don't* stare at me, here or in the shower."

"Damn it, Laura, I've had it with—"

She cut him short by turning around. He had chosen to overlook the humor in her taunt, but the fact that she was smiling caught him by surprise. That was not, however, what struck his words from him.

Laura's eyes had always been bright and alive. Even through the pulsing lights of the dataflow, her nearly luminous blue eyes made the letters and numbers that filled Aaron's world seem to fade. But from the moment he'd come face to face with her, those eyes had always been drawn inward, studying the flaws and inconsistencies of her fissuring life. Sitting on the rock now, facing him, her eyes were looking outward for the first time, in front of her, at where she was heading. For one small, perfect moment, Aaron was lost in them.

"I'm ready to get the hell out of here," she said, hopping from the rock with a sprightly spring. "Our first step is going to have to be finding Mal."

"What? Are you serious? Did you hear what the Librarian said?"

"Yes. And I considered it, like I said I would. But if someone offered you your father back as he was — flawed, troubled, and real — or a perfectly functioning, flawless robot version of your father, which would you take?"

She didn't bother waiting for his response, but walked past him and back toward the car.

"But, Laura, you can make this new life the real one," he said, as he fell into step behind her. "That's your choice."

She spun on him again, in the middle of the empty street, and this time her eyes were bright with rage.

"I *already* made my choice, and this Remak asshole tore it away from me."

"Or you chose to leave it behind."

"I didn't," Laura said simply, and turned back toward the car.

Aaron followed her in silence until they got to the car. He stopped at the passenger side and watched her go around.

"It may be," Aaron said over the roof, "that the only thing of value the Librarian actually said was that you should take this opportunity and make it work for you. If you choose to ignore that, that's your prerogative. You should know that, as a completely impartial observer, I believe you're being an incredible fool. I just wanted that out in the open between us because"—he bit down hard before he could get it out of his mouth—"because I owe you that much. That said, just drop me off at the nearest town with a bus station. I've already bought my tickets."

Laura gaped at him over the roof, her face blank with surprise until, like paper tossed into a fireplace, it combusted with rage.

"You child," she said, her volume escalating. "You fucking child. You can't blind yourself with your own tiny little interests, all your digital *shit,* now that you got what you wanted." The curse rang off the storefronts around them, and Aaron could imagine the bookstore owner and the pharmacist leaning toward their windows with prurient fascination. Laura herself was storming around the car toward him now.

"You got the truth you were looking for," she hammered on, approaching him like a furious parent. For his part, Aaron backed himself up against the car, flinching as she loomed above him. "Dealing with that truth means growing up. And what do grownups do?" She glared at him. "What do they do?"

"Face their problems? Is that the idea?"

"The idea is that grownups take responsibility for more than just themselves. Do you remember what the Librarian said? Remak could change things *inside my head,* and the Old Man knows about him. Imagine what the Old Man could do with that kind of power. Grownups make a choice not to let a monster devour everything good just because they can shut themselves in a room and pretend they won't get hurt."

Her breath was coming so hard that he could feel it on his face, hot and angry.

"This Remak and Mal are already fighting that fight,"

he said, but even in his own ears, his voice was that of a weak child's.

Laura's body relaxed. She stood back on her heels and stopped looming. Those luminous eyes of hers played across his face like a spotlight.

"Sometimes," she said in a voice born of concern, of knowledge rather than rage, "people have to do things together. Last time it took four of us to beat this thing, apparently. Now, for all we know, Mal is by himself." Her voice caught on something sharp that threatened to open it up and make it bleed tears.

"You know what people do when they're together, Laura?" Aaron said, finding his own strength as she allowed her vulnerability to the surface again. "They lie to each other. They abandon and betray each other."

"They do that. That's true. That's the choice your father made. You can choose a different side, because people also teach you and fight for you and offer you a hand when you don't think you can hold on a second longer."

Aaron couldn't remember the last time he wanted to vomit so much.

"You're in love with this Mal guy, aren't you?" he said. "You're in love with some guy you don't even know."

Her eyes went into herself again, for just a moment.

"I *do* know him," she breathed, barely loud enough for Aaron to understand it. Then she walked back around the car and got in.

So . . . how did one capitulate to Laura's demands without appearing to have backed down? Devising a stratagem, Aaron reached down for his door as the lock snapped shut.

The window slid down two inches.

"If you want to go to the next town," Laura's voice issued forth, "you can walk."

For an instant, just a bare instant, he was struck dumb by her ability to actually take a hard line.

"For God's sake, Laura," he countered. "Who's being a child, exactly? Open the damned door."

The lock clicked, and he pulled open the door and slid in.

"You're worse than the Librarian," he said, buckling his seatbelt. "Won't even come face to face with me."

"You did come face to face with the Librarian," Laura said, starting the car and pulling out.

"Not Ms. Hubert," he corrected. "The Librarian."

"Ms. Hubert *is* the Librarian, jackass."

"She's— Wait. The Librarian is a guy."

"A guy would think that," Laura said, guiding them

slowly back the way they had come, around the town square and up through the residences.

"That coward," Aaron said, shaking his head. "That goddamned coward."

"Did you want to go back and have a word about it with her?"

Aaron turned back to see the library disappear around the corner.

"Just drive," he said sullenly.

THE CONTRACT

MAL OPENED HIS EYES AND looked through a groggy haze at a room he didn't recognize. It was illuminated in the color of low rage, moist with heavy humidity. Portraits on the wall looked down with judgmental eyes on the bookcases, the long table, the chairs, all in deep, old wood. Mal flexed his arms, his chest, his back, muscles popping and twitching as though he had been asleep for days.

What had woken Mal up was a tight pressure on his arm. He blinked his eyes until they cleared of gummy sleep and saw Rose's hand, fingers digging into his bicep through the bloody sleeve of his sweatshirt. But Rose wasn't looking at him.

A surge of voltage lit up Mal's spine. Sometimes, in a fight, you took one too many shots to the head, and you left yourself for a while. What brought you back was the sense, beneath a truly conscious level, that danger was close to you. That was what Mal felt now: danger, close to him.

He sat up fast, shaking off the hum of his swirling senses, got his feet on the floor, and stood. Arms surrounded Mal, squeezing tightly with shaky strength. Rose pressed up against him as if he were a life preserver in a roaring sea.

Just two or three long strides away, there was a wheel-chair. Within it hunched a figure that was impossibly ancient. Its body was gnarled, its face cracked with the deep lines and folds of untold age. As Mal watched, the figure—the monster—rose. Standing, it straightened its crooked body to reclaim a dignity it hadn't known in many years.

The Old Man came toward them, his face still a gro-tesque chaos of fissures, his frame still a frail parody of a functioning body. But in his step, in the roll of his arms, in eyes that nearly lit up the room around him, there was a ter-rible and perverse vitality.

Mal pushed Rose aside and lunged forward, his right fist firing out in a devastating cross. Mal didn't know how he ended up in this place, but here was the solution to every-thing in one good, clean punch.

The snap of flesh against flesh rang off the walls, but to Mal it felt as though he had struck an oncoming truck. Shock waves rang up his arm, emanating from his fist, which had been stopped flat by the Old Man's upraised hand. The skeletal fingers closed around Mal's fist and held it tightly. He could feel the bone-splintering pressure of the fingers in his knuckles.

"This is the strength of a dozen minds, boy," the Old Man said, his hot, rotting breath scrabbling up Mal's nostrils, the sick intimacy of a diseased lover. "Imagine how powerful I'll be when it's a thousand. Or a million."

With a sudden jerk, the Old Man twisted his wrist, and Mal's arm was wrenched violently to the side, his body following in a mad tumble across the floor. The Old Man turned and looked down on him.

"Your mind is difficult to penetrate. It's hard and gray, like metal." The ancient, cracking lips split into a carnivorous smile. "Nevertheless, I'll wager you're very, very scared of me right now."

Rose threw herself onto Mal, one arm raised up to fend off the Old Man's vibrant eyes.

"No," she said. "You promised you would let us go."

"Did I? I feel like a new man since I agreed to that, a different man. However, I still understand the value of a contract. I will honor the word of it as stated. I said I would not stop you from leaving. So, leave."

Rose pulled at Mal, but he was heedless of her. He came to his feet slowly, appraising his enemy. Once he stood tall, he didn't move.

"Mal," Rose said, grasping his arm like a child. "We have to go. We *have* to."

But Mal was stone, immovable. It was only a matter of time before he found the right line of attack.

"Mal," she said through tears of frustration, "Remak sacrificed his life so you could live."

He looked at her.

"He died for you," she said, still pulling. "You can't throw your life away like this."

Mal looked back up at the Old Man, the hideous face taking the scene in archly. Then Mal let himself be tugged backwards, toward the large double doors. The Old Man watched every step of their progress. Rose heaved the doors open and pulled Mal out into the carpeted hall, into the relief of the amber light.

Roarke, sitting in a chair, rose to immediate attention. Mal instantly shifted his stance to account for the new threat.

"I told them I wouldn't stop them from leaving, Mr. Roarke," the Old Man's commanding new voice reached out into the hall. "So it falls to you. Kill them both."

Roarke took in the strength of the voice, the glimpse of the impossible figure he got through the doorway with analytical dispassion, and came toward Mal and Rose.

"You're not with your partner now, Roarke," Mal said. "You're not ambushing a man with a concussion anymore."

The gray man nodded and stepped in.

An ample amount of Rose's time and concentration over the last year had been devoted to studying Mal. He was broad in the chest and shoulders and slim at the waist, but his bones seemed heavy under the dented flesh and smooth muscle. He seemed at times to lumber when he walked, to tread through life with difficulty, as if constantly pushing against a heavy wind.

She had seen him, too, before his fights, wolfing down a meal before pushing out into the twilight, headed for the space beneath the old stone bridge in the park, where he would bloody his knuckles and do worse to the face of another boy who had put money on his own skill and capability. She had seen him often enough after fights, creaking slowly into bed, favoring bruised and battered limbs, muscles, bones. But she had never actually seen Mal fight.

She wanted to see him wired and ready for a fight, or return triumphant or, at least, alive. She did not want to see the work, the pain, the *reality* of the violence itself.

What shocked her now, what swept her away briefly from the soggy fear bleeding through her body, was how beautiful Mal looked when he fought. The lumbering, the burden, the weight—all of it was gone. He came unbound, looked nearly—what an alien word to apply to Mal—*joyful* in his movement. His strength was still there, but he had transformed from the weight and heaviness of lead to the supple, graceful movement of mercury as he slid past Roarke's whipping thrust, slipped beneath his lateral chop and rose up at the man's side, his own fist flickering like a wasp, catching Roarke across the cheek, leaving a burning welt behind.

Roarke didn't register the blow. He feinted with an open-handed strike toward Mal's chin, and when Mal moved in one direction, Roarke's knee came up to cut him off. The knee caught Mal in the side of his torso, and Rose saw his body rock from the impact, heard him cough out a jolt of pain. He recovered instantly, snapping out two jabs, both deflected by Roarke's viper-quick hands. Roarke threw back a strike that cracked into Mal's chest and sent him backpedaling. Roarke pressed in.

Mal threw three humming punches; Roarke beat them

all aside with his open hands and struck back with another hammering blow that caught Mal in the chest. Mal backpedaled again, threw a retreating strike, had it deflected, and took a blow to the gut. Roarke, despite his girth and the wedges of muscle straining at the material of his suit, was too quick; inhumanly quick.

Mal flicked his head to the side, tossing off the pain. He threw a strike, but instead of backing up farther, he moved to Roarke's side. Roarke immediately matched the move, keeping Mal to his front, circling.

They circled, looking for openings, their feet moving carefully, carrying them in slow loops as their hands sped up, flickering. Mal's shoulders and head darted down, up, under, around. Then, when the circling brought Roarke's back to Rose, Mal scored a stinging jab off Roarke's face, followed with a hammering cross.

They continued to circle, probing, striking, parrying, dodging. Again, when Roarke's back was to her, Mal landed, twice, on Roarke's head. She could see Roarke working harder to shake it off, trying to stop the circling. But Mal slipped too quickly around, pressed his advantage, forced Roarke's back to Rose a third time, and landed again.

Rose realized only now what Mal was doing. He kept putting Roarke between the two of them. What had the Old Man said? Fighting to her was a fiction, a story she could scarcely wonder at. Mal knew that, of course. But Roarke did not. Every time his back was to her, he had to take her into account, and his attention would slip just far enough for Mal to come in.

The last blow had shaken Roarke enough that his ripostes were wider, larger. His fist swung, the force of his entire body behind it, a heavy whoosh of wind cutting over Mal's darting head. Mal came back with two quick jabs, splitting Roarke's lip and reddening his jaw with blood. But Roarke's next attack was already set up, and his stiffened hand swept down and chopped into the junction between Mal's neck and shoulder, bludgeoning him to the ground.

Mal went down but caught himself on hands and knees, immediately rolling forward to avoid Roarke's kick, then came up so that, once again, Roarke was forced between him and Rose. Mal looked dead in her eyes for just an instant, just long enough to give her a nod.

Her body stiffened; she imagined grabbing a chair, a vase, something to attack Roarke with. But in the end, all she could do was imagine it.

Roarke imagined it, too, though; saw Mal's signal and imagined her sweeping up from behind with the killing blow. He was forced to split his attention down the middle and blocked Mal's head strike, but couldn't stop the pile-driving uppercut from landing in his gut.

Roarke coughed loud, spat blood, and took another shot to the head, and another, three, four. His hands came up to block, made it only halfway. The machine-gun sound of the punches ricocheted off the walls of the hall.

Roarke stumbled and found his balance just in time to catch Mal's fist, cracking against his temple. He lurched forward, grabbing at Mal's sweatshirt, looking for an anchor to drag his opponent closer. Mal grabbed the hand, twisted it so that Roarke's arm was locked in an awkward line. Then Mal brought his fist hammering down on Roarke's elbow.

The flesh-muffled snapping of arm bone made Rose shriek. Roarke did not. No sound issued from him. He sank to his knees, his eyes holding on to Mal as the arm dropped and dangled uselessly.

Mal's fist cocked back, ready to shatter Roarke's face in an explosion of red. He held it there and gave his own somber gaze back to Roarke. Their eyes held each other for just a moment. What, Rose wondered, were they finding in each other?

Mal dropped his fist.

He looked up to find Rose but instead looked past her. She followed his line of sight. The Old Man was standing in the doorway now, close enough to reach out and clutch.

"Run, Mal." She ran forward and grabbed his hand, pulled him out the door they had entered through. They raced down the tidy hallway, out into the service entrance. Two men in coveralls looked up as Rose and Mal came barreling out.

"Yes, run," one of them said, with the Old Man's vibrant voice. "Run if you want to live just a little longer."

They were out on the sidewalk, careening through crowds of suited people talking on cells, attending their own concerns.

"Run," said a tall, thin brunette, looking up at them from her cell conversation. "Run to a place where I am not."

"Soon," said a child, holding his mother's hand, "I will be everywhere."

They ran.

THE VISITORS

UNDER THE BLUISH LIGHT OF an overcast morning, Laura and Aaron walked up to the door of a small house set at the edge of the road. Behind the house was a tangle of brush and plants leading toward a distant mountain. Laura tapped the door with her knuckles.

Footsteps approached from the other side and, without the customary questions, the door opened. A girl, barely older than Laura, stood on the other side. Her pert, pretty face was framed by short blond hair. She had five silver rings in her left ear.

"Hi," she said, in a lively voice that suggested she was eager to receive visitors out in this fairly solitary place.

Aaron opened his mouth to speak, but Laura spoke quickly, to head him off.

"Hi," she returned brightly. "My name's Laura Westlake. This is Aaron. Is this Tommy Jericho's house? Are you Annie?"

"It is and I am," she said. "How can I help you?"

"That's kind of complicated, actually," Laura answered with an exasperated smile. "We're looking for someone, and I think you might be able to help us. Kind of."

"Well, why don't you come in, and we can find out?" Was there a note of apprehensive hopefulness in such quick hospitality, or was this just the country way?

"Thank you so much," Laura said with sincere weight as they followed Annie the few steps it took to get to a small kitchen table.

Drink offers were politely refused, and Annie settled down across from them at the table. Aaron fidgeted in his chair, uncomfortable in the spare rural setting of the house.

"Are you two from New York?" Annie asked.

"How did you know that?" Aaron shot back, immediately suspicious.

Annie tapped her own forehead, then pointed at Laura, indicating the Mets cap that sat snugly on her head.

"I'm from New York, too," Annie said. "Tommy is a Yankees fan, but you're welcome here, anyway," she said with an irresistible gleam in her eye. Laura felt instinctive warmth for Annie and searched her face, looking for a long-lost friend. There was humor and hope there, but melancholy as well, a fluttery gratitude for unexpected company. Such a large field with such a small house and a small girl in the middle of it.

"So, who is it you're looking for?" Annie asked, finding the scrutiny just the slightest bit unnerving, perhaps.

"Mal," Laura said, short, sharp, and direct.

"Uh . . ." Annie was obviously hesitant to dash anyone's hopes. "I'm sorry, I don't recognize that name. Do you know a last name?"

Laura hesitated, chewing on the word as though letting it go might cost too much.

"Jericho," Aaron said in a terse voice that matched his impatient look. "Mal Jericho."

"Well, that's Tommy last name. Is that why you came here? I'm sorry, I don't think he knows anyone named Mal. You don't mean Max, do you? That was his father."

"Well, that's about it for here," Aaron said, setting his body to stand up. "Can we get going now, Laura?"

"Doesn't Tommy"—Laura pressed on, ignoring her companion—"have a brother?"

"No," Annie said, becoming more unnerved by the second. "No brother. Tommy works at the garage in town. You could certainly go down and ask him about this. But, honestly, there's no way he's kept a brother from me. He doesn't even speak with his mother anymore, and his father's gone. I'm basically what he's got now." She offered a quick, self-deprecating smile.

Laura leaned back in her chair, suddenly exhausted. Despite her unease, Annie did not seem ready to let them go yet.

"Did you guys come all the way from the city to speak to us?"

"Poughkeepsie," Aaron answered.

"Do you live there?"

"No." Aaron's face made it clear that he couldn't have imagined anything more distasteful.

"College," Laura said. "I go to college there."

"Vassar, right?" Annie said. "What do you study?"

"Psychology."

"Aren't classes in session right now?"

"They are. But finding this person is" — she cleared her throat gently — "really, really important. I took a leave of absence."

"You left college on purpose," Annie said, unable to keep the quiet sorrow out of her voice.

"Are you looking at colleges?" Laura asked, a soft interest coming into her face and dismissing the fatigue of a moment before.

"No," Annie said wistfully. "There's a nursing school over in Oneonta. We're saving up for it now." An idea seemed to bloom in her brain. "Us and a mysterious benefactor," she said to herself.

"Sorry?" Laura said.

"Listen," Annie said, suddenly energized with excitement. "This is going to sound crazy, but there's someone doing us favors now and then, and we sort of don't really know who he is, not his name or anything."

"What do you mean?" Laura asked, her voice vibrating with anticipation.

"Someone wires us money. It's inconsistent, different amounts, no schedule, but it's been happening for more than a year."

"But you don't have a name," Laura said, working the facts through.

"I could . . ." Annie hesitated, her desire to help struggling with her common sense. "I could put you in touch with the bank. I mean, if I vouched for you, they might be able to—"

"Can you give me your cell number?" Aaron broke in, his patience just about worn out.

"Pardon?"

"Your cell has a number that people use to call you, right? Give it to me."

"Social cues, Aaron," Laura chided with a sidelong glare. "Social cues."

Aaron's eyes swiveled from Laura, back to Annie.

"*Please* give it to me," he corrected himself melodramatically.

Annie recited her number.

"Is that going to . . ." She watched Aaron's eyes glaze over, stare into nothing.

"It's coming in through a floating code," Aaron reported, his gaze distant and ghostly. "But it's underwritten by a fake LLC, but it's got Silven Holdings code styles all over it." Laura's eyes were riveted to him, as were Annie's. "The deposits are being made—whoa, in *cash,* do you believe that?—in New York City, at an ATM on Twenty-Third and—"

"Stop," Annie said, louder than she needed to. "Stop, please. I don't want to— It's just that . . . things are working okay for us. I don't want to push it off balance or anything."

"Of course, Annie," Laura said. "Of course." She stood up. "Thank you so much for helping us."

"I barely did anything." That same self-deprecating smile passed across her face.

"You did, Annie. You trusted us."

Annie looked down, her face growing hot for some reason.

Laura had to nudge Aaron, still working something in his head, to get him up and to the door. Annie opened it for them, and Laura propelled Aaron toward the car sitting in the driveway. Before she followed, Laura turned to Annie, seemed to be searching for something to say. Their eyes found each other, some understanding, some strength flowed between them, and Laura swept her into a hug that nearly stole the breath from Annie's chest. Annie hugged back as hard as she could.

"Good luck," Annie said, strangely fighting back tears.

"I'd wish you luck, too, Annie, but I know you don't need it. I can see you're strong enough to make it through."

She took in Annie's face for a last moment, then turned and went to the car.

"They made the transfer at an ATM on Twenty-Third Street and Eighth Avenue in Manhattan," Aaron told her as she got into the driver's seat.

"Will you be able to find out what we need if we get to the ATM itself?" Laura asked, doing a poor job of remaining calm and collected.

"If I don't have an address for this Mal guy before we

hit the highway," Aaron said, "you can kick me out of the car without stopping."

"Are you — "

"Drive."

She did, pulling away from the small house and onto the street. In her rearview mirror, she could see Annie standing in the doorway, watching them go.

"MCT surveillance cams picked up the spot at the date and time the transfer was made," Aaron told her as they moved through the town. Laura noted the garage and the thin young man in the stained overalls bent into an open hood. "I've got him crossing Twenty-Third and going down into a subway. The subway cam has him going downtown."

There was quiet as they passed out of the town and headed for the highway entrance in the distance. Laura's fingers tapped impatiently on the steering wheel, her hands becoming damp. Her eyes kept flickering to Aaron, his face slack, all the effort happening within him.

She steered them onto the highway, heading south to New York.

"Well?" she said hotly.

"I picked him up on five different MCT cameras all the way home," Aaron said, his eyes refocused and a grin breaking on his face. He'd had it minutes ago but was making her wait just to amuse himself. "He's at an apartment building on Orchard and Delancey."

"Which—"

"Number 17C. Registered to someone named Rose Santoro."

Why did it drive a pit into Laura's stomach to hear that?

"I could send you a capture of him," Aaron taunted, "*if* you still had your cell."

"You could do something else for me, instead."

"Oh, please tell me. I'm dying to do something else for you."

"Make a deposit into Annie's account."

"What? Why?"

"Didn't you see how desperate she was? How hard she was trying? No." Laura shook her head. "Of course, you didn't. She's giving this everything she's got. Her entire future depends on her going to that nursing school. It will change their lives massively."

"Are you feeling okay to drive? Because you're apparently in the middle of a psychotic break."

"No, Aaron, I'm serious. The money would mean nothing to you, and it would change her life."

"*That's* your best argument?" He closed his eyes. "Wake me up when we get to New York. Or don't, actually."

"Aaron, if you do this, I will never mention how you were spying on me in the bathroom ever again."

The pondering silence was cut only by the buzz of cars moving on the highway around them.

"You swear?" he said, looking at her again.

"I do."

"How much money?"

"One hundred thousand dollars," she said easily.

"One hun— I know you aren't serious."

"Come on. One hundred thousand dollars would barely even show up as a decimal place in your accounts. And that's enough to stake Annie for the rest of her life."

Aaron was gone again for a moment. When he came back, he had the tone of an accountant.

"The state school she was referring to has a two-year program to become a registered nurse, the total tuition of which is less than half of what you suggested."

"Fifty thousand." Laura made a show of turning it over in her head. What she was really doing was cataloging the fact that the old strategy of doubling your initial bid to ultimately get the amount you really want worked on sneering adolescents as well as budget-conscious parents. "Okay."

"It's done."

Just like that, Laura thought. *Aaron will forget about this in ten minutes, and Annie will never forget it as long as she lives.*

"Aaron," she said levelly. "Thank you."

"Whatever."

She sighed.

"Why don't you go ahead and take that nap," she suggested dryly.

She brought them into Manhattan and around to the East Side Highway, headed for the Lower East Side as directed by Aaron, who was amply baffled that anyone might not know their way around New York.

"This is weird," Aaron said on their approach. "The data here is really quiet. Usually New York data can't shut up. But it's like everything is asleep. Even the newsblogs are intermittent."

It figured that Aaron would be studying the dataflow to learn something he could have looked out the window to see. There was almost no traffic around them. As they paralleled the city streets, Laura could see very little foot traffic where she expected the usual throngs. She might have pursued it, but then, glancing out the other window, she caught sight of the East River, shimmering in multifarious hues from its constituent chemicals.

"I didn't think it would actually look like a rainbow," she said.

"The campaigns are true," Aaron confirmed. "You must be the only person in the free world who hasn't come to see it."

"Is it true about how it got that way?"

"Which truth?" Aaron replied with apparent seriousness. "The one about how chemicals leaked in there during construction and are eroding the island?"

"Yeah, that one."

"True. In about twenty-five years, the edges of this island are going to start crumbling away."

"That's it? That's all you've got? Too bad for an entire *island?*"

"Someone will do something about it," Aaron said with total assurance. "When they need to."

"You, Aaron. *You* do something about it. Your father—"

"Don't."

"Your father died because he chose the wrong side. You want to avenge him, honor his memory? Break the system that killed him. Become more than he was. Make your own choice, not the one he made for you."

In consideration or peevishness, almost certainly the latter, Aaron remained silent.

As they moved South past the Fifteenth Street exit, Laura caught sight of the spear-like points attacking the sky above the glimmering mirrored dome. The Lazarus Towers. She had only ever seen them on HD. She never would have believed anything could pull an observer's eyes away from that hideous dome, let alone turn it into a tourist attraction.

But that was the whole point, wasn't it? Make mistakes look like successes. Cover the terrifying truth with shiny lies. She looked at Aaron, studying the towers himself. Where she might once have expected admiration, his face was captured in a look she couldn't identify.

The apartment building between Orchard and Delancey was a dull white, its opaque windows sending the reflection of the sun shearing back into the world.

There was something wrong on the streets here, something beyond the fact that poverty was being hidden with shiny paint and corporate smiles. There was barely anyone out, and those who were glanced up with edgy glares and quickly pulled their eyes away, scurrying into doorways or around corners.

"What's going on?" Laura asked, praying that this was not just what the city was always like.

"I'm . . ." Aaron's voice was low and edgy. " . . . not really sure. It feels like everyone sees something we don't."

"Why would—"

"Look," he interrupted her. "This is the building. Let's go."

He walked into the building as though he owned the place himself, which, in fact, he may very well have, for all she knew. The plain white façade was easy to overlook, to take for granted. This was probably the point, because anyone venturing inside would have entered a wash of grime and dirt that had turned the lobby into a gray smear. The elevator doors slid open with the hiss and grunt of equipment reaching its last legs.

"Wait," she said, her stomach queasy with doubt. "We can't just go up."

"That's what we're going to do," he said, not breaking stride.

"Aaron, please, what if . . ."

He stared at her from within the elevator.

What if I'm not supposed to be here? What if this was all a—

She stepped onto the elevator and stabbed the seventeenth-floor button before he could.

After a rumbling ride, the door wheezed open on a hallway that had lost the battle to filth and lack of care long ago. The metal doors in front of every apartment were etched with obscene pictures, curses.

Her hands were trembling as they came to 17C, and Aaron knocked at it with short, angry blows.

When there was no answer after several moments, Aaron studied the lock with easy disgust.

"It's a standard lock," he said with contempt. "I could get us through a cellock with no problem. Honestly, how do people live like this?" He pushed the door once, hard, out of annoyance, and it opened, revealing the torn internal lock mechanism. "Well, that's convenient."

"What happened?"

"I don't know. Someone broke in or something. Maybe they forgot their keys." He pushed the door open the rest of the way.

"What are you doing?" Laura asked urgently.

"Do you want to have your reunion in this hallway, Laura?"

Laura paused on the threshold, then, her throat clenched with some sort of indescribable dread, she stepped in and closed the door behind her.

The place was tiny. There was a bed, a cinder block that served as a nightstand, a small refrigerator, an aluminum chair positioned before the window, the bars of which, Laura noted, you couldn't see from the outside.

Aaron plopped himself into the chair as Laura studied every inch of this grimy little place for a clue, just as she had been studying the details of her life for the last year and coming up short.

There was nothing really personal here, and perhaps Laura was relieved. She couldn't test herself to see if she recognized what might have belonged to Mal. But as she waited, she could feel the fear inside her grow, from the pit of her stomach up through her throat, making her want to vomit. Her fingers and toes were suddenly tingling with it, and her head began to pound with surges of panic; panic and something else besides.

She spun around to face the door just an instant before it opened.

A girl, her shaggy hair nearly hiding her nervous features, jolted in surprise. With her was a large boy, moving slowly, his face bloodied and scarred. Scars Laura recognized, a face Laura knew, had known forever and ever and ever. The boy's face froze in shock as Laura's brain split apart, spilling out memories.

JESSE KARP

PART III

LOVE AND FEAR

/

ARIELLE KLIEST'S FATHER HAD BEEN an older man, a Swiss banker who had emigrated from Germany earlier in life. Rumors followed Arielle throughout a childhood spent predominantly in a rigorous Swiss boarding school that her father had not emigrated from Germany but fled it when the Allies had come in at the close of World War II. This was a theory shared both by students and faculty alike, and Arielle could scarcely avoid hearing it. She never asked her father, and not out of fear, but merely for the fact that she didn't particularly care.

Her mother was a much younger Swiss woman, a vice

president of the bank at which her father worked. Her mother was graceful and elegant and possessed of the sort of beauty that belittled rather than enchanted those around her. The union of the two was an efficient and profitable one, and Arielle herself was raised—when she was allowed home—in an environment where acts of ostensible affection and acts of horrific greed and amorality were undertaken with equal dispassion.

On the verge of attaining the presidency of the bank, her mother was torn down by a scandal involving the siphoning of funds into the accounts of a young man she had, apparently, taken up with and planned to abandon Arielle's father for. Her mother stepped down quietly and, in less than a week, had vanished, passing utterly from the grasp of her family and friends. Arielle never bothered making the effort to search her out. It was not out of hatred, but rather for the fact that she had never been able to summon any sincere feelings of love for her mother to begin with.

The effort of dealing with the scandal and the financial difficulties it brought with it wore her old father away. By the time he died, Arielle had acquired degrees in economics, comparative languages, and semiotics. She was heralded as a genius and accepted the compliment with her family's signature dispassion. This was the greatest way she could imagine to honor her father once he died, to the extent that she thought to honor him at all.

Since she had been a child in boarding school, among the progeny of the wealthy and the influential, she had heard and repeated stories of the Old Man, a figure that had haunted the dreams and daydreams of these children of the wealthy and influential from their earliest memories. Arielle's mind gorged on the ripe fruit of stories about his manipulations, theories about which world events bore his fingerprints. Throughout her studies at university, her passing interest in this figure had become a fascination, and much of her spare time was spent researching him. It proved a frustrating pursuit as the so-called facts of his existence traveled by word of mouth and almost nothing was written down, cataloged, stored in any way. Stories blurred into one another, sharing elements, changing shape, until you could grasp nothing solid at all.

To her, that slowly became the Old Man's nature, his power. He was mist, smoke, always at the corner of your eye, but never quite observable. This ghost haunted her. As she built financial empires and shattered others, there was always this figure of mist and shadow, her inability to grasp him always keeping satisfaction, *true* satisfaction, out of her hands.

Plagued at no time in her life by the vulnerabilities of either love or fear, she stepped off the path she had been blazing through the business world and stepped onto a dark, shadowy path far less traveled.

She moved from city to city, country to country, searching out the rumors. She went from sweating, stinking tents in the hearts of fetid, filthy bazaars to pristine climate-controlled corporate conference rooms seeking anyone, *anyone,* who would even claim that he or she had laid eyes on the Old Man, heard his voice, was in the room next to his, knew someone who had spoken to him. Anything.

The second attack on New York City, the power plant explosion the world would come to call Big Black, made something shift. Allegiances flowed, power structures slipped, and different ones rose. Suddenly, there were power vacuums that needed to be filled.

One day she was having lunch with a young, back-stabbing vice president who bragged with a malevolent smile that things were changing at his company, *things were changing,* and did she know who was going to end up on top? The arrival of a man with gunmetal gray hair and the bearing of a soldier interrupted their meal. Arielle immediately sensed something, and not only because the back-stabbing vice president deferentially excused himself and departed the restaurant. This new arrival didn't bother to sit down;

he merely told her that a car was waiting outside. The Old Man had proffered his hand.

On the other end of that car ride was an apparatus unlike any she had ever seen. She was put in a coordinating position, gathering information from an array of agencies, organizations, and corporations, and from this vantage point her predilection for pattern recognition honed by her study of semiotics allowed her to see something indescribably vast taking place. Like small snapshots of distinct locations that you fit together to create a huge image of an entire city, she saw how a project that belonged to one corporation in France fit into the project of another corporation in Japan, and that the results of each individual project had consequences, profits, rewards on a global scale. The hostile takeover of an obscure company in Dubai, the trading of bonds between a company in Berlin and another in Stockholm, and the introduction of laws preventing civil litigation against corporations in the United States, when all pieced together properly, suddenly explained how vast acres of protected land in Alaska were suddenly opened up for drilling to an American corporation. Pieces fit together, but only if you could see the whole, only if you could see the world as the Old Man did.

Her time in this service was spent, by virtue of the very few employees who traveled in her circle, in the company of the man who had come to collect her in the restaurant that day. Orin Roarke was possessed of a dispassionate air that she had come to rely on both practically and, to her profound astonishment, emotionally.

Thus, the irony was not lost on her, as she looked into the face of the man she loved and spoke frankly.

"I'm afraid of him."

"That's how he works," Roarke replied from the other side of her desk, his face that comforting mask of stoicism. Beneath the steel-gray crew cut, the face was bruised and puffy, and the soldier—as she had come to think of him—had a cast and sling on his right arm.

"It's different." For no reason she could quite define, she was nearly whispering.

"The difference would be hard to deny," Roarke allowed. "He's walking. Hell, he's practically hopping. He's like a teenager in an old man disguise now."

"I don't even mean the physical differences. It's the way he looks at things now, at us. We're not even like tools anymore." She knew she was speaking in the unfamiliar terms of instinct and emotion, a world Roarke had no truck with. "Set aside his health. Have you noticed any changes?"

Roarke looked at her just that one telltale moment too long. It had been the ultimate undoing of many she had faced.

"What?" she pleaded in a harsh whisper. "Tell me."

"The boy, Mal," Roarke's voice had lost its clipped military tone. "He was nearly dead, his body was falling apart. And then . . . it just wasn't. He beat me down. I knocked one of his teeth out a few days ago, and he had it back. The things that are happening here; they're not . . . *human* things."

She could scarcely believe it when the next words came out of her mouth, in a lower voice even than before, a voice vibrating with urgency and terror.

"We could leave now," she said. "Get out and never look back."

"You will come to me now." It was the Old Man's vibrant hiss of a voice, though he was nowhere apparent. Kliest heard it, like a snake trapped in your eardrum, and when she looked at Roarke, it was clear that he had heard it, too.

Roarke looked at her, his soldier's face holding strong, but his eyes breaking open for just a moment, asking her which way to step.

She looked back, words caught in her throat. The Old Man was everywhere now, in every hallway, in every room, in their *heads*. This business they had started—God is dead, who will replace him?—she had carried out the details as she always had, without question. Only now was it dawning on her that the consequences might fall just as heavily on her as the rest of the world.

She stood up, smoothed her jacket and skirt, and led Roarke out of her office, down the short hall, and to the double doors she had stood at with a sense of wicked anticipation so many times over the last few years.

She stepped in, and where, for her, it had been like entering the treasure-packed cavern of a dying monarch, it was now like stepping into the lair of a beast.

The Old Man stood perfectly still in the center of the room, facing away from them, hands clasped behind his back. The dim red light deepened the crevices in his flesh, exaggerating the skeletal sharpness of his fingers. Even standing there, though, his pernicious vitality pulsated like a heart.

To the side, the figure of Castillo stood sentry, enveloped in shadow. His chest rose and fell, laboring with heavy breaths, his gleaming eyes whipping from figure to figure. He was a bull trapped in a pen.

"I am whole now," the Old Man said with his back to her. She couldn't see his thin, cracking lips move, but the voice, quiet and vibrant, reverberated inside her skull. "And, whole, I am ready to begin my ascension." He turned and his eyes flickered, and he seemed to notice Roarke for the first time. "First things first."

The Old Man stepped forward, and Roarke immediately sidestepped, interposing his body between Arielle and the approaching monster.

The Old Man didn't break stride. He moved forward with what in a much younger man would have to be called a spring in his step. The Old Man stopped before Roarke. Directly in front of her, Roarke's body twitched, a gentle flutter as a body might experience fading off to sleep. But for the fact that coursing adrenaline was hyperfocusing all her senses, she wouldn't have even noticed it.

"When you see them, when you can reach out and actually touch them, minds are so delicately balanced, so precarious. It's such a simple matter to submerge the man"—he nodded at Castillo's hulking, animal form—"and untether the beast. Or to push even farther, until the mind is gone altogether. This is empty now"—the Old Man gestured at Roarke. "Come, see." He extended a hand, and she stepped forward, compelled by dread, until she could see Roarke's face.

But it was not Roarke's face anymore, not really a face at all. While its structure of bone and flesh remained the same, its animation, its life, was gone. Whatever could be said to actually *be* Roarke was gone from it, as clear as the difference between a mannequin and a real human being.

She stifled a shriek, choked it down with all the dispassion she had accumulated over the course of her life. That much she could still do.

"Consolidation is a gratifying pursuit." He regarded

her with a measure of excitement. "You will mobilize the MCT. Things will be very different soon."

She pressed her fingernails into her palms so hard that she felt the hot trickle of blood. She could not bring her eyes up to look at him.

"Don't fret, Arielle. Your work has not gone unappreciated. There is a reward for you."

"This body still functions." It was Roarke speaking, his lips moving, but it was the Old Man's voice coming out of him. "If the last of your duties are performed to your consistently high standard, I will let you have Roarke's body. It can be with you, talk to you. Touch you."

She saw it in her head, perhaps because he put it there: Roarke, reaching out, caressing her cheek, her neck with his strong hands. But the nerves, the feeling, led into a festering, monstrous brain, and beyond the face, the Old Man looked out from Roarke's eyes.

She could hold back her shriek no longer.

JESSE KARP

MADE OF MEMORIES

FOR AN IMPOSSIBLY LONG STRETCH, the depth of realization in Laura's eyes held the room in a motionless, soundless amber of indecision. The world spun around them, flying off on its own way as the room remained frozen, trapped.

"Laura," Mal finally said, two syllables laced with such anguish that they brought a knife of ice slicing through Rose's heart.

Laura, for her part, remembered. Everything the Librarian had told her, everything since Mike's sacrifice, since they had run out of the crumbling edifice that had been Man in Suit, Remak's reappearance as a bizarre, ghostly observer.

She remembered the future she had made, sweated and cried and bled to build with Mal. She remembered it all not as a giant tidal wave held back by a dam that had suddenly crashed in, but merely as a sleeper remembers the world when she awakens, a simple reemergence. She wasn't thinking about it, and then she was. It was as though Mal had simply been in another room and she had been concentrating on something else, and then Mal walked back in and, oh, there was Mal.

She remembered everything up to the point where Mal had laid a gentle kiss on her lips as she closed her eyes and they went to sleep and she woke up in her parents' home, with scrambled eggs and tofu bacon cooking and an application in to Vassar after taking a year off between high school and college.

Some malicious surgeon had grafted a mockery of a life onto her real one and given her a lobotomy to accommodate it. The anger swelled in her once again, even as the thumping of her heart pushed the realization into her brain: Here was her *real* life. Here was Mal.

Mal.

Her lips twitched, unable to quite hold back the smile that the solemn moment wanted to forbid. Her feet strained forward, her arms fought to come into an embrace. But it wasn't just Mal. It was Mal with a girl at his shoulder. Aaron, of course, finally defused it.

"Mal, right? Aaron Argaven. I understand you and your girlfriend here screwed things up badly, and now Laura and I need to fix it."

Mal's dark eyes lit on him, confused, then returned to Laura.

"The Old Man," she said. "We think he's after Remak, to learn how he manipulates minds."

Mal simply looked back at her, his expression still, but she knew him well enough to see the wild currents passing behind his eyes.

"How do you know about that?" the girl next to Mal asked in a small voice. She was a small girl, and it was her bearing as much as her stature that made her small: voice, gangling limbs, shoulders and torso bent in such a way to suggest a fetal curve.

"I'm Laura," Laura said to her. "What's your name?"

"Rose," she said in a quarter-voice from behind her hair. "I'm Rose."

"Rose, we learned all of that from the Librarian. The Librarian is —"

Rose was nodding.

"I know who the Librarian is," she said. Was this what

had happened? Laura had demanded her own memory be erased because Mal had found someone else and the pain was too much to bear?

"That man Remak," Rose said. "He sent Mal into the Old Man's tower, to find out what he was trying to do."

"And?" Aaron was used to the instant gratification of his dataflow. He pressed for information the only way he knew how: impatiently.

"He's going to make a big move starting here, in the city. The MCT is a part of it," Mal said. "He wants control. That's all he's ever been about, and now he wants more of it. *All* of it."

"Through Remak," Laura said. "Through his access to the neuropleth."

"Neuropleth." Aaron turned it over in his mouth. "'Many minds'? What's that supposed to mean?"

"Remak's body was converted into neurological impulses," Laura said as if reading from an advanced biology textbook without missing a beat; or as if she were quoting Remak from memory. "The neuropleth was where he interfaced with other people's nervous systems."

"You remember," Mal said.

"I remember. Now I remember," Laura said, and she saw Rose flinch as she did.

"Our time running from the Old Man. What Remak

became, what the neuropleth is. How Remak helped us. And didn't help us."

"Remak saved Mal," Rose said, struggling to look Laura in the eyes. "But he's gone. Really gone. For good."

How did she feel about that? Considering that it was Remak who had obliterated her memory and created the false life that she had finally escaped, she felt only the dullest ember of grief for him.

"I'm not sure that's a bad thing." Laura was surprised to hear herself say it.

"He saved Mal," Rose said, her voice finding the slightest edge of commitment.

"He stole my memories," Laura said, turning on her sharply.

"But he gave you your life back." Rose was clutching at Mal's hand with angry propriety.

"We *are* our memories," Laura said, anger crackling in her voice.

"So Remak is gone," Aaron commented archly, derailing the argument. "And so is this ability he had to control minds. So the Old Man can't get it, and we're safe. Relatively speaking."

The room was silent in tension. Rose and Mal did not seem prepared to offer comfort regarding the state of their safety.

"The Old Man has it already, doesn't he?" Aaron said, the world, as usual, conforming to his lowest expectations.

"Yes," Mal confirmed.

"So what does—"

"Wait." Laura cut him off. "How did he get it?"

"The same way he gets everything," Mal said. "He took it."

"Yes," Laura said, staring at Rose, her instinct—or perhaps just her sense of resentment—kicking in. "But took it from whom? Wasn't Remak gone?"

"Yes," Mal said. "But in his interactions with Rose and me, he left a . . . I don't know, a doorway to it in our heads."

"So the Old Man took it from you?"

Mal's eyes were resolutely not shifting toward Rose.

"No," he said, finally.

"Then why do you keep answering?"

"Laura." Aaron had sidled closer to her. "What difference does it—"

"Why do you keep answering, Mal?" Laura pressed. *Why are you protecting her?*

"Rose told me," Mal said.

So, with the evidence clearly supporting her now, Laura turned full on to Rose.

"You gave it to him," Laura said. "Is that what happened?"

"I . . . I didn't *give* it to him." Rose looked as though she were about to buckle. Her hands were clenched, her arms trembling to hug her own body. "He *took* it."

"How does someone take a doorway out of your head?"

Rose's eyes flickered manically beneath the strands of hair, from Laura, to Mal, to the floor, back and forth, back and forth.

"How?"

"You weren't there," Rose said hotly. She had clearly meant to shout it at Laura, but it came out as a hiss. "Remak died to save Mal, and I let that diseased thing go into my head and rip out what he wanted to save Mal." She was angry but didn't know how to make it come out of her, like an actress so overcome with stage fright, she couldn't own the part. "We did what we had to, to save Mal. Where were you, Laura? Where were you?"

Laura's offense instantly dwindled. Her eyes went straight to Mal. *Where was I, Mal? Not where you needed me. Goddamn Remak. God*damn *him.*

"So what does it mean, exactly?" Aaron cut into the tension with characteristic obliviousness. "The Old Man can do what Remak could?"

"The Old Man's mind is . . . I don't know . . . bigger than Remak's was, more powerful," Mal said. "He can control people without inhabiting them the way Remak could.

And he can draw strength from the minds in the neuropleth into his own body. He's only had access to it for about half an hour, but he can already do that. He hasn't mastered it yet. I think the world would look very different now if he had."

"Screwed things up is right," Aaron said. "Looks like we got here just in time. Laura, we're going to need to —"

"Stop." Laura bowed her head and held her hands up. "Just stop for a goddamned minute."

They watched her, Rose consciously or unconsciously sidling closer to Mal.

"Could you excuse us, please?" Laura said. She was looking at Aaron, but it was clear whom she wanted to be with.

Rose's eyes became instantly desperate. It was not lost on Laura that she was asking to speak to this girl's (maybe) boyfriend alone, and in her own apartment on top of it. But her personal quest could not end, no new mission could be undertaken, until she and Mal had their moment.

"Uh . . ." The awkward syllable filled the room for too long as Aaron expelled it. "Okay. You might want to, I don't know, make it quick or something, since there's some sort of important stuff going on."

"Shut it," she told him. "Just give us an hour."

Shaking his head in bewilderment, Aaron started toward the door.

Rose wasn't moving, but Mal touched her shoulder, and

when she looked up at him, he nodded stoically. Gripping
her own arms across her chest so hard that Laura could see
the tendons straining, Rose went to the door.

"Listen to me," Aaron said as he came to Mal. "You
have no idea what she's gone through to get to you." He
looked up into the giant's melancholy face. "Don't screw this
up."

Aaron walked on, opened the door, ushered Rose out,
and followed, closing the door behind him.

Laura and Mal looked at each other across the empty
room.

MAKING A FUTURE

"ARE YOU WITH HER NOW?" Laura asked, and it sounded painfully childish in her ears. Were they in junior high? Had she just spotted him coming into the cafeteria with another girl? Or was this actual life and their love had once been the most important thing in it? She immediately corrected herself, nearly tumbling over her own words. "Are you in love with her?"

"No." Mal was a stone statue, his unreadable countenance cracked with scars.

Her own face was held together with no small act of will. She didn't let tears come, kept her lower lip from trembling. But she could not outwait his silence. This moment was supposed to be filled with joy. It was all she had right now.

"Was there anything else you wanted to say?" she asked. "Because, you know, we've got like fifty-nine more minutes to fill here."

Nothing specific changed in his face, but something in her perception of it adjusted. Perhaps a small but crucial memory slipping back into place, a formula for how to pull from Mal's granite expression some meaning. She found the muscles in his jaws, saw them clenched like he was bracing for a blow, saw the line of his shoulders harden. Mal, as ever, was fighting. What he was fighting, and why, was still out of her reach.

"Mal, it's me. You don't have to fight yourself around me. You don't have to hold anything back. We built a life together, made a future all by ourselves. Stop fighting and remember me. *Are* you in love with her? If you are, I need to know it."

Mal held his tension, and it was such a struggle, she could see the muscles of his stomach starting to quiver. He was holding something in with all his might, and why would he hold it back unless it was her worst fear realized? Then, just before she could bear it no longer and her own internal dam was about to crumble down, his dark eyes suddenly seemed to become liquid. His jaw and shoulders relaxed, as though an enemy had just left the room.

"There's only you, Laura," he said in a cracking whisper. "There's only ever been you."

She was in his arms, his strong, gentle, protecting arms: *home*.

"I don't work right without you, Laura." His face was pressed into her hair, and she could feel his breath on her temple when he spoke. "Everything is in a fog. I don't move right or think right. Things . . . things fall apart."

"Mal . . ." She breathed the word out like it was the secret of the universe. "I was living in a dream. I was buried so deep in a lie that I didn't even know it. I didn't even know you. And you were still what kept me going, what pulled me out of it. You drove me on against everything in the world so I could fight my way back to you." She looked up into his beautiful, sad, imperfect face. "That's how much I love you."

She felt his arms clutch her tighter. It was almost painful, but she wanted him to hold her tighter still.

"Laura, I—"

"No," she said. "We don't need to talk anymore right now." She took him by the hand and walked him to the bed and put her hands on his firm chest and pressed backwards until he sat and then lay back.

　　　　　　　　　　　　　　　JESSE KARP

She climbed in beside him, crushing up against him in this tiny little bed that was barely large enough for him alone. The warmth and firmness of his body brought back sense memories and sent waves of joy coursing through her, a joy more genuine, more immediate than she'd had in a year, maybe ever. She rested her head on his chest and listened for the quiet thunder of his heart. The thunder slowed as they lay there, calmed her as it had from the moment she first heard it in a tiny motel room on an obscure highway outside of a nowhere town, and as it had kept her world together all the time since, until it had inexplicably vanished.

His powerful arm, wrapped around her, drew her to him, and they found each other again, with an intensity and passion that astonished Laura.

Afterward, she found his heart again and lay there, sinking into a happiness that had been so distant, she didn't even know it was gone. But it was hers again. Somehow or other, she and Mal would cast their future from it and never lose each other again.

Her head clogged with happiness, she faded into a welcoming darkness.

"Laura." Mal's voice pulled her from the edge of the world. What a wonder it was to have *his* voice bring her around. "Laura, I have to tell you something."

"Tell me," she said drowsily.

"Your memory," he said, his voice heavy. "Your life. *Our* life."

"You don't have to say it, Mal. It didn't take much to figure it out. We always knew Remak could be ruthless. Did he use me as a bargaining chip, promise to bring me back if you cooperated with him?" She could scarcely imagine Mal's pain. She'd thought her own life had been an agony over the last year. "He's gone now, and I'll never be able to have it out with him. I don't know if it makes me sad or angry or . . . or what."

Mal sat and swung his legs over the side of the cot. His movement forced her into a seated position, too, and they sat there, side by side, in the empty room.

"Laura. He didn't."

Needles of ice raced down Laura's back.

"No," she said. "Don't say anything else, Mal."

"Remak was the one who went into your mind and changed things. You and your parents and everyone who could help bring your old life back. He even went into your dog."

"Stop, Mal. Stop now."

"But it was me. I made him do it."

Laura's heart clenched and froze solid.

"Our life was a ruin," Mal said. "We couldn't keep

things running straight. Every time we had a break, took a step forward, someone or something would come along, and we would have to stop everything, to fix it, to manage the world's problems, because the world didn't even know it had them. We weren't living a life. You were so sad, Laura. Every day I woke up and saw your pain. I would come home and see you watching movies of your parents."

Laura glared at the floor, terrified to look up, to move her body an inch.

"I couldn't bear that happening to you," he said, barreling on. "But what we were doing, it couldn't be abandoned. And I had no life to go back to. We were trying to keep away from Remak, keep away from his demands, his endless tasks. But I found him and I promised him that I would take on any one job he asked if he would fix your life. Give you back what you had once, what made you happy. He said it would be hard, that it might not work, that it wasn't what you would want. But he knew he would need my help someday. I made him do it. To make you happy again."

Laura's muscles tensed, twitched, wanting to move in every direction at once. She came up from the cot, walked across to the wall, her fists clenched, her body hunched. She stood there just a moment, staring at the cracking, water-stained wall, and then she spun on him.

"I *was* happy. I was happy with *you*." She was beyond

rage. "And that sham of a life Remak created, it nearly drove me insane. We fought together every day, Mal. We became adults together. And you sent me *back?*"

"I didn't—"

"How *could* you?" Her eyes were hot with tears and hatred. "How could you take away my choice? Life isn't about being happy all the time. Life is finding out how you can make the world better and turning yourself into that. Sometimes that's happy and sometimes it's miserable, but you get to choose how you do it and who you do it with, and you *took that away!* You might as well have raped me."

Mal's head bent and his body shrank beneath the onslaught. But the embers of her rage only burned brighter.

"Don't you see what you took away? Do you remember Isabel? Isabel who died in the mountains, shot by your friend Brath? Do you remember Mike, who gave up his life for all of us? They're gone, and my memory is all that honored them. I thought about them every day. Every *day*. Did you? Without me, you made them disappear. Them and me.

"We *are* our memories, Mal. We *are* our memories. By taking mine away, you destroyed me."

Life had gone from Mal. He sat there, inert and empty. She would have laid a comforting hand on anyone else in the world who looked like that.

But for Mal, she did not.

"THAT'S THE PRICE"

ROSE AND AARON SAT IN a booth in the back of the diner. Erica, the waitress who alternated shifts with Rose, delivered their food with a weary tread, forced a smile out for Rose, and slunk back into the kitchen. The diner was empty but for the two of them. It was filled with an uncomfortable silence that echoed that of the street, cleared of people, the air heavy with something imminent.

Aaron examined his eggs with a half-absent contempt, much as he had taken in the diner itself. Part of his attention, however, seemed focused elsewhere, forever internal, as if he were here, but also somewhere else much more important at the same time. It did not stop him from laying into his food with the appetite of a starving man.

"Is he your boyfriend?" he asked between hurried bites. Such was his eternally diverted attention, Rose was not sure at first that he was speaking to her. She started when she realized she was meant to answer.

"No," she said, staring down at her own food that had, and would, go untouched.

"Lucky thing, that," Aaron said. "You do not want to go up against Laura." He shoved more eggs into his mouth, chased it with toast. He was putting it away so fast, there was no way he could even be tasting it. "Underneath all the soft, touchy-feely crap, she's a serious pain in the ass."

Rose's sense of Laura was only that Laura was better. Prettier, stronger, smarter. Willing to stand up for herself. Rose shrugged, a barely perceptible wisp of a movement.

Aaron's attention was consumed completely by something inside him then, and it was as though he left the table altogether. Rose sat uncomfortably across from him. Mal had no cell phone and was subject to deep, sullen moods, but his attention did not wander with such random, jerky abandon. Aaron was the first person she had spoken to at any length who had one of those cellpatches. Without an object that visibly claimed his attention, talking with him was almost like talking to someone who fell into narcoleptic seizures.

Her eyes wandered. An MCT truck rumbled by outside. Had her mind not been overcome with other concerns, Rose might have pondered its strangeness. The MCT only brought heavy ordnance like that out when there was a large-scale operation going on — "urban pacification," as their spokesmen often called it.

"Weird," Aaron said from inside himself, and then, suddenly, was talking to her again. "So how are you involved in all this?"

"I . . ."

"I got the whole business with Mal and Remak and the Old Man. What I mean is, how did you get pulled into this in the first place?"

The words formed in her head, but she held them back as she always did, afraid to give a part of herself up to the world. With luck, Aaron's attention would wander again before she had to.

"Hel-*lo?*" he said, bothering to look up from the last of his meal and trying to catch her eyes.

"Mal helped me once."

"Helped you what?"

Her eyes flickered up, caught him staring, hurried back down to her dish.

"Helped you eat a meal? Helped you cross the street? Helped you knock over a liquor store? Helped you what?"

"There was a man." Fighting her desperate grip, the words escaped her as little more than whispers. "Mal stopped him."

"Really?" Aaron threw down his crumpled napkin on his plate. "Why'd you need his help?"

"What do you mean? Why wouldn't I?"

"You've got two arms, two legs. A brain in your head, I'm assuming. You look like a fully functioning human being. Why do you need somebody else's help?"

The words lit her up like a live current. She had always assumed that her failings were apparent on her face and body like a disease. As the shock passed through her, she looked up to find Aaron's eyes, to look in them, only for an instant, and see her reflection there. But when she did, his attention was once again gone from her.

"There's something going on," he said. "It's all over the place, suddenly. There's too much happening to be a— " His eyes clicked back to her. "Are you seeing this? Christ, pick up your damn cell."

She took her cell out, keyed it for a newsblog. The latest headlines sprang up on her screen.

At three different subway stations throughout the city,

five different people were pushed in front of oncoming trains at exactly the same second.

A child and his mother had pushed the boy's father out of a fifteen-story window in Midtown.

A group of firemen fighting a fire simultaneously broke off to grab one of their own men, strip him naked, and lock him in a burning room.

On the Giuliani Bridge, five people got out of their cars just to haul a sixth, unrelated person out of her car and throw her over the side.

Rose looked up from her cell, her eyes gleaming with terror.

"I'm getting other stuff off private feeds," Aaron said. "A paramedic broke off a resuscitation to — what the hell? — to strangle his partner. That's in Jersey City. A group of office workers in Pittsburgh are pulling random people from their desks and drowning them in toilets and sinks. It's spreading outward. Whatever the Old Man is doing, it's happening now." His full attention came back on. "We've got to tell Laura." His face suddenly curled into a scowl. "She doesn't have her cell. What's Mal's number? *Quickly*."

"Mal doesn't have a cell."

"He — Are you joking? What the holy living *fuck* is wrong with you people? Come on." He was out of the booth and moving toward the door before he had even finished speaking. "Come *on!*"

Rose hurried after him. In the kitchen, Erica didn't even watch them go. Her eyes never came away from her own cell.

The one thing the owners of these prison-like slum apartments had spared no expense on was the soundproofing of the doors. This may well have been to keep the sounds of pained cries and agonized pleas for help from ringing up and down the hallways. At the moment, however, it left Rose and Aaron standing before the door, straining to gain some kind of clue as to what was going on inside. Rose was certain she could hear the rising and swelling of a voice, and the implication of it clenched her gut with cramps.

Aaron paused before the door, brought his hand up to knock, and, apparently having heard the strains of sounds as well, winced as his hand fell against it.

After a moment of waiting, he knocked again, harder. A moment later, rolling his eyes and expelling a gust of disgusted breath, he pounded hard enough to send echoes down the hall behind them.

"This is ridiculous," Aaron said when there was still no answer. "Just open it."

Rose held her position.

"Open it, for the love of Christ. There's more going on here than Laura's sweaty little assignation." He stepped to the side and gestured wildly at the door. When she did not move, he grumbled in disgust and yanked it open himself.

She squeezed her eyes shut tight as it came open.

"What?" Laura's voice, angry. *"What?"*

Because Aaron did not speak, and Rose couldn't imagine what would give him pause, she opened her eyes. Laura stood in the middle of the room, her face red with anger. Mal slumped on the bed, looking more haggard than Rose had ever seen him, even after the worst bare-knuckle fight of his life.

"There's . . ." Aaron surveyed the scene, scouring the room for some clue. He, like Rose, could not have missed the disarray of the bed (*her* bed) or the disheveled and untucked look of hastily re-attired clothes. "The Old Man's plan is happening. It's huge. And it's spreading."

Mal's head cocked up.

"Say it," Laura directed him, like the babysitter of a reticent child.

"It's some kind of mass homicidal mania. Complete strangers are cooperating to murder people they have no connection to. It's happening all over the place, and it's getting . . . wait. There's more."

Mal was standing now. He took a step closer to Aaron. Laura's eyes were riveted on him.

"This is coming in from New Haven, Connecticut," Aaron reported. "There's . . . This is . . . there's a group of people breaking down doors in apartment buildings and throwing occupants out the window. Police are —*Jesus!*—police are helping."

"The Old Man is tearing everything down," Laura said. "Why? How does this help him?"

"He's not tearing everything down," Aaron said, never too distraught to correct someone. "He's being very choosy about whom he kills."

"Just like with the Idea, though, there are some minds he can't control," Mal said, cataloging his opponent's weaknesses. "He would have gotten me by now, if he could have."

"It's a hostile takeover," Aaron said. "That's all it is. He's using the people he can control to kill the people he can't control. All of them."

"Soon it will be our turn," Laura said. "Then there won't be anything left but him."

Rose looked at Mal, at Aaron, both of them stopped short and staring at Laura, waiting for her to explain. Why? What was it about Laura that filled these two with such confidence in her?

"I have to go," Laura said. "To stop him."

"No," Rose said, with a harshness that made her voice unfamiliar in her own ears. "There's no way. Mal tried, but the Old Man, he's too strong now."

"*He's* not strong," Laura insisted. "It's his connection to people's brains through the neuropleth. We have to strip it from him."

"Laura." Mal's voice was soft, but immovable. "You can't."

"*No!*" Laura nearly screamed, making Aaron and Rose both jump in their spots. "*No.* You don't tell me what I can do."

Mal committed to the fight, took a step toward Laura as if he were stepping into the ring.

"I fought him myself. The minds are powering him now. He's too strong. You can't beat him."

"Wrong," Laura said, with a suddenly quiet determination. "*You* can't. You fought him the way you know how to fight. But you're not prepared to die for it, Mal. I am, if that's the price," she said. "Me, for everyone else."

Mal took a quick, dangerous step forward.

"No."

"Laura," Aaron threw in with a dubious tone, "I've got to say, I don't think that's the best—"

"Yes," she said, and Rose watched as, right before her, a girl became something far, far greater than herself. Laura's voice was suddenly light, easy with certainty. "I know you can't see it, Mal. For you, sacrifice is just another way to give up a fight. That's why you couldn't save Tommy when we were inside the Idea, when it offered you Tommy's and Annie's lives for your own. But you couldn't do it. Or you wouldn't."

Mal wrestled with the words, the accusation.

"But that's how Mike beat the Idea and that's how Remak saved you," she continued, heedless of the pain she was causing. Or, perhaps, well aware of it. "And that's how I'll beat the Old Man. People like him, they don't understand the power of sacrifice. Sacrifice isn't giving up the fight, Mal. It's just saying that the fight is more important than you are."

A dark, impenetrable silence locked the room down. Rose felt unable to move. Her awe for Laura weakened her knees, made her eyes moist and her chest hollow.

"Where is he, Mal?" Laura demanded.

"Oh, come *on*, Laura," Aaron said, exasperated. "You don't need him for *everything*. The Old Man is in the Lazarus Towers."

She nodded.

"Then I'll go there. I'll find a way to tear *him* down." She turned to the door without anything further. The others watched her with drowning eyes.

"Wait," someone said, and Rose was astonished to find that it was her.

Laura turned to her, waiting.

"You can't just walk in there," Rose said. "That almost killed Mal. They'll stop you before you get anywhere near him."

She turned to Aaron.

"It's true," he confirmed from within the dataflow in his head. "Security has it locked down."

"Fix that," she told him.

"Fix it," he mumbled. "I could hack in, get you clearance. But they're not robots; they'd know a teenage girl doesn't belong there."

"You could—"

"An escort," Aaron charged ahead. "I'll get you an escort to the top, like you've been summoned. But that won't get you to the towers themselves. There are a lot of streets between here and there."

"It looks quiet," Rose said, looking up from her cell. "The newsblogs are saying that the MCT is restoring order in the city."

"They're 'restoring order'?" Aaron said. "That's not good news. Do you remember what Mal said? The MCT is working for the Old Man."

"He can't control unlimited numbers of people at the

same time," Mal said. "He's not that powerful yet. That's why he needed to arrange things with the MCT and to make sure government forces were taken unaware."

"He needs to keep things safe and orderly for himself," Aaron said, "until he *is* that powerful."

"I'm coming with you, Laura," Mal said.

"No," Laura and Rose said simultaneously.

"If you're going to beat him, to tear him away from the minds that are giving him his power, you have to do it in the neuropleth."

"Then I'll find a way —"

"Me," Mal said. "I'm the way. I told you, when Remak was in me, healing me, he opened up a doorway in my head, a doorway to the neuropleth. I can do the same for you. It's the only way to meet the Old Man on equal footing. And I'm the only one who can put you there."

"So do it right now." Every word Laura uttered to him was a challenge.

"That won't —" Rose cut herself off when faces turned toward her. "That won't work. If you want to confront the Old Man in the neuropleth, you have to have . . . Remak called it neural sync. It means your nervous systems have to make physical contact." The echo of physical contact with the Old Man shivered through Rose's body as she said it.

"And that means," Mal said, "that while you're battling

him in the neuropleth, your body will be right there next to him, where he can . . . You need someone there to protect your body."

The necessity of it was inescapable, but Laura clearly didn't like yielding.

"Come, then," she said brusquely.

"Wait," Rose said. "Remak told me that you can touch other minds while you're in the neuropleth, but if you try to go into another body like Remak did, you'll become like him—your own body will turn into what Remak was."

Laura and Mal cataloged this, added it to their arsenal.

"Laura," Aaron said, gracing her with a rare glimpse of his full, unadulterated attention. "Are you sure you can do this?"

She looked at him, and, impossibly, a smile broke across her face, soft and deeply sad.

"What's happening now? Out there."

"The MCT is mobilizing special squads. They're shooting people down in the street."

Laura looked back at him, the inevitability of this out where everyone could see it.

"Laura," Aaron said, and something unfamiliar and uncomfortable rode his face. "Thank you." He hugged her ferociously, like a baby animal about to lose its mother. Suddenly, even to Rose, he looked like a child.

Just as suddenly, he released, stepped back, and nodded.

Laura stood before him like a big sister seeing her younger brother off to college. Then, without another word, she turned and went out the door. Mal followed, but at the threshold he stopped himself. He stepped back to Rose, stood directly before her. For the first time, he took her hand in his.

"Find your strength, Rose," he whispered to her. "It's in you. Just find it."

She took in every inch of him carefully, as though he were the most precious thing in the world and he was about to shatter.

He released her hand, turned, and was gone.

THE FORGOTTEN PLACES

THEIR FEET BEAT THE PAVEMENT as they moved uptown, holding as best they could to niches and recesses. MCT jeeps stalked up the streets like predators. In the distance, plumes of smoke rose into the sky, distant shouts echoed upward, stray gun shots cracked between the buildings. But around them, the concrete canyons resounded with Laura's and Mal's lonely footsteps. The city seemed haunted now, by the thing up in that tower, and the MCT was clearing away the last remnants of the living.

"They're going to see us eventually," Laura said.

"I know," Mal replied. "Just one more block."

Distantly, the Lazarus Towers slashed out of the skyline, its central spire wounding the sky. It was much farther than a block away.

Mal took her by the hand, prepared to sprint the last length. She pulled her hand from him, glared back into his eyes. He turned away.

"There." He pointed to a spot on the far corner and ran. She followed after him and came to a stop beside him, in front of a grocery store, its doors barred and its window slivered with cracks.

"We have to go in," he said, holding his hand out to her tentatively.

"In here?" she said, ignoring his hand.

"No. I can't show you unless you take my hand."

She put her loose hand in his, offering no message or emotion through it. He pulled her to the edge of the grocery store, toward the stairway of the next building over. Until, suddenly, he was opening a door, and they were walking into a building that hadn't been there a moment before. It was a single large room, its walls covered with bookshelves. Everything here was gray, not just in its appearance, but in its nature. The books had lost their pigment, the writing on the bindings fading into an illegible blur.

"One of the forgotten places," Laura said, a memory she was not pleased to have back.

"Yes. Bookstores are slipping away fast now. There's a network of them throughout the city. There's a forgotten alleyway behind this one that cuts to another one. I can get us safely to the towers from here."

She followed him through the heartbreaking rows, a haze of ghostly dust clinging to the air, kicked up by long-absent customers, and now never to fall because gravity forgot its hold on the particles.

He took her through the stockroom, out the back door into an alleyway, the concrete walls oddly rubbery as she brushed by them. He took her through these pale byways that cut through the city, made out of absences; soundless, no wind to blow the dead papers from the places where they lay, slowly receding from existence.

The quiet between Mal and Laura was dreadful. It felt to her like walking down the street with a stranger, her mind churning for something to say, but also firing with the wild anger of what had been done to her.

He pulled them out of the last forgotten place within sight of their destination.

The towers seemed to swallow up her field of vision, rendering even the gleaming carapace of the dome all but invisible to her. She could see Mal's entire body straining toward the central tower, in the shadow of which he had nearly died. He looked as if he wanted to lift his fists and duke it out with the very structure itself.

She could almost feel the Old Man here: the air seemed thick with the sense of something prodding, probing, an itch just beneath her senses, bugs crawling beneath her skin.

Why was she not terrified? She was walking to her doom with the full intention of never returning. Did she not believe she was really going to die? Or was it, in fact, that she had somehow always been headed for this, for sacrifice? In the most mundane of miracles, her parents had made a strong child, and the child had made a strong woman, a woman who would become what she needed to in order to fight.

Mal's strength was that he would never bend, never change. But hers was that she could.

And this, this bastion of humanity, this beneficent doomsday machine, was what she needed to be now. What everyone needed her to be.

The tower sheared up, higher and higher as they approached it, Laura leading the way.

JESSE KARP

AARON AND ROSE

A HEAVY AND UNWELCOME QUIET had fallen in the apartment, too. Rose sat, hunkered on her bed, her knees hugged to her chest, her brow knit in a deep concentration that had no room for Aaron.

Aaron had tried to chat at her in a futile effort to gain a response. He preferred a hum around him, a crackle of motion and sound.

He was responsible for expediting Laura's entrance to the tower, which required slicing their system and placing false orders, which themselves required code signatures, which required him to slice even deeper down. This was busy work to him, a mindless chore of running probable algorithms based on their code styles until he found one that allowed him to slip through. He had been told he was a genius at this sort of work. His father had once even brought him in for a shareholder demonstration, a sort of PR event about the limitless potential of Argaven leadership. But the truth was that Aaron's genius was far beyond this stuff; it lacked challenge. It was the mental equivalent of twiddling his thumbs, and it did not eat nearly enough of his concentration to shut out the burden of solitude around him.

So he went to look out the window, to see some motion, some life. As it turned out, with the bars placed inside the window, he could not get his face close enough to the surface to have a look down there. He could see only across to another shining, featureless façade. It struck him only then how like a prison this place was, and he wondered what the people trapped living in these boxes did with the knowledge that they were being treated as cattle. Or, worse yet, did they not even know? Did they simply *feel* it, and were their lives, in some way, unconsciously guided by this feeling?

He patched into the MCT's visual security net, looking through the eyes of various security cameras for the life and motion he craved. The streets, though, were weirdly empty, with only scurrying shadows at the edges of view and giant, rumbling MCT vehicles lumbering slowly along the avenues. Even the wondrous flow of information—the ones and zeroes of binary code that created the music of Aaron's world—was plodding in an unprecedented funk, slowed in some kind of sympathetic fugue with the human world.

He was not getting what he wanted, and he was struck with a pang of realization: that all of this equipment was suddenly, epically unsatisfactory to his needs. Because what he wanted, what he really needed, was Laura. Just to tell him to shut it or to scold him for being so monomaniacal or to put her hand on his arm. But none of that was ever going to happen again, because she would soon be quite dead and would leave Aaron with a hole that was even emptier than the one she had filled to begin with.

Goddamn her.

He spun on Rose as though he were going to take out his frustration on her frail and yielding emotions. But the moment he locked her in his sights, when the words were welling up, there was a hurried pounding on the door.

Rose lurched off the bed, clutched at the door, and yanked it open—assuming, no doubt, that it was Mal.

Instead, waiting on the other side was a tall, slim woman so perfectly honed in the line and balance of her sharp features and the tailoring of her sharp suit that she seemed to have been machined into existence, molded and refined from a flawless alloy. Her blond hair was in a tight bun, and the perfect silver dot of her cellpatch gleamed even under the dull light offered in this dreary place. Her eyes were hidden behind cellenses, and her face was so smooth and unlined that it was impossible to tell what age she could be, or even what decade of her life she was in. Her poise, framed in the doorway, was well controlled, giving nothing away.

Rose, whose poise was quite the opposite, took a stumbling step back at the alien figure in her midst.

"I need to speak to Mal Jericho right now," the woman said in a voice that chimed like crystal ice.

"He's not here," Aaron answered when Rose remained silent. "Who are you, exactly?" As he asked, he sent a proximity code and found that her cellpatch security was tighter than the security of both the Lazarus Towers and the MCT.

Cracks began to form in her poise.

"I *need* to speak to Mal Jericho. Do you— Wait. Are you . . ." She held her question in a moment longer, clearly not believing. "Are you Aaron Argaven? How are you . . . What are you doing here?"

Knowing that she knew of him and the way she reacted to his presence there revealed certain things about her: the line of work she was in, her level in the hierarchy respective to Aaron's lineage. This knowledge pumped confidence into Aaron's voice.

"Look, don't dither in the hallway," he said. "Come in and explain yourself, and then we'll see about answering your question."

Her head jerked about with shock that she was even still in the hallway, and she stepped into the apartment, distaste for the uncouthness of her journey nipping at her heels.

"Your name?" he asked, shutting the door behind her.

"It doesn't— My name is Arielle Kliest." Her voice was becoming shriller and her delicate, sculpturesque fingers with their gleaming jewel-like nails were fluttering in agitation. "I work for the Old Man. I've been his right hand for years. But he's gone over the— No. He's just gone. It's not even him anymore. Or it's more him than it ever was. He's going to tear us down. He's going to tear everything down. Mal Jericho is the only one who can stop him."

"How's that exactly?" Aaron maintained his own poise, not because he was immune to the effect of her words, but because after a lifetime of privilege, he knew how you acted in front of a menial.

"The Old Man has fused with a—a—a thing. Mal is the only person who knows what it is, I think, or knows how to get it out of him."

"And what gives you—"

"Listen," she said, and were she not pressing down on

it with all her control, her voice would have been a shriek instead of a hiss. "There's no time. Someone's been sent after me. You need to tell me where Mal is right now."

With impossible punctuality, as if by merely giving it the shape of words made it true, the doom that had followed Arielle Kliest from the Lazarus Towers bore down upon them.

The door did not bother with a knock this time but was instead flung open with such force that one of the hinges audibly cracked. The shape of a man shattered the precarious safe haven of the room. His form was low and wide, like a bull. His face, though, was not altogether a man's. It was missing something inexpressible, something no civilized face should have. Shadows seemed to gather unnaturally at the eyes.

To her credit, Arielle Kliest regained her poise and stared her fate in its inhuman face.

LAURA AND MAL

THERE WAS NO MOTION AROUND the base of the central tower. A stray car chugged out dirty smoke from its exhaust, abandoned in the street. Laura plunged ahead, pressing toward the main gate of the central tower, Mal pushing after her, before an MCT squad turned a corner and saw them.

A small group stood before the sprawling courtyard that was the main entrance to the central tower, two men in black and gray jumpsuits and a man in a charcoal suit.

Their lenses followed her approach like automatons, like cameras that never stopped tracking you.

They came to the gated entryway of the courtyard, and the man in the suit stepped forward. He was of indeterminate age, his hair was styled in a generic wave, his eyes were hidden by cellenses, and his face was a thing of placid neutrality.

"Ms. Westlake, Mr. Jericho?" the man said. "This way, if you please." He tripped the cellock, and the gate swung open. He motioned into the courtyard and fell in beside Laura as she entered, Mal following behind. The uniformed men, both carrying weapons in holsters at their belts, flanked them.

The man in the suit guided them silently through the courtyard's characterless benches and concrete urns of plastic plants and past the fountain with a stone bird appearing to rise, as if resurrected, from the running water.

They entered the climate-controlled expanse of lobby, whose vast tiled reaches echoed with their footsteps. Guards were stationed at doorways and elevators, but none of them moved, and only a few suited men walked from one passage to the next, their eyes stale and their faces musty with apathy, despite the Armageddon about to fall on all of them.

The man took them through passages that wound behind offices and finally came to a stop at an elevator, the

JESSE KARP

doors waiting open for them. He motioned them in, but Laura stood, staring at its mirrored insides.

"Orders came down just half an hour ago to take you two up to the very top," he encouraged, offering a plastic smile by way of further invitation.

Thank you, Aaron, she thought, not in fact all that grateful at the moment.

She entered, and Mal and the suited man stepped in behind her, though the guards did not. The man slid a card into a slot on the button panel, and the top light glowed softly. The door closed, and they moved upward.

"If you don't mind my asking," the man said quietly, his voice hesitant if not his expression. "What's up there, exactly?"

"Sorry?" Laura said, shaken from her own thoughts.

"On top," the man said. "Who's up there?"

"I'm sorry," Laura said. "You don't know who you work for?"

The man tilted his head in mild surprise at this.

"Certainly I do. I work for the Lazarus Corporation."

"Yes, but that's not a person; that's a corporation. You don't know who owns it, who's in charge of it?"

The man shook his head, a child confronted with an indecipherable geometric proof.

"I don't actually work for a person," he said, in a tone that suggested he was the one making sense. "I work for Lazarus. The corporation is its own entity, you understand. I was just wondering who signed the bills and such."

Laura nodded. She understood perfectly. He was nothing more or less than his function, just a man in a suit.

"Just a greedy old man," she said, "with a swelled head."

The door slid open.

"Just around to the stairway and up two flights," the man said. When she hesitated, watching him, he added, "I'm not allowed to go any farther."

She took a final look at him and tugged the Mets cap on her head snug, a totem of her past. The she and Mal walked out onto the white landing, the door closed, and they were alone.

"He's just above us," Mal said. "This is how I got in before."

"Do you think he knows that we're here?"

"Maybe. If he could get into my head, he would have already. It's like with the Idea before, there are some brains that aren't open to him. That's why he's killing all those people, isn't it? But even if he knew we were coming, I don't think he would care."

She looked across the white landing, toward the stairs,

but before she took a step, Mal reclaimed the lead. He led them up two white sets of stairs and found a white door waiting, slightly ajar. There was a slot for a card, a camera above. Obviously, you would normally need clearance to come through, though Aaron apparently had hacked all the way to the very top of the monster's lair.

They went into a hallway done in deep browns, from the rich wood of the walls to the plush carpet beneath. Intermittently along the wall was a spotlighted painting or a niche containing an ancient stone bust of an ominous, cracking marble head gazing down at them balefully.

There was no doubt at all which direction they needed to go. The world throbbed with a heavy, powerful heartbeat, though whether it was moving through the hallway or just through her own head, Laura couldn't say.

At the end of the hall, there was a set of double doors. She felt the heat from beyond, the choking heaviness of something that reeked with age.

"He's in there," Mal said needlessly. Expectation hung in the air between them, something waiting to be said, a last opportunity.

"Let's do this, then," Laura told him tersely.

"We have to make"—Mal paused unconsciously —"physical contact."

Laura held out her hand. He looked at it somberly for just an instant, then reached out and took it.

She looked straight into his eyes, unwilling to be intimidated by the weight of what he had done to her, unwilling to give him that power. The eyes looked back at her, in the midst of that young-old face, filled with longing.

Suddenly, she felt that longing, too; she was in those eyes, looking out at herself from the other side. She was in that brain and *in* that longing.

Through his eyes, she did not see the same Laura she saw every day in the mirror. She saw herself through the prism of Mal's longing. One facet glowed with his awe of her: her ability to feel so openly and earnestly, her connection to the world and the people around her, her willingness to give herself to them. Another facet shone with her fragility, which bred in Mal the fierce, indestructible need to protect her, to make sure her open and earnest heart was never, *never* tarnished or tainted or bruised, because, to him, it was the only good, true thing in the entire world. Another facet flickered with the fiery red of her anger and the deep gray of his crushing sense of guilt over what he had done and his flailing lack of understanding over why it had not been the right thing to do. A final facet reflected her as an opportunity, a last chance for happiness. It was not Mal's own happiness, she realized, but any happiness. To him, she was the hope that real happiness of any sort could exist in the world.

The sight of it all drove down into Laura's heart, and a realization overcame her now-distant, simmering rage. Of course, Mal didn't understand that life wasn't about happiness. The only true happiness he'd ever known were the glimpses of it he'd had with Laura. Happiness was a fairy-tale word to him, a holy grail at the end of a quest, a goal rather than a road you traveled on, often taking detours and side roads and hopefully finding your way back to it eventually. He thought it was his job to find the happiness for both of them, to hold it and to wrap it around them and to keep it there forever. Mal had come home and seen Laura tearful over a life she had left behind and thought that they were fighting a battle against her misery. So, true to who he was, he found a way to beat it. Or so he thought.

She was swept, then, from this realization as Mal pulled her deeper into him, deeper, deeper, until she was not in him at all, but through the opening within him, explod-ing outward onto a burning pathway dividing into millions of coursing branches that connected into—God, how many were there?—all the brains on the planet, luminous with their own crackling currents of neural life.

She was in the neuropleth and could feel the doorway to it spring open in her own mind, a glorious gift Remak had left Mal and that Mal had now shared with her.

Then, with heartbreaking abruptness, she was in her body again, in the hallway, looking up at Mal from her own eyes. She staggered, gasping to catch her breath, and he steadied her with a firm hand.

His touch instinctively lit her up, and, looking at him, she saw the echo of herself in his eyes.

"Oh, Mal," she said, putting her hand up toward his cheek.

He flinched away, unable to keep his eyes on her.

"This is it, Mal," she said. "This is what we've got left. We're not going to see each other again once we walk into that place." The words sounded bizarre, fantastical in her ears, like she was performing in some child's play. "Whatever's left to say . . ."

His neck was corded with the strain of holding the words down—or trying to force them out. He could not even bring his gaze to her. So she put her hand gently on his chin and turned it, and when his dark eyes found hers, they were streaming tears. In her newly recovered memory, she could find perhaps four instances of Mal truly, fully smiling. There were none of his tears. She had never seen Mal cry.

"Mal," she said. "Over the course of time, I would have found a way to forgive you. But that's time we're never going to have. So instead I'll tell you that I love you. I never stopped loving you, even when I didn't know who you were."

Mal's chest was shaking with the force of his emotion, and she felt the heat of tears start down her own cheeks, as well. She took his hand and squeezed it.

"You showed me who I am, Mal, and who I could be. I'm strong because of you."

He was shaking his head, squeezing her hand back, and her fingers throbbed with the pressure of his strength.

"No, Laura." He got it out in a strangled voice between sobs. "You were always strong. Stronger than me."

She pulled herself to him, put the side of her head against the hard muscles of his chest, and found his heartbeat, which was her very center.

"Maybe I was strong," she said. "Maybe. But you taught me how to use it. You taught me how to fight. Sometimes you need to fight, but there are a lot of ways to do it. Please remember, Mal, *please*. Sometimes you need to have the strength to fight in a different way."

"I love you, Laura. You were always what I was fighting for."

She came away, pushed to her tiptoes, and kissed him

hot and hard on the lips. They stood like that, together, in the silent hall of the monster's tower, for just a moment.

"Protect me long enough to kick the shit out of him," she said, finding her fire again.

"I will, Laura." Mal's body was relaxing, his face hardening. A fight was nearby. "I promise."

She tore herself away from him and shoved open the doors, marching in to face the Old Man, or whatever he had become.

FIND YOUR STRENGTH

CASTILLO ENTERED ROSE'S APARTMENT WITH the juggernaut force of a charging bull. Without even looking over, his concrete block of a fist blasted into Aaron's chest.

To say that Aaron had never been struck so hard was to belittle the experience. Aaron had rarely been struck in his life and never harder than when his father had cuffed him as a child for spilling soda on the office laptop. It was more accurate to say that Aaron had never imagined you *could* be hit so hard, that a human appendage could contain such force or a human form could sustain it without being torn apart. Aaron was snapped back as if a chain attached to his back had suddenly been pulled taut. His head crashed against the wall and, such was the nuclear Armageddon of pain radiating from his chest, that he did not even register it.

His vision swam with lights and refracted figures that could not possibly have existed, until his cellenses corrected for him and put the world back into shape. The attacker was advancing on Arielle Kliest, who made no move to escape, but impassively watched her fate barrel toward her.

"There. Is. No. Out." Each word came out like a killing blow, not meant to convey meaning, but as another way to pulverize. Something had lobotomized this man, excised the human and left only a beast. The beast took Kliest by the arms and, as though grasping a child's toy, lifted her from the floor and flung her down on the dirty ground, where her skull thudded and she folded. The beast's foot lifted, a bludgeoning weight poised to come down on Kliest's delicate neck.

There was nothing Aaron could do. He could not even find enough air to expel a scream from his lungs. What surprised him, though, was that he wanted to stop it, desperately, ragingly, more than he had ever wanted to find the Librarian, to have his father back, *anything*. He did not want to see this woman killed before him.

"You leave her *alone*."

The beast stopped and turned, now encompassing the third occupant of the room.

Rose had spoken, though Aaron knew this only because she was the last choice left. He certainly did not recognize the sizzle of determination in the voice, since he had barely heard Rose's voice rise above a fluttering whisper.

As the beast turned, there was its face again, with all the features of a man but somehow not a man's anymore. Aaron's cellens grabbed those features, and Aaron put them into his Face Recognition program, and almost instantly a military record came up.

Castillo, Lee. Marine, infantry, special ops, honorable discharge. It buzzed through Aaron's head with a comforting rush of information, telling him all about his enemy.

The figure advanced on Rose, who held her ground, faltered, pressed herself hard into the wall behind her.

"Castillo," Aaron gasped from the floor.

Castillo's head snapped around, a glare cutting through the shadow of his eyes, and he broke off from Rose as though he truly were an animal, a bull, merely pursuing whatever irritation struck him most recently, and that the sound of his name, for some reason, was the greatest offense.

What else did the record say about Castillo? He was thirty-six, six feet three inches tall, three hundred ten pounds. His medical records showed he had a history of high blood pressure and—

Castillo's shadow fell over Aaron, and the concrete hands took Aaron by the throat and lifted him up.

—a serious injury in his right knee, a piece of shrapnel lodged there from an exploding mine.

"Rose," Aaron called. "He's got—" His next syllable was strangled away by the pressure of thumbs on his throat. His air cut off immediately. He was going to die. Die before Laura, even.

He did a proximity ping with his cellense, locked on to Rose's cell, mentally keyed a call.

Amidst the grunts and strains of violence, Rose's cell sounded a stupid little wheedle.

Aaron's cellenses held back the darkness that was trying to claim his vision, showing him Castillo's face in hideous clarity.

Pick it up, Aaron screamed silently at Rose. *Pick it up.*

She must have seen his eyes flicker to it. She snatched it from its place by the bed, looked at the screen that held the text Aaron had just sent through: ***HIT HIM AS HARD AS YOU CAN IN THE RIGHT KNEE NOW!!!!!!!!!!!!!!!!***

The flesh of Aaron's face, tingling with blood loss as the flow of oxygen to his brain dwindled, felt Castillo's hot, reptile-dry breath. It would, perhaps, be the last human interaction he ever had.

Rose swept the aluminum chair from its spot and swung it around in a full turn of her body and brought it whistling into Castillo's right knee with perfect accuracy.

Castillo's body lurched, his grip released, and he crashed down to one side, never uttering a sound.

Aaron tumbled back to the ground himself, sucking in ragged breaths.

How do you like that, *Laura? Technology just saved my life.*

Castillo's hand whipped out from the floor, caught Rose's ankle. Before he could steal her balance, though, the aluminum chair whistled down and buried itself right in his face. The hand held firm on her ankle, but the chair rose into the air once more and, with all the strength those gangling arms could muster, came down again. And again.

Blood and splinters of teeth sprang away like shrapnel at every blow. Through the obscuring hair, Rose's face was hideous with rage. A dam had broken in Rose, and a bottomless reservoir of fury was being disgorged at Castillo. It was a primordial fury licking up from the lizard brain, unfettered and unstoppable and utterly alien to Aaron, because it could only have been born of a lifetime filled with helpless oppression and cruelty.

Castillo's face was distorted, malformed, the shape of it lumpy and swollen, the bones of the cheeks, the jaw, the nose concave. Yet, from its bottom center, beneath those dwindling bestial eyes, the coursing blood split apart to show a smile, blood running over the torn lips and tracing between the jagged teeth, delineating each ruined enamel tablet in liquid red.

The smile drove Rose on, her anger animating a frail body that was far beyond its limits. Who, Aaron wondered, was Rose striking in her mind? Who was this revenge actually meant for?

The chair came up and down, her entire body trembling with exhaustion until, finally, the hand at her ankle loosened, released, began to twitch.

The chair came up again but dropped backwards, clanging to the floor, followed presently by Rose, her spent frame huddled on the floor, her chest rising and spasming, gasping for air.

Aaron's eyes studied her closely, studied the aftermath of pure, unadulterated emotion that would never overcome him. The pain did not subside from his body, but thinned and spread into an evenly distributed throbbing that made his bones and organs vibrate.

He surveyed the room, four fallen figures in various

states of disintegration. That, at least, he could do something about.

"Are you all right?" a soft voice asked after minutes had passed.

Aaron focused in again, saw Rose coming to a seated position, the chair lying next to her flecked with blood and strands of gore.

"Superb," he said in a soggy voice. "Are you all right?"

"No," she said. "But I never really was. You should call an ambulance."

"Like I'd trust a city ambulance," Aaron replied. Even with the wet sound of internal bleeding in his voice, he still managed to sound smarmy. "I've already called for a private medical service. They should be here any minute."

She nodded, then leaned back against the bed, holding her hands up, flexing the chafed and swollen fingers before her eyes, studying the ruin of Castillo between them.

Aaron watched her for a moment, then closed his eyes and waited for help.

WE FIGHT TOGETHER

THE ROOM WAS LIT IN red, and the air felt thick and hot. Beads of sweat trickled down the small of Laura's back.

The thing sat on a throne of sorts, a large wooden chair behind a massive, antique wooden desk. The face creased into a smile at her arrival. It looked to Laura like a nightmare figure out of a fairy tale; one of the old, old fairy tales the way they were before history polished them up and gave them happy endings and made them fit the expectations of happy children. It looked like an old grandfather, sitting in the corner of a dark room, who greeted his young arrival with feral eyes and a smile of sharpened teeth, saliva running down his chin.

"Laura," the room around her seemed to say as the Old Man moved his mouth. "Little Laura." His eyes did not even flicker up toward Mal, who stood at the door, his posture loose and prepared.

Laura could feel the Old Man trying to crawl into her, and she held tight to the gasp of fear that wanted to explode from her chest.

"You're here to destroy me." The voice vibrated from the walls of her skull as the Old Man rose from his throne. There was a fluid, lithe energy in the decaying limbs as he walked toward her with an easy, rolling gait. "But I am the quiet agreement between interested parties," he said, standing before her. "I am the invisible lever upon which governments shift. I am the secret in the minds of powerful men. I am the glue that holds your civilization together." His hand came up, the brittle fingers touching her cheek. Physical contact. In a moment, the hand would move to tear her apart.

"You're greed and corruption," she countered, "the tiny secret that scurries for darkness. And it's time for civilization to run itself without you."

She threw herself at him, not with her body, but straight

through the doorway in her head. The last thing she saw was the moldering flesh of his face split apart, deformed by a twisted shriek of rage. Then there was the pathway of the neuropleth, coursing with voltage.

She shot through the neuropleth, until it bloomed before her, the Old Man's greatest weapon, greatest power: his brain. If the other brains were bright, sparking things, the Old Man's brain was a star, hissing and snapping with cracks of synaptic lightning. Umbilicals of neural electricity stretched out like tentacles from a kraken, connecting to every brain Laura could see. As they pulsed, the Old Man pulsed brighter, swelling with the life that belonged to them.

The Old Man's hand came away from Laura's cheek and swept back, prepared to strike her with all his impossible strength. Mal sprang forward from his place and launched himself into the air, clasping his fists together and bringing them over his shoulder like he was cocking a baseball bat. His arc carried him to his enemy, and as he came down, Mal swung his clasped fists with all his might.

The fists connected with the Old Man's ancient face, filling the room with a resounding crack, as if someone had fired off a rifle. The Old Man's head snapped to the side and whipped directly back without any sign of pain, without a flicker in the gleaming eyes. His gnarled hand came up, and he swatted as though trying to rid himself of a fly. Mal was flung off his feet, sent tumbling to the floor, where he rolled off his back and up to his feet again, teetering on unsteady legs, blood pouring from his nostrils, from his lips. He shook the pain from his head and charged in.

The Old Man's hand swatted again, but Mal slid beneath it, and it passed over his head with a heavy rush of air. Mal fired two uppercuts into the torso and a clean hook to the chin. Rather than respond to the attacks, the Old Man's hand reached out toward Laura, her body standing in a helpless fugue before him.

"No." Mal gritted his teeth, throwing his arms around his opponent, wrapping him tightly, and plunging his knee into the Old Man's kidneys. It struck as if against a stone pillar, and the Old Man opened his arms, tearing effortlessly from Mal's embrace. Staggering, Mal was not able to dodge as a hand struck his chest and threw him into the heavy ornate desk.

Mal spun and grasped the edge of the massive desk. A roar tore from Mal's throat as he lifted the impossible burden, and then, his muscles bunching into knots beneath his flesh, he thrust the load like a battering ram at the monster.

The Old Man reached out and took hold of the desk's leading edge and, almost daintily, tossed it aside. The desk spun into the air and splintered with a deafening report straight through the ceiling as, amidst a shower of plaster and shards of masonry, the room was exposed to the sky.

The force of having the desk wrenched away catapulted Mal halfway across the room, where he hit the floor with such impact that he felt bones grind together within him. He coughed out the pain, choking on a swell of his own blood, and pushed himself agonizingly up. He rose just in time to see the Old Man's hands grasp Laura's body, lift it, and hurl it like a missile at the wall.

Laura's electrical life buzzed around the Old Man's vast brain, a gnat by comparison. His strength was, as it had always been, the minds of others: how he could manipulate them, what they could be made to give him.

She fired the lightning of herself outward, toward the captive brains, and spread her energy wide. She found in herself the prism of Laura that she had seen through Mal's eyes. She plucked from it the sense of hope for true happiness in the world that she represented to him. She saturated the captive minds, hitting them with millions of volts of pure, unadulterated hope.

In the throes of this inexplicable rush, the countless brains—for just one instant—rejected the Old Man's touch. In that instant, the blinding orb of the Old Man's brain flickered and diminished, became a sick and desiccated thing once again.

Laura saw it, even as—so distant that it was less a sensation than a notion—she felt her body shatter apart.

As the neuropleth faded from her senses, Laura sought out one mind. She found it before she was gone, just beside her, a thing of gray fire, as if made from iron.

We were always together, Mal. Always.

Laura's body met the wall with unbearable force. Mal saw the neck twist and the limbs break apart, and felt the world slip inescapably from his grasp.

A life of anger, of rage, of *fight* that coiled always within him sprang loose as he turned back to the Old Man.

The Old Man looked up at him, the vitality siphoned away like blood from an open wound. The creases of his flesh held sway again, swallowing his moist, malignant eyes. The legs creaked; the torso went flaccid. Teetering on legs that couldn't hold him, he looked at Mal and gulped in enough air to speak.

"You . . . mustn't," he said.

Mal's fist struck, ending the Old Man forever.

WHAT WE BECOME

WE WERE ALWAYS TOGETHER, MAL. ***Always.***

Mal collapsed to his knees before Laura's mangled body, squeezing his eyes shut. Looking at it would drive him mad, like seeing the world itself bent out of shape and twisted into a grotesque aberration.

"I can't do what you can, Laura," he said. "You can fight in a way that I never could. You taught me . . ."—he made himself look at her—"that sometimes the fight is more important than I am."

He put his hand down on her cooling skin, felt the last

of her life trickling away, and he stepped up to the doorway in his head. *If you try to go into another body like Remak did,* Rose had said, *you'll become like him—your own body will turn into what Remak was.*

And if I'm like Remak was, Mal excoriated himself, willed his words to be true, *then I can do for Laura what he did for me.*

Mal let his anger fall away and found his feelings for Laura, his very heart. He rode that emotion, let it carry him like a bolt of lightning into the neuropleth and straight to the mind he wanted, fiery silver and burning from within like the bright blue of Laura's eyes.

He poured himself into her brain, felt his body shift, melt, coalesce. He turned into what Remak had been, a being of energy, of will. That will coursed through Laura's brain, through her nervous system, into her body.

He *became* Laura—her broken bones fused together by his hope; her dying heart strengthened by his love; her dimming life fired by his will. He remade Laura and, in becoming her, unmade himself.

In the middle of the ruined floor that was once the monster's lair, its roof exposed to the sky, Laura opened her bright blue eyes. For an instant, just an instant, there came a fleeting sense of Mal.

She reached out fast, tried to grab it. But, empty, her hands turned to fists and her face broke into anguish, and she beat her own chest in anger, in misery.

"*Mal!*" she screamed, beating at her own chest. "*Mal!*"

She screamed until the anger was gone and only the grief was left.

"Oh, Mal," she said through tears.

Laura walked amidst dazed people, reemerging onto the streets as if in a stupor. Their heads swiveled slowly about them, gathering in a city that was somehow unfamiliar. Their eyes found the buildings, the sky, one another. What they did not seem to be doing was folding themselves immediately back into their cells. Few that Laura passed were focused on, or even held, a cell. Eyes found Laura, saw her, gathered her in. One person, a man in smart business attire, stopped her to ask if she was okay. They were not invisible to each other; at least, not for the moment.

In the distance, the top of Lazarus Towers dwarfed the skyline around it. But the tallest of the towers, the central one, was rent open at the top, blown out from the inside. The twisted metal looked like a hand stretching upward, pleading to God.

Laura found herself in front of Rose's building, hesitating before the entrance. Her hope was not gone. Mal had shown her hope, and she had given it to all the minds in the neuropleth to free them for a moment. The people rushing around her, alive with vitality she barely recognized, showed her that it had meant something.

She spared the building one last look, her eyes gliding upward toward the floor Aaron and Rose waited on. Then she turned away from it and joined the flow of people around her.

Her hope was not gone, but now she was alone.

PART IV

FIGHT FOR THE FUTURE

WHERE TO BEGIN?

This was the question Aaron Argaven asked himself. He found his answer, as he did with so many personal dilemmas these days, by conversing in his head with Laura, imagining her shining eyes filled with righteous indignation, a sarcastic lilt to words that sprang forth from her preposterous, naive, and utterly invincible good intentions.

So he walked briskly and confidently — Laura, of course, would have said arrogantly — into the office of Intellitech's new CEO. He laid out his eight-step plan to recall the current cellens technology, provably dangerous to human brains as they were. It was a solid plan, as it included the PR campaign required to guard them from liability during the initial steps all the way through to profit projections for the last steps, which involved a safer, more efficient cellens technology that Intellitech would, naturally, patent.

Roderick Van Allen had been recruited to usher Intellitech through the difficult times following Alan Argaven's unfortunate passing. Van Allen was a trim, dignified man who maintained an athletic physique through tennis on the weekends and who had a gift—he felt—for feigning vast reservoirs of patience even when he was struggling to hold his temper in check.

"I'll take it under advisement, Mr. Argaven," Van Allen said.

"I'd appreciate a more considered response," Aaron replied, his posture straightening.

"I see," Van Allen said, no longer bothering with the pleasant smile of—so he had hoped—dismissal. "You are familiar with the current financial climate?" It was absurd that anyone old enough to read a newsblog would not be. Corporations had entered a suddenly dangerous and uncertain age, facing a swell of regulatory thinking from communities and governments. Corporate bodies were now at each other's throats for their space in a reduced power pool. Smaller or less cautious corporations were being pulled apart as if by wolves, and even the larger ones were girding themselves for a long, cold winter. It was as if some basic agreement between the corporations, some invisible foundation upon which they worked and tacitly cooperated for their mutual benefit, had fallen out from under them overnight; as if some invisible force that impelled the world to look away from the control they had handed over to faceless corporate agendas had dried up and withered away without warning.

To Van Allen's question, Aaron replied with a curt nod.

"Then you should have no trouble understanding," Van Allen said, "why your plan does not fit Intellitech's strategic profile at this time."

"Intellitech is a tool," Aaron said, disappointed though not surprised that he would have to condescend to explain this. "You are the person charged with applying it. But it is such a powerful tool that you have a responsibility to wield it with compassion and care."

"Intellitech is not a tool." Even as he said it, Van Allen was shocked that he had allowed himself to be pulled into an argument of semantics with a child. "It is an entity unto itself in the employ of its shareholders. I am the man charged with guiding this entity, and my sole responsibility is to those shareholders." He struggled to find a properly patronizing tone to end on. "Is that perfectly clear to you, son?"

Aaron considered him as he might a pile of trash that had inexplicably wound up in the middle of his living room.

"What's clear to me," Aaron said, "is that Intellitech no longer serves a useful purpose. My promise to you, Mr. Van Allen, is that within five years, I'm going to send this company crashing down around your shareholders. Is that perfectly clear, sir?"

Aaron didn't wait for an answer or for further comment of any kind. Instead, he walked from the office as he had entered, briskly and with confidence.

Aware that he was more capable than any ten CEOs currently presiding over corporate bodies, but also aware that people in the business of corporate finance had difficulty taking a fifteen-year-old seriously, Aaron determined that he needed help. It was a tricky business, because the help in question needed to be capable of carrying out his orders — that is, allowing for his superiority — but at the same time must have a singular talent for the work in his own right. After three weeks of carefully parsing electronic resources and following an indistinct trail, he found the help he wanted sitting in a tiny, gloomy basement apartment in a suburb of Chicago, surrounded by computers and other electronic tools of the trade.

JESSE KARP

At Aaron's appearance, Arielle Kliest displayed an uncharacteristic show of fear. She quickly gathered herself, collecting her hard, beautiful face into a mask of resignation at whatever her fate was to be.

Aaron explained his five-year plan for the downfall of Intellitech and several of its ilk, through an aggressive strategy of community and environment improvement, which included the exposé of the ozone satellites and the dangers of current cellens technology, as well as the refurbishment of New York City's East River; a plan that would fall directly in line with the country's current push for corporate regulation and community responsibility. At the same time, the plan would create a financial base that would fund similar projects and carry the two of them into a limitless future.

"Every corporation in the world wants me dead," she said coolly. "They don't quite know who I am or what I was to them yet, but they're figuring it out."

"Consequently," Aaron extrapolated for her, "it's only a matter of time before someone finds you. It only took me three weeks, though I am, admittedly, quite good at finding people. Wouldn't the most sound strategy for survival be to head them off before they came at you?"

Kliest had long ago come to this conclusion. Immediately intrigued by Aaron's five-year plan, she sat back on her lumpy, uncomfortable couch and considered it with the mathematical precision she had once used to decide the fates of corporations and countries.

"Impressive and ambitious," she concluded. "But impossible."

Which was what Aaron had been waiting for. It was a test, really, because anyone who believed his plan as presented could work was not worth his time. So he pulled out his big gun, his nuclear weapon of world corporate realignment. He had been planning on offering it to Intellitech if they had fallen in with his plans, but it was clear now he had waited until the right time.

"A little while ago," he said, "I had a conversation with a librarian. She mentioned something to me that piqued my interest. Naturally, I pursued it with all the resources at my disposal. Even so, I've really only been able to piece together its rudiments. Nevertheless, I'm certain you'll agree that it is a sufficient foundation to begin our campaign upon. It's called the Global Dynamic."

He explained it to her, a theory of social interaction that could predict trends on a global scale. Its seed, Aaron's research had revealed, was in Jung's theory of the collective unconscious, which posited a measureless, ineffable connection between all of humanity. The Global Dynamic, however, was, to Aaron's outlook, far more practical in application. It recognized seemingly small, disassociated behavior in relatively tiny social samples as part of a much larger, integrally connected tapestry that, when taken with other apparently disparate trends, created a massive indicator of where the world was headed. The example Aaron used was of a precipitous rise in the sales of action figures in the United States serving as an indicator that the nation was headed inevitably into a war. This, he explained, was merely the tip of the iceberg. Sales of certain resources could be tracked to predict or conceivably even manipulated to alter the course of human relations the world over.

"The Old Man employed the Global Dynamic. I guess he didn't share very well."

Kliest shook her head absently, her icy eyes distant.

"How do you feel about the five-year plan now?" Aaron asked, unable to mask the timbre of childlike pride in his voice.

The power inherent in accurate cultural forecasting was vast, and when wielded by someone with her experience, her knowledge, the implications were . . . absolute. She nodded slowly and with a dawning hope that felt positively alien to her.

"Less than five years, I think."

• • •

When will it end?

This was the question Maddie Grant asked herself, staring up at the cold, sterile emergency room lights as the doctor probed with professional thoroughness. He was doing his job, just as the policewoman had been doing hers, asking an endless litany of quietly agonizing questions, each repetition with the words strategically rearranged in order to catch any discrepancies, any slips, any lies.

The doctor's face—young, bleary-eyed, wildly uncombed hair, five o'clock shadow—reappeared in her vision. Her right eye was blurry with tears; her left was swollen closed, though no longer caked with dried blood, thanks to the doctor's alcohol-saturated swabs.

"That's all finished," the doctor said, snapping off the rubber gloves and sending them into a nearby garbage can. "I have to go speak to the officer. Are you okay?"

He meant, of course, was there anything he could immediately do for her, though the further-reaching implications of his question rang through Maddie's thirteen-year-old body like a hammer blow. She was not okay. She would never be okay again.

She nodded.

"Someone will be here in a minute." He lingered for just an instant longer than he needed to before leaving her alone with her pain. She did have her choice there, though:

Dwell on the shredding physical pain, and she could hold the emotional pain at bay. Focus on the emotional pain, and the physical pain dulled briefly.

The corporation her father worked for had folded, robbing him of his entire existence. He had become redundant. Binges of liquor, stammered whispers about how he got what he deserved, after years of tearing apart other people's lives like they were just numbers on paper. His guilt was eventually transferred to Maddie's mother, now a statistic on a police blotter, and then to Maddie herself. Then there was a foster home for Maddie, and a boy there who seemed like he might offer comfort. A boy who turned out not to be what he seemed at all.

His angry hands, his mean, probing fingers, had torn her last hope away. She would allow the hospital to patch her up, the police to escort her out, and she would survive just long enough to . . .

The metal rings of the curtain slithered along the rod, foretelling an entrance. A shadow fell over Maddie's face and held for a moment before it moved closer, and a face came into view. It was a girl's face, and it seemed impossibly young, even to Maddie. The honey-colored hair was so short it was nearly a crew cut, revealing a delicate, scrubbed face and a pair of brown eyes so large they seemed like they should be staring out of a Japanese cartoon.

"Hi," the girl said. "My name is Rose Santoro. I'm a volunteer advocate." Her voice was gentle and quiet but not in the least tentative. "May I sit down with you?"

Maddie didn't respond, thinking perhaps that would be indication enough of how she felt.

The girl sat and filled the silence with more soft words. "I'm here to help you any way I can."

Help her? It was almost—*almost*—enough to make Maddie laugh. Maddie turned, found the brown eyes, intending to show Rose what was left of this girl on the hospital bed, to show her how much *help* she could be. But then Maddie saw something in the brown eyes. She saw the pain within those eyes even as she saw her own reflection in them, one and the same. She saw the pain in Rose's eyes and saw that Rose was alive, here, in the business of helping.

"You can find the strength to make it through this," Rose said. "I promise you, you can find the strength."

A young woman named Laura drove into a small town. The towns had it harder than the cities. The corporations were so tied into the infrastructure of cities that the companies couldn't afford to abandon them. Even in the face of regulation, they fought to cut corners while remaining crucial to the survival of cities. Towns were easier to abandon, up and move factories out, like the proverbial rats scurrying from a burning house.

Laura had driven through more than one of these towns. This was her life for the time being, driving from place to place, seeing the people who lived there and how they lived. She shared a day with them, or a week. She shared their food, walked their streets, learned their names, and spoke to them. Her face and her voice became familiar for a time, in restaurants, bars, stores, town meetings—a friendly presence with a kind word to offer. Many of the people would later comment that, when they spoke to her, they felt like the strangers here and that they were speaking to someone who was at home, who knew where she was and what she was doing, even though it was their town and she was the visitor.

Sometimes, in a few of these towns that she passed through, things might begin to change. A month later a motion might be made at a meeting to rally support behind a local farmer, to tie the fortunes of several local businesses together such that they could support one another and profit from each other's business, or an ordinance would be passed that an hour a week of community service was now required to graduate from the high school. A decision might be made to lean the town toward one sort of merchandise—automotive parts, say, or canned vegetables—and that the town get behind this one industry and make its existence valuable to a nearby city. Or a library might be put up. Or a park might be built. Or volunteerism might see a steep rise.

Sometimes this would happen, though it would seldom be directly attributed to anything Laura said or did. They mainly remembered her after she was gone, not just for her friendly manner, but for something that fluttered just beneath it: a sense of quiet inside her, a melancholy. Some of the more astute people called it a longing, and their sense was that it was built deep into her bones, as much a part of her as her blood or her heart, and that it would never leave her. It was, in fact, part of what made her so easy to be around, this idea that she was holding on to some of the trouble in the world and keeping it at bay.

They might mention her in an offhanded conversation during lunch break or in a wistful reminiscence over a beer after work. They mentioned her and kept on going with their lives.

And Laura, she just kept on going.

Lippincott for his masterful guardianship and for swooping to the rescue when a rescue was sorely needed.

My insightful editor Julia Richardson, whose precise and perceptive suggestions put the final, indispensable touches on *What We Become* with grace and subtlety.

All the folks at Houghton Mifflin Harcourt, including Jennifer LaBracio, Karen Walsh, Kate Greene, Jeannette Larson, and the fleet-footed Amy Carlisle, who put their time, resources, and greatest effort into both *What We Become* and *Those That Wake.*

The Jefferson Market branch of the New York Public Library, if acknowledging a building is allowed, for providing the quiet atmosphere and evocative architecture necessary to writing large portions of both this book and the last.

Always and forever to Maren, Zoe, and Verity for inspiring me to find the best in myself and, sometimes, even a little bit more. And a special thanks to V, for coming up with the name "Rose."

h

a

den